Praise for
Kathleen Y'Barbo

"Y'Barbo gives us a solid story with characters who lead the way to laughter and danger."

— LINDA MAE BALDWIN, *RT Book Reviews*

"Kathleen Y'Barbo has written a high-spirited novel about the kind of woman we'd all like to be: spunky, creative, witty—and a good shot."

— DIANN MILLS, author of *A Woman Called Sage* and *Sworn to Protect,* commenting on *Anna Finch and the Hired Gun*

"I love Kathleen Y'Barbo's deft hand at combining romance, comedy, and suspense. Her books are pure fun to read."

— MARY CONNEALY, author of *Doctor in Petticoats*

"A fun read. Delightful, engaging, charming, and yes, funny. Humor in the characters, and humor in the events, as she dreams of and heads on an adventure in the west. I thoroughly enjoyed this romp of a read."

— LAURAINE SNELLING, author of the Red River series, Daughters of Blessing series, and *One Perfect Day,* commenting on *The Confidential Life of Eugenia Cooper*

"With excitement, romance, and humor, Kathleen Y'Barbo spins a tale that captures your mind. The author's enthusiasm for writing spills out of every scene, creating, as it should, enthusiastic readers."

— STEPHEN BLY, award-winning western author of more than one hundred books, including *One Step Over the Border,* commenting on *The Confidential Life of Eugenia Cooper*

The
Inconvenient
Marriage of
Charlotte Beck

A Novel

OTHER BOOKS BY KATHLEEN Y'BARBO

The Confidential Life of Eugenia Cooper
Anna Finch and the Hired Gun

The Inconvenient Marriage of Charlotte Beck

A Novel

KATHLEEN Y'BARBO

WATERBROOK
PRESS

THE INCONVENIENT MARRIAGE OF CHARLOTTE BECK
PUBLISHED BY WATERBROOK PRESS
12265 Oracle Boulevard, Suite 200
Colorado Springs, Colorado 80921

All Scripture quotations or paraphrases are taken from the King James Version.

The characters and events in this book are fictional, and any resemblance to actual persons or events is coincidental.

ISBN 978-0-307-44482-0
ISBN 978-0-307-72964-4 (electronic)

Cover design by Kelly L. Howard; cover photography by Joel Strayer.

Published in the United States by WaterBrook Multnomah, an imprint of the Crown Publishing Group, a division of Random House Inc., New York.

WATERBROOK and its deer colophon are registered trademarks of Random House Inc.

Library of Congress Cataloging-in-Publication Data
Y'Barbo, Kathleen.
    The inconvenient marriage of Charlotte Beck : a novel / by Kathleen Y'Barbo. —
1st ed.
        p. cm.
    ISBN 978-0-307-44482-0 — ISBN 978-0-307-72964-4 (electronic)
    1. Marriage—Fiction. I. Title.
    PS3625.B37I53 2011
    813'.6—dc22
                                                    2011001515

Printed in the United States of America
2011—First Edition

10 9 8 7 6 5 4 3 2 1

To Senior Master Sergeant Robert Turner, USAF ANG,
My hero in combat boots.
Thank you for finding me!

Author's Note

Wherever possible, I have remained true to actual historical events. In a few cases, however, the dates of certain events or the locations of certain landmarks or buildings have been altered slightly to fit the story. And though there never has been an observatory in Leadville, I still think the idea is a fine one.

In England, the American woman was looked upon as a strange and abnormal creature with habits and manner something between a red Indian and a Gaiety Girl. Anything of an out-landish nature might be expected of her. If she talked, dressed, and conducted herself as any well-bred woman would...she was usually saluted with the tactful remark, 'I should never have thought you were an American,' which was intended as a compliment... Her dollars were her only recommendation.

—*Jennie Jerome Churchill, Lady Randolph Churchill*

Train up a child in the way he should go: and when he is old, he will not depart from it.

—*Proverbs* 22:6

Part I

The Rules of Engagement

1

A lady carries herself with great poise and the sense
that an egg sits atop her head.
                                        —*Miss Pence*

June 9, 1887
London

What Charlotte Beck wanted, Charlotte Beck generally got.

Thus Charlotte stood on the doorstep of Fensworth House, poised
to make her unofficial debut into proper society despite the fact that she'd
not yet reached the age of introduction nor been presented to the queen.

Won't Gussie be surprised when I write her about the evening? The
thought of her best friend, Augusta "Gussie" Miller, bolstered Charlotte's courage and reminded her why she'd insisted on being included
tonight. After much pleading, Charlotte had convinced Gennie, her
stepmother, that she needed to practice her social graces before her first
official events of the New York and London seasons.

As the door opened, Charlotte swallowed a flutter of nerves. A uniformed servant nodded at her, and she worried she would forget the
litany of instructions on proper decorum that Gennie had again gone
over with her on the carriage ride here.

Charlotte slid a glance that she hoped conveyed thanks to the man
whose duty it had been to escort the Beck ladies tonight. The same man

who'd successfully lobbied on her behalf. Colonel William F. Cody, who was not only her father's business partner but also practically family, responded with a wink, then adjusted his lapels.

Her gaze swept past the colonel to the room a level below them, which glittered as much from the chandeliers above as from the jewels the nobility wore. The light was perfect for painting. She closed her eyes to memorize the scene then opened them quickly when Gennie touched her arm.

Had she any breath left, Charlotte might have sighed at the loveliness of it all. But under Gennie's instructions, the maid had pulled her corset strings so tight that even mild exertion would likely send Charlotte plummeting to the floor.

Perhaps rushing her debut was not such a wise move after all. The combined effect of nibbling at almost nothing all day and then squeezing into the lace-covered instrument of torture was not Charlotte's idea of a grand time.

Colonel Cody shifted positions to move beside her, and she glanced up to see him giving one last swipe to his well-tended mustache. A fellow clad in the livery of the Fensworth household stepped in front of them and cleared his throat. "The distinguished Colonel William F. Cody, Lady Eugenia Cooper Beck, and Miss Charlotte Beck."

A hush fell over the room as Gennie allowed Colonel Cody to take her arm. "Show time," he whispered to Charlotte before linking arms with her as well.

The name of the famous American showman had caught the crowd's attention, and several dozen men and women moved toward them. The famed "Buffalo Bill" released Charlotte and escorted Gennie down the stairs to greet their hosts.

Left alone at the top of what seemed an impossibly high vantage point, Charlotte reached for the banister then thought better of it. *A lady carries herself with great poise and the sense that an egg sits atop her head,* said Miss Pence, the tutor who'd spent the last few weeks whipping Charlotte into some manner of good form.

Find a focal point and walk toward it, looking neither up nor down. Easily done in her grandfather's drawing room, but not here with half of London watching her performance. Charlotte took a shallow breath and focused on a lovely Adams mantel across the room. Leaning against the mantel was a much more interesting focal point: an impossibly handsome, dark-haired gent who appeared quite amused at her plight. He had the audacity to lift one corner of his mouth in a taunting grin.

A child might have stuck her tongue out at him, but a lady did no such thing. Shifting her focus back to the fireplace and, above it, a rather lovely Watteau painting of an idyllic countryside setting, Charlotte took her first successful, if halting, step. And then another, and another, keeping in mind the wobbling imaginary egg, until she'd reached Gennie's side. Only then did she brave a look at her one-man audience, who applauded.

"Darling," Gennie said, drawing her attention, "say hello to our hosts." To the fellow in noble regalia and his strikingly beautiful wife, she said, "I'm so happy to present our daughter, Charlotte."

Our daughter. Charlotte squeezed Gennie's hand, and her stepmother returned the gesture. That the Lord had given her Gennie to fill the gaping void of living without a mother was still a blessing that brought tears to Charlotte's eyes.

She shifted to balance the imaginary egg then offered her host a smile. Slowly her attention turned to the earl's wife. Again, Charlotte smiled in greeting as Miss Pence had instructed her. *Speak when spoken to and do not assume nobility cares one whit for your ramblings* had been a favorite saying of the sour old tutor.

Lady Fensworth, resplendent in a gown of deepest blue, leaned forward, and her appraising gaze swept Charlotte's length. "You're quite lovely. Perhaps I should introduce you to my Martin. After he's finished speaking with Colonel Cody, of course."

"Martin?"

The question was met with instant disapproval on the face of their hostess while their host seemed to be off in a world of his own. Charlotte looked to Gennie for guidance on how to repair what was obviously some sort of damage.

"The future earl," Gennie whispered.

"Oh, yes, thank you. I would very much like an introduction," Charlotte managed. The woman's cool stare kept Charlotte off balance as she turned to find the man in question. She spied the colonel's silver hair and then, by leaning just a bit to the right, found a partial view of his companion. "Is that Martin?" she quietly asked Gennie.

At Gennie's nod, Charlotte studied the dark-haired man. When he turned his head her direction, their gazes collided. It was the same awful fellow who'd taken great delight in mocking her as she made her entrance into the ballroom.

This was Martin Hambly?

As Charlotte contemplated this fact, the man in question winked.

Of all the nerve.

"Come dear," Gennie said.

But she was too stunned to move. Rather, Charlotte's eyes narrowed. Whatever sort Martin Hambly was, he certainly was not a gentleman.

"Charlotte, do join me." Gennie's insistent tone caught her attention.

"Yes, of course." Charlotte offered a hastened version of a bow then scurried off a step behind her stepmother.

As she made her way across the room, she kept the dark-haired man in sight. She saw him duck behind a group of party goers, and though she searched for him, Martin Hambly was nowhere to be seen.

Gennie joined several society matrons engrossed in a conversation regarding the queen's upcoming Golden Jubilee, and Charlotte found her tolerance for this event, as well as her ability to take a decent breath, waning. The room began to spin, and she searched for a remedy. Colonel Cody stood against the far wall, a crowd of men surrounding him. He gestured animatedly with his arms, no doubt telling an exciting story about his time as an army scout. She longed to join the conversation, but Miss Pence would find it most improper.

She took another shallow breath, and her vision shimmered at the edges. To sit was unthinkable, especially given the limitations of the contraption that held her not only captive but upright. Escaping back up the stairs to freedom and the carriage that delivered her was also an impossible dream.

Charlotte sighed. She now knew without any doubt how a horse felt when it had been hobbled. Surely the New York parties would be much more fun.

As for the Pence egg, she'd been amusing herself for the last half-hour by imagining it as a ruined mess on the lovely ballroom floor, one that certain guests found too slippery to avoid. It was an evil way to pass the time, but any amusement was better than fainting dead away.

"Are you unwell?" one of the matrons asked her.

Charlotte once again looked to Gennie for the proper response.

"Perhaps a bit of fresh air might help," Gennie whispered. She nodded toward a large bank of windows overlooking what appeared to be a lovely garden. Heavy curtains lifted slightly at the edges, indicating the promise of a breeze. Gennie caught Charlotte's wrist. "Mind your manners." She pressed her lips to Charlotte's cheek. "And don't get caught," she whispered in Charlotte's ear.

Charlotte gave her stepmother an incredulous look. Had she just been instructed to climb out a window? When Gennie winked before returning to her conversation with the ladies, Charlotte had her answer.

"Excuse me, please," Charlotte said to the wagging tongues. She set the Pence egg back in its imaginary place and moved toward the makeshift exit as if she owned the place.

As few knew her, no one impeded Charlotte's progress. She spent only a few moments standing at the edge of the room to assure she'd gone unnoticed before turning to slip behind the curtains. Then it was a simple matter for Charlotte, who had been sneaking out of her second-floor bedroom since she was eight years old, to disappear under the open sash and out into the fresh night air.

Or it should have been simple. But her slippered foot caught on the sill, and the stupid corset kept her from bending. She hit her head on the sash, tipped over, and plummeted off the edge of what turned out to be a balcony with an extremely low and unsteady railing.

The stars above tilted and whirled as she grasped blindly for something to stop her fall. Only when she ceased tumbling did Charlotte realize that she'd not landed on the ground. Rather, she'd been caught by a man.

Worse, a second look confirmed it was Martin Hambly, the awful mocker who'd previously been posed beside the Adams mantel.

Charlotte's mouth opened to order the awful man, who stared at her with that insolent grin, to release her at once, but instead she gave in to her strangling corset and fainted dead away.

๑๑

Even when Viscount Alexander Hambly didn't go seeking trouble, it found him. This time trouble had come in the form of a girl playing dress-up. Or that had been Alex's opinion from afar as he watched the would-be Cinderella descend the staircase to join the ball.

Up close, however, Miss Charlotte Beck gave a different impression. While he determined her to be of an age at which some men preferred their companions, Alex didn't find the woman-child type to his liking. Worse, she was American, and not one of those interesting Yanks like Colonel Cody. No, from head to toe, it was apparent this was a female of the pampered variety.

He considered disposing of his duties by offering the vapid Miss Beck up to the frontiersman. Surely one man to another, Alex's explanation that he'd been minding his own business, watching for the appearance of Jacob's Comet on the western horizon, when a flying guest landed in his arms would be taken seriously. But then he remembered that the girl had arrived with Colonel Cody, making him a close acquaintance at least and possibly a dear family friend, and that Colonel Cody tended to shoot things for a living.

Indeed it was a predicament.

Voices on the balcony above sent Alex toward the hedge. Unfortunately, he'd not considered the limp bundle in his arms when he slid into his hiding place. A slight whack on the head from a tree branch was all it took to awaken the sleeping beauty.

And she didn't appear the least bit happy about her predicament. "Release me this—"

Out of necessity and self-preservation, he pressed his palm to her still-moving lips with his free hand. "Shhh," he hissed with as much authority as he could muster. The ploy seemed to work. "All right, then," Alex whispered. "What do you think you were doing?"

The woman in his arms merely glared at him.

"Well then," he said slowly as he stared down into the loveliest pair of green eyes he'd seen in some time, "while I can say with all honesty that I was watching for Jacob's Comet to appear, my guess is you have no such excuse."

Her eyes widened and then slowly narrowed. A moment later, her teeth clamped down on his hand and he let out a yelp. Taking her advantage, the woman slid from his grasp and bolted from the hedge.

"Why, Charlotte Beck, is that you?" a man called.

Alex froze. Following at this point would only invite scandal. While he cared not a whit about the wagging tongues of London's elite, his parents were much more sensitive to such matters.

"I'm sorry," the Beck woman said. "Do I know you?"

Alex couldn't hear all of the man's response, but it appeared he was explaining just how they'd come to be introduced. At a tea, perhaps? Or was he saying at sea?

"I see," Miss Beck said quite clearly to the unknown man. "I was just taking the air and hoping to catch a glimpse of Jacob's Comet."

Jacob's Comet? Had the Beck woman just stolen his alibi?

The rest of her conversation was lost on the breeze as the two moved back inside, though her laughter floated through the hedge to settle somewhere between his heart and that place where irritation arose.

And rise it did, especially when he took a step and found the American's fan beneath his foot. Alex picked up the crumpled piece of finery, ruffled and covered in the same pale fabric as Miss Beck's dress. Shaking off the leaves but not bothering to remove the smears of mud, Alex went off in search of Charlotte Beck.

ⓒⓒ

For the first time that night, Charlotte was thankful for the awful corset. Without the instrument of torture, her spine might have turned to jelly somewhere between the stairs leading from the back garden to the ballroom and the spot on the edge of the dance floor where she almost literally ran into Uncle Edwin. At least this way her back remained straight and her shoulders square. Only the best posture for a woman properly dressed.

"Do take me home," she said as she linked arms with her uncle, then offered her cheek for his kiss. The orchestra struck up a waltz.

"Home?" His laughter reminded her of Papa, as did the way he made her feel that anything she said was of great importance. "After all the fuss you made to be allowed to attend? I'll do no such thing. Gennie would have my head. Now perhaps a dance?"

He gave her a look that told Charlotte her ruse had not worked. He knew her too well. She needed a stronger excuse for leaving Fensworth's home post haste. Or at least before the fellow she'd landed on could catch up and tell on her.

"All right then," she said. "Escort me back across the room to Gennie so no more of these awful men accost me."

"Accost you?" He halted and lifted a brow. "Explain yourself."

Charlotte took a breath, or what passed for one whilst imprisoned in the corset, and offered a downcast look. "Promise you won't tell Gennie this, but…" She paused for effect then slowly swung her gaze up to meet her uncle's stare. "Suffice it to say one fellow has received an injury for his trouble."

As she spoke, Charlotte slid a peek around the edge of the crowd in case the fellow from the garden had appeared. Her conscience prickled at her uncle's change in expression.

"What happened?"

"I, well, that is, the room was warm and the garden lovely, so…" She looked down at the mud on her slippers then back up at Uncle Edwin. "I was merely trying to catch a glimpse of a comet." At her uncle's confused expression, she paused. "I admit I bit him, but he deserved it. Thus, there truly is no further cause for action."

"Where is the scoundrel? I'll have his—"

"Forgive the intrusion, Miss Beck," a decidedly familiar male voice called.

Charlotte looked past her fuming uncle to see the man from the garden moving toward them. In his hand he carried the mangled remains of her fan.

"Hambly," Uncle Edwin said in an ugly hiss. He touched her arm. "Is that the man who accosted you?"

"Well, actually…" She grappled with an answer as her conscience began to sting.

"Just a moment of your time," the man said.

"Charlotte?" When she couldn't find any words, Uncle Edwin turned to face the dark-haired man head-on. "You'll speak to me and not her, Hambly."

Martin Hambly held up his hands, the fan still dangling from his fingers. "I mean no harm."

"Uncle Edwin, please don't make a scene." Charlotte moved between her uncle and Hambly. "I must confess that I might have instigated the situation by—"

"Move," her uncle said as he pressed past her. "This family's been asking for…"

And then Uncle Edwin punched him.

2

Speak when spoken to and do not assume nobility
cares one whit for your ramblings.

—*MISS PENCE*

"I don't care if he was Fensworth's prize pony," Uncle Edwin said as he
helped Gennie into the carriage, then climbed in beside her. "Hambly's
son walked through the ballroom with your ruined fan out for all to see."
He paused and seemed to be considering what to say next. "A gentleman
would have considered Charlotte's reputation."

"The same could be said for Charlotte. Still, Edwin," Gennie said
as she settled her skirts, "your behavior was simply barbaric."

"Barbaric, was it?" He turned his attention to Charlotte. "Tell her
what you told me."

What had she told her uncle? "I, that is…" She paused to think, an
impossible task with two sets of eyes staring at her and the awful corset
biting her ribs. "I believe I might have mentioned that—"

"That he accosted you," Uncle Edwin supplied. "You were simply
out looking at a comet."

At that statement, Gennie's brows rose. "When did you develop an
interest in astronomy, Charlotte? Other than the painting you made for
your grandfather, I've seen no indication of any affinity for stargazing."

Several answers came to mind. "I'll send a note of apology to our
hosts," Charlotte said instead. She lowered her eyes. "Please don't tell Papa."

"You'll do no such thing, and I'll make no promises as to your father." Gennie paused. "Of all the noblemen in London, you two had to offend the earl and his son. Do you have any idea how difficult it has been for Lady Hambly and me to arrange even the most tenuous of truces between our families?" She crossed her arms and looked out the carriage window.

"But, I—"

"Driver, please turn the carriage around," Gennie said sharply. "We're going back to the Fensworth home."

Charlotte shook her head. "We can't go back there."

Uncle Edwin joined the protest until Gennie held up her hand to silence both of them. "*We* aren't going back. Charlotte is."

"I am?"

Gennie nodded. "You are." She swiveled to face her husband's brother. "Edwin, you have amends of your own to make, but as this entire incident began with Charlotte, it shall end with her. You may either wait with me or find another means of transport."

"You can wait alone." He called to the driver. "Stop here and let me out." Charlotte watched as her uncle bounded from the carriage without looking back.

"Stubborn man, that one," Gennie said as she settled back against the seat. "Now, as to *your* Beck stubbornness, shall we discuss it now or once you've completed your errand?"

"I'd rather hear it now, if you please," Charlotte said, "though I doubt it will be news to either of us that what some see as self-assured, others might call stubborn."

"Self-assured, is it?" Gennie chuckled. "I supposed I might have been accused of that a time or two in my youth." Her expression sobered. "However, you've a decision to make, and you'll make it right now before you leave the carriage."

"Goodness, Gennie, you sound—"

"Irritated? Annoyed? Completely exhausted with your antics?" Gennie's eyes narrowed. "Yes, yes, and yes!"

The starch went out of Charlotte's argument as she took in her stepmother's reaction. "Well," she said softly, "I had no idea you felt so strongly about this."

"Whoso diggeth a pit shall fall therein: and he that rolleth a stone, it will return upon him." Gennie paused. "From the twenty-sixth Proverb."

Charlotte swallowed hard and studied the battered and stained fan dangling from her wrist. For once, no witty comment or smart retort came to mind.

"Your fan isn't the only thing you've ruined tonight." Gennie leaned forward to cover Charlotte's hand with her own. "A lady's fan is easily replaced. A man's reputation, however, is precious and fragile. As to your reputation…" She paused and looked away. "Perhaps you'll be excused as just another American. However, I'm sure your grandfather would wish a remedy of some sort."

"A remedy," Charlotte echoed as Gennie once again met her gaze. "Yes, of course, but how?"

Gennie leaned back against the cushions and contemplated the question. "I don't suppose we can depend on stargazing to become all the rage. That would certainly excuse your behavior." She shrugged. "We shall simply have to pray nothing further happens to raise eyebrows."

Gennie spoke as if she had little hope of seeing this happen.

"I promise I'll behave," Charlotte said. And she meant it.

The carriage slowed to a halt, but Charlotte's heart did quite the opposite. Crossing the street before them was the very man she'd wronged. *Thank you, Lord, for not making me go back inside.*

"Go on," Gennie said as the liveried servant opened the carriage door. "I'll wait here."

"But that isn't proper," Charlotte argued, recalling Miss Pence's admonition against unsupervised walks with unmarried gentlemen. "And I've just promised to behave."

"Very well then." Gennie looked at the servant. "Follow her, please. Keep your distance but see that propriety is maintained."

"Yes'm," he said with a nod.

Far too quickly, Charlotte found herself at the curb with the Fensworth heir moving away at a fast clip. As he had not seen her, Charlotte had not only to catch his attention but, failing that, catch him.

And in the ridiculous corset, no less.

Forgetting Miss Pence's egg, she lifted her skirts and darted as best she could across the traffic on Grosvenor Square. At the opposite curb, she turned back to see Gennie watching.

Now what?

Gennie shook her head and pointed to the retreating Englishman.

With a groan, Charlotte turned back to her pursuit. "You there," she called to the broad back of the Hambly fellow. "Please slow down."

He kept walking, oblivious to her situation. Or perhaps reveling in it. Stepping in and out of deep shadows and brilliant streetlights, the nobleman appeared fully aware he'd been summoned and fully resistant to respond.

Charlotte picked up her pace, breathing as deeply as she could so as not to faint from lack of oxygen or the stench that permeated the city. The man's stride was long, his agility quite good, for they had reached a section of sidewalk crowded with people. She too wove in and out of strolling Londoners, keeping the back of the Hambly heir in view. When she glanced behind her, Grandfather's servant was nowhere to be seen. He had either blended into the crowd or abandoned his post.

And yet she could not turn back. Gennie would require her to complete her mission, be it now or tomorrow. And *now* was Charlotte's time of choice. She never had learned the gentle art of patience. Nor did she relish the thought of offering her apology in front of others—chief among them the earl and his wife.

"You, sir!" She darted around a trio of lads. "Slow down! I wish to speak with you."

"Hey, there," one of the young men called. "You're a pretty thing."

Ignoring the bawdy laughter, Charlotte pressed on. If only she could remove the corset. Then she could catch this man without once again making a fool of herself by passing out.

"Mr. Hambly," she gasped. "Truly, you *must* stop."

"Ooh, she's a *lay-dee*," one of the street toughs singsonged.

"A fine American *lay-dee*," the other added.

"Looks like she's *a-feared* of us," the third said. "See how she runs after that bloke. Or maybe she's not a *lay-dee* a'tall."

Well, that did it. Charlotte halted. She palmed the ruined fan that still dangled from her wrist and pointed it at the trio.

"Come one step closer and I shall be forced to show you exactly what happens when a man goes too far," she said. One of the three jerked his hand to his pocket, and Charlotte swatted at it with the fan. "Don't," she said through clenched jaw.

"I recommend you listen to the lady," came a deep voice from behind her. "Look what she did to me."

Charlotte glanced over her shoulder to see Hambly had returned, sporting the beginnings of a nasty black eye. A clamoring of boot heels on the sidewalk told Charlotte the men had chosen to retreat. Unfortunately, so did the earl's son—in the opposite direction.

This time she easily caught him. "Look, if you'll just stop a moment," she said with what little breath she could manage, "then it won't be so hard to say what I need to say."

He halted so quickly that Charlotte slammed into him. A fortuitous accident, given her childhood talents.

"Go home, little girl." He took off again at a faster pace. "I'm trying to find my—" He swiped at his forehead. "Just go home. I'll hold no grudge, nor do I hope to recall your face. How's that?"

"That is not acceptable," Charlotte said. "Not acceptable at all."

The earl's son kept walking, but Charlotte smiled. He wouldn't get far now.

"I advise you to return and hear me out," she called. "I've quite a heartfelt apology planned, but I cannot give it to a moving target."

"Not necessary," he said curtly.

"I assure you it is," she protested. "And besides, you'll need your pocket watch eventually." The Hambly fellow turned to face her, his hands moving to his pockets, and Charlotte dangled the gold timepiece at arm's length. "Fair trade, sir. One lovely watch for one heartfelt apology."

Shaking his head, he moved toward her. "How did you do that?"

Charlotte waited until he reached her then dangled the watch over his outstretched hand. "A lady never divulges her secrets. Now, about that apology."

The Englishman met her stare with his good eye, the bruising under the other eye continuing to darken. "Go on."

"I'm terribly sorry," she said. "My uncle, well, he has a temper."

He snatched the watch from her hand. "As do I."

"Look, Martin." She paused to look up at him. "I can call you Martin, can't I?"

"Martin?" His laugh held no humor. "How did you learn my name?"

Charlotte toyed with the fan then shrugged. "Your mother thought we should be introduced."

Out of the corner of her eye, she noticed her grandfather's carriage roll to a stop across the street. Gennie appeared to be watching but seemed in no hurry to join them. Beside the driver sat the servant, his head down.

"Of course." The Englishman shook his head as the beginnings of a wry smile dawned on his face. "And Martin Hambly was called out right in the middle of Mother's ballroom with Father watching." Another chuckle, and this time Martin truly seemed amused. "Almost worth it, I'd say."

Odd that he referred to himself in such a way. But then, nobles could be an odd bunch, including certain members of her own family.

"Again, I do apologize. And you'll likely hear from my uncle as well." She paused. "Or at least you should."

"Miss Beck, you've accomplished what you came for." He adjusted his hat then gave her a curt bow. "Apology accepted and duly noted. I'd be much obliged if you'd forget what happened tonight. Now if you'll excuse me, I'll—"

"Forget?" She shook her head. "Unlikely. You see, I'm not in the habit of ruining reputations. I warrant I'll never forget you, Martin Hambly."

"A pity you didn't get to meet my brother, Alex. He's quite unforgettable as well. And definitely the more handsome of the two, current injuries notwithstanding."

Charlotte squared her shoulders. "I would say perhaps another time, but I doubt the Hamblys and Becks will spend much time together now that I've caused such a fuss."

He looked at her. "I must admit you're not at all what I was expecting when I turned my attention to the sky tonight. Thank you for a most entertaining, albeit painful evening." He gave Charlotte a wink. "Beginning with your performance on the staircase and ending just before my face was pummeled."

"You're a cad."

The Englishman gave her a scathing look. "If you were fully grown, I'd kiss you and prove it so."

She crossed her arms. "I'm not at all sure I like you, Martin."

He shrugged. "There are times when I don't much like Martin either, but what can I do? He's my brother." And with that, he left Charlotte standing on the sidewalk.

"What in the world did that mean?" she muttered as she made her way back across the street and into Grandfather's carriage.

"Did things go well?" Gennie asked as the carriage lurched forward.

"I suppose so. He accepted my apology."

Gennie patted her arm. "Of course he did, darling. He's a gentleman."

Charlotte didn't have the heart to tell her that Martin Hambly— or possibly his brother, Alex—did not appear to be anything of the sort.

A lady should find a focal point on the opposite side
of the room and walk toward it, head held high. If
that focal point has a title and a hefty bank account,
so much the better.

—*Miss Pence*

The house was blessedly dark when Alex turned onto Grosvenor Square,
a testament to just how long he'd paced the streets circling Hyde Park and
the surrounding area, waiting for either his brother to appear or his anger
to disappear. Of all the women who might have fallen into his arms, why
had it been her?

Edwin Beck had been itching to punch a Hambly for years. At least
since the day Martin won Edwin's favorite polo pony in a race Edwin
claimed was fixed. It wasn't, of course, but the younger Beck brother had
never been a good sport or a good loser. That Alex had been the one to
offer an excuse for fisticuffs irked him almost as much as the slight to
the Hambly name.

The only bright spot in the evening was the fact that Beck and
everyone else thought Martin had been the one to land on his trousers.
That alone would someday be worth at least a smile. Not that he wished
his brother ill, for he did not. Martin had been through enough, while
Alex had, somehow, returned from the war unscathed both physically
and mentally.

When he allowed it, Alex wondered why, as twins, he had not shared equally in the suffering that plagued Martin. He paid his penance for returning whole by taking Martin's place at society functions, as the older Hambly twin no longer handled crowds or strangers well. And always, when playing his brother, Alex was a perfect gentleman.

Which begged the question of why tonight this slip of a girl had caused him to do what he'd never once done in public since returning from Africa: misbehave. He'd contemplate that question someday.

Someday but not tonight, for once again his twin had disappeared. And though Martin usually returned home on his own, he rarely reappeared without some sort of unexplained injury or loss of coin. Then there were the times when only the considerable donations made by Father kept Martin from landing in jail.

If Alex didn't love his brother dearly, he might hate him for the trouble he caused.

He spied Martin emerging from the fog up ahead. "Perfect."

Biting back a greeting lest he chase Martin away, Alex clenched his fists and walked on. With each step, his mirror image—minus the swollen eye—came closer. Apparently he'd been slumming, for Martin's usual gentleman's attire had been substituted for something the stable hands would have cast aside. And yet Alex could only feel relief that once again Martin Hambly had come home relatively unscathed from whatever nightmare precipitated tonight's excursion.

"Finally the good brother comes home looking like the bad." Martin Hambly's laughter and his footsteps bounded toward Alex across the cobblestones. "What's the matter? Can't bother to speak to me?"

How the Lord could create two such similar people who were so very different was one of life's unanswerable questions. Even before the war and their experiences in Africa separated them, Martin had never been mistaken for Alex once one of them opened his mouth to speak. Where Martin had been friendly and outgoing, it had always been Alex's lot to hang back and allow his brother the spotlight. Not only did Martin prefer it, so did Alex. The arrangement worked for both of them.

Until the war.

"Hello, Martin," he said wearily. The gate swung open, and Alex offered a nod and a quick word of thanks to the smiling servant. "Coming in or just passing by?" he said when he noted Martin had paused just outside.

"Still deciding." He cast furtive glances, first to the right and then the left. "I'm not certain it's safe."

A weariness had settled all the way to his bones, and Alex had less patience for his twin than usual. "I doubt it is. Father's had more than his share of the Yorkshire pudding, and you know how that affects him. I'm sure Mother's beside herself, listening to him moan from the bellyache. Still, I recommend you come inside the gate. It's safer inside than out."

Martin inched forward enough for the servant to slam the gate shut and lock it tight. "Thank you," Alex told the fellow as he skittered away. He waited just a moment before giving his brother a curt nod. "Good night, then."

Alex had almost reached the stairs when something—or someone—hit him between the shoulders. He landed hard on the ground and then rolled away just as Martin pounced. Alex fought to stand, his brother's hand around his throat. Enraged by an enemy only he could see, Martin fought like a madman.

After a few glancing blows and one hard punch to the midsection, Alex had had enough. "Stop it, Martin," he demanded, but his words and, apparently, his identity went unheeded as the future earl kept swinging. It was a pattern all too familiar and yet one Alex had little patience for that night.

Especially when his brother, who could come out of this odd rage at any moment, actually drew blood.

Finally Alex bested him with a blow that sent Martin staggering backward against the garden wall. His head hit first and then his body crumpled. Before Alex could reach his brother, he saw the elder twin struggle to a sitting position and swipe at a dark smear of blood on his forehead. Alex found a handkerchief in Martin's pocket and held it against the source of the bleeding.

"The soldiers," Martin said in a gasp of air. "They're coming for us. To kill us."

Not again.

"Be still," Alex told his brother. "Exertion will make things worse."

For possibly the first time in his adult life, Martin complied. He lay very still and appeared to study the sky while Alex continued to press on the wound.

"They're beautiful." His brother's eyes found Alex. "Never understood why you so fancied the stars. But look." He attempted to lift his hand.

Alex obliged by glancing up in the direction Martin pointed. Streaking across the eastern sky was what he'd been waiting to see all evening: Jacob's Comet.

"It has a tail," Martin whispered.

"That's because it's a comet."

"See, that's where we differ," Martin said in a long breath. "I wouldn't have known it was…"

"A comet." Alex pressed harder. "I warrant we differ in more than just the study of astronomy." He searched Martin's face, trying to ignore the fact it was the same one he saw daily in the mirror. "You do under-stand there's no one trying to kill us, don't you, Martin?"

"Of course." Martin's laughter held no humor. "It isn't you they're after." He met Alex's stare, his eyes vacant and his expression blank. All familiar signs of the angst that plagued him. "They want me."

Alex sighed as he handed the handkerchief to Martin then settled back on the ground beside him. Overhead a canopy of stars peered through wisps of clouds, which ringed a pale moon. He climbed to his feet and offered Martin help in standing, steadying him when he fal-tered. "Let me help you to bed."

A statement Martin neither acknowledged nor likely heard as he stumbled inside. He rarely did.

A lady cares neither for public opinion nor
the accolades of others. Rather she cultivates the
approval of those who truly matter and discards
the remainder.

—MISS PENCE

June 10, 1887
Earls Court, London

Charlotte turned her face to the rare London sun and allowed the warm light to create patterns beneath her eyelids. Had she possessed her canvas and pigments, she might have attempted to paint the colors she saw, the shifting swirls of red, amber, and periwinkle. Today, however, she'd set her paints aside to endure a performance of Colonel Cody's show.

She wished she were sitting with Grandfather in his library, quizzing him on the well-worn book on commerce and economy she'd read into the wee hours. Wouldn't Miss Pence be horrified to know Charlotte much preferred returning to her place in Adam Smith's *The Wealth of Nations* rather than donning her corset to make yet another social appearance?

Were it not all the rage and quite the coup to garner an invitation to ride in the carriage during the performance, Charlotte would have declined. It was all a bunch of silliness to her, pretending to bring a bit of the Old West to London. What sort of Old West Colonel Cody had seen, Charlotte couldn't say. There was nothing wild about the West where she lived. For all its proximity to the prairie, Denver strongly resembled London in its modern conveniences. She'd found nothing much there to call exciting since Papa became enthralled with the country life and purchased that awful ranch.

But Gennie had embraced her adopted home in the West with great enthusiasm, and because she loved it, she thought it a great adventure to accept Colonel Cody's offer to participate in a dramatization. Their coach was to be set upon by actors pretending to be ruffians and rescued by the great Buffalo Bill himself.

Charlotte's gaze swept the close confines of the carriage and recognized a prominent politician and at least two members of Queen Victoria's extended family. All wore expectant smiles and uniforms decorated with medals and sashes.

Gussie would have exclaimed her pleasure to the rafters had she been included. Charlotte, however, seemed to be the only one who wished the ordeal would hurry to an end.

"You know," she whispered to Gennie, "I'm sure any number of people would love to have my seat. Why don't I offer it up to someone who will appreciate the honor?"

Gennie shot her a look that told Charlotte exactly what she thought of the idea. "You'll do nothing of the sort. You know your father made me promise to keep you in my sight at all times since the *incident.*"

Charlotte swiveled to face her. "Why did you cable him? You knew he'd be upset."

Her stepmother met Charlotte's stare. "And you know I withhold nothing from my husband, especially when it concerns the family." She paused. "Why do you think we visited the House of Worth, Charlotte? It certainly was not so you could flaunt your as-yet-untamed nature by such a display. No, your father and I hope your wedding dress and trousseau will be used sooner rather than later. You *do* want that, don't you?"

She did, but only if she could manage an arrangement whereby she was wed but not shackled. "Yes, I suppose."

Gennie patted her hand. "Then you must continue to take training with Miss Pence and learn as best you can the behavior of a lady."

Sighing, Charlotte leaned back against the stiff springs of the ancient coach. "Yes, of course, I'm such a source of scandal."

"Watch your tone, young lady." Gennie leaned in closer.

Charlotte shrugged. "I was only doing what you told me and moving discreetly toward the window to get some air."

Gennie stiffened. "I do not recall telling you to fall out that window and into the arms of the Hambly heir."

Charlotte's brows rose in spite of her vow to keep her countenance neutral. "How do you know I fell?"

Her stepmother's chuckle held no humor. "Even you wouldn't go so far as to jump, Charlotte."

The gentleman seated across from Charlotte was taking far too much interest in the conversation. After giving him a pointed look, she shook her head. "I am innocent of any reason for gossip."

Gennie snorted. "You are anything but." She offered the man a smile then reached over to pinch Charlotte. "Now cease your arguing and pretend you're enjoying this."

"I won't." She rolled her eyes then reached for her newly purchased fan. "It's all too much."

"No," Gennie said with deadly calm. "What's too much is enduring the companionship of a girl who has no idea what she wants in life or how she might fare should her father cease paying bills for her escapades."

Charlotte pointed the fan at Gennie. "You're hardly one to say anything. Your purchases in Paris easily matched mine, and I've not seen you go without since we arrived in London. And for your information, we are staying at *my* grandfather's home, which will someday pass on to Papa and then to me and Danny, not you. What I have, I am entitled to. What you have, you got from marrying Papa."

Not true at all, for Gennie came from people just as wealthy as the Becks, but the words had slipped out so easily that they were said before Charlotte could think better of them. All eyes were now on them, and Charlotte knew her protest at being accused of scandal was causing yet another one.

Gennie's eyes narrowed. "Are you quite sure of what you've just said, Charlotte?"

She looked away and pretended disinterest in the fact that the attentions of the other passengers were focused on her. From what little she knew of the German language, at least two of the coach's occupants were discussing her quite freely, and not in a nice way.

"Very well, then," Gennie said as she adjusted her gloves. "Since you're so well set, I'll cable your father and let him know you won't be needing his assistance any longer. Perhaps it is not too late to stop the order from Worth. Seeing as you'll be taking care of your own trousseau and wedding gown. Oh," she said with a lift of her brows, "wait. You have no money to pay for such things. I suppose you'll just have to find work somewhere. I know governess work was not beneath me when I first arrived in Denver."

Charlotte jerked her attention from the Germans to Gennie. "You cannot allow Papa to take away my support."

Gennie gave Charlotte a satisfied look. "I can."

"You wouldn't dare."

"Wouldn't dare do what?" Gennie asked with an innocent expression. "You're obviously not above considering scandal and ignoring the things your father has done for you, so I'm merely removing an impediment to whatever it is you want." Her brows rose. "Remind me again, Charlotte. What is it you want?"

The fact that she couldn't think of a single pithy response irked Charlotte as much as it concerned her. What did she want? To marry? Have children? Perhaps someday. To see her paintings hung in some great gallery, perhaps the Louvre or Metropolitan? That would be nice, she supposed. To read more books like Mr. Smith's and perhaps dare to consider a course of study at university? She'd certainly discussed the option with Anna Finch Sanders, her longtime neighbor and family friend, though never with much enthusiasm.

Until now. Once she left the prison of this carriage, she would return to Grandfather's home and write Anna immediately. If Wellesley did not have a course of study to pique her budding interest in the world of business, perhaps another university would.

Someone gave the signal and Mr. Godfrey's band struck up a chorus as the coach lurched forward. Charlotte braced herself as the wheels rolled over deep ruts caused by the frequent London showers. A gate swung open, and with it came a wave of cheering that made hearing anything else impossible. The temptation to cover her ears was overcome only by the idea she might tumble out the window if she released her grip on the edge of the seat.

"I wish Danny were here. Isn't this fun?" her stepmother shouted.

"Fun," Charlotte echoed without enthusiasm. She'd happily trade places with her young half brother if it made Gennie happy. Even a nursery would be better than this stifling coach.

Then she spied a trio of handsome fellows, each dressed in an outfit of honor and attempting to catch her attention from the royal box.

"Apparently you're causing quite a sensation," Gennie shouted into her ear. "Aren't you going to respond? Remember, Major Burke instructed us to be enthusiastic in our acting."

"What would Miss Pence say?" Charlotte quipped. "Likely she'd find it scandalous. A lady is neither seen to be enthusiastic nor—"

"Oh forget about that old biddy." Gennie leaned forward to wave at the onlookers as if she'd been playing the part of a damsel-soon-to-be-in-distress all her life. "Even she couldn't resist this."

Despite her anger, Charlotte found Gennie's antics amusing. Her gaze scanned the grandstands. Behind the admirers sat a dozen more, all waving or making some kind of motion to cause her to look their way. And all, apparently, with sufficient pedigree to have secured a seat in an area reserved for royals. When she lifted her hand to wave, a cheer went up, and so did Charlotte's spirits.

Let Gennie make her threats. She was not without options in this world, even if it meant smiling and waving at a royal or two to make her point.

Then came a noise so loud it sliced through the crowd's din and rendered them almost silent. The cry of the Indian braves was so fierce that Charlotte instinctively withdrew from the window. Leading the charge was Red Shirt, a regal fellow who had entertained Charlotte only a few minutes ago with their shared skill at sleight of hand. As he raced past, feathers flying, Red Shirt offered Charlotte a broad grin.

Behind him, several dozen men in war paint rode seemingly wild ponies that less than an hour ago Charlotte had petted and hand-fed apples. Several of the braves made a point of winking or offering up a silly face to her as they rode dangerously close to the coach. It made for great theater, however, and Charlotte laughed and clapped for the performers in spite of herself.

When Colonel Cody and his men galloped past and scattered the tribe, Charlotte was almost disappointed. Another circle around the arena, and the performance was done.

Charlotte piled out of the coach along with the others to join the colonel. While the excited participants chattered and laughed and the throngs in the stands cheered, Colonel Cody pulled Charlotte aside.

"What say you to a little extra fun?" He grinned. "A postscript to our performance? Perhaps something I taught you when last I visited your father's ranch?"

She looked up at the showman and tried to recall just which trick he was considering. "Would my father be horrified?"

He considered the question a moment. "Possibly."

"Count me in, then."

The colonel whispered quick instructions then lifted his hat to slyly signal the performers. As the crowd continued to cheer, a whoop went up from the Indian camp.

Gennie looked Charlotte's way and offered a smile. "I told you this would be great fun."

"I suppose," Charlotte said with what she hoped was bored indifference. "I've had wilder rides back home. Remember the time the horse got spooked by the rattler and—"

"That is quite enough, Charlotte Beck." Gennie fanned herself. "Colonel Cody is our host and I'll not have you speaking like that in his presence."

"Well, all I know is it's awfully hot here for London." Charlotte retrieved her fan and hid her giggle behind it.

After one more cross look, Gennie turned her attention to the matron on her left who apparently found great excitement in associating with Yanks and especially with Gennie.

Catching sight of the lone Indian heading her way, Charlotte waited until the appointed time then pretended to drop her fan. As she reached for it, she gave it a discreet kick, sending it into the path of the rider.

She cast a casual glance at Colonel Cody, who winked, and then Charlotte stepped out to retrieve her fan.

5

A lady's steps should be slow and purposeful,
but certainly not giving the impression she might
actually be going anywhere of any great importance.

—*Miss Pence*

June 11, 1887
Beck House, London

The third step on Grandfather's wide staircase always made a peculiar
sound, so Charlotte tucked the leather-bound volume of *The Wealth of
Nations* under her arm and skipped over it. Unfortunately, the help had
been generous with the furniture wax, and she lost her footing and
skated the rest of the way down the stairs on her posterior.

"What's all the commotion?" Grandfather called from his library.

"Just me," she said sheepishly as she scrambled to her feet. "I missed
a step."

"More likely danced over the third one." Her grandfather appeared
in the door, a gray-haired but well-aged version of her beloved Papa.
"There's a reason I don't allow that plank to be properly nailed down."

Charlotte smoothed back a stray curl then hurried into her grandfather's embrace. "Good morning," she said. "Is there tea enough for me?"

"Always." He released his hold on her. "Come and join me, dear.
We've something to discuss."

She followed him into the library and inhaled the familiar scent of oak and leather that seemed to permeate every inch of the cozy space. While Grandfather's London home was as grand as any other on the exclusive block, Charlotte doubted the others held a room quite so cozy.

Despite the June temperatures, a fire had been laid. She returned the book to its place on the shelf, then took a seat, leaving her slippers on the floor and tucking her feet beneath her. Grandfather tamped down the flames until only the orange glow of embers remained.

"They think I'm so old I must freeze even in the summer." He turned to her, blue eyes twinkling. "Don't get old, Charlotte. It's ever so bothersome."

"I promise." She grinned.

"Now, to get right to the heart of the matter." He settled into his favorite chair and reached for a folded copy of the *London Times*. "I don't suppose you've read the paper today." Without giving her a chance to respond, he continued. "No, you young people have much to do and couldn't possibly slow down long enough to read about the day's events. Though I warrant you'd be better for it if you made the attempt."

"Yes, Grandfather," she said as she tried to decide exactly what he meant. "I shall endeavor to adopt the habit."

He leaned forward and thrust the paper toward her. "No time like the present to begin."

"Yes, of course." Charlotte opened the paper.

"Start with that headline just below the middle crease." He pointed to her. "You'll recognize the subject matter right away."

"'Society Suicide, Saddle Scandal: Beck Heiress Performs Hair-Raising Stunt at Wild West Performance.'" Charlotte gasped. "Oh, Grandfather, I—"

"Please." He gestured to the paper. "Continue reading aloud."

"All right." Her heart hammered. "'The lovely Miss Charlotte Beck, American granddaughter of the Earl of Framingham and daughter of Daniel Beck, the Viscount Balthorp, somehow managed to save herself from sudden peril by vaulting into the arms of a rider atop a careening pony. She then not only fit herself neatly behind the rider, but also retrieved his rifle and shot a hole straight through Colonel Cody's best hat.'"

"Which had, of course, been tossed into the air for the occasion," Grandfather said as if he'd memorized the passage. "Continue."

Charlotte swallowed hard and blinked back the tears that stung her eyes. "'This reporter had the honor of speaking with several of the attendees seated in the royal box, and received the same comment from each of the highly regarded persons. One wonders what Miss Beck might have been thinking to consider such wanton behavior in full display of the international press gathered in anticipation of Queen Victoria's upcoming Jubilee celebration. To quote the Prince of San Renik, "It's one thing to play at riding in a coach and quite another to ride behind a galloping Indian brave with your skirts flying. I do, however, applaud the young lady for agility and accuracy with a weapon."

Charlotte looked up, tears rendering her unable to continue. Unlike Papa, who would've stomped around the room, making a great show of his displeasure, Grandfather merely sat quietly and watched her.

The gravity of the situation settled on her, and Charlotte ducked her head under its weight. "I've made quite a mess of things, haven't I?"

He nodded, and his image swam in the tears that fell freely from Charlotte's eyes. She heard them plop on the paper, felt them stream down her cheeks to saturate the front of her morning gown. And worse, she felt the burn of humiliation at being such a disappointment to her beloved grandfather.

What must Papa think? Surely he'd heard of her scandalous behavior by now.

Which meant she must repair the damage.

"Already invitations have begun to be rescinded." Grandfather shrugged. "Personally I'm happy to be relieved of any reason to dress in my Sunday best and make polite conversation with people I barely know. You and dear Gennie might find the unexpected lapse in your appointments a bit more upsetting, however."

"Oh no." Charlotte pushed the soggy paper aside. "Even the garden party at the palace?"

Grandfather shrugged. "I've not been so informed. It's possible that I, as one of Victoria's oldest acquaintances, might be spared the wrath others will inflict on the Becks. The other hosts, however, will not open their doors to scandal—quite literally—even if it comes from an American."

Charlotte's bottom lip trembled. "I must repair the damage."

Grandfather rose. "Dear, I fear there's no repair for this. Now, perhaps you should wash your face and then join me for breakfast."

"What's this about damage?" Gennie stood in the door, her smile radiant. It disappeared when she saw her stepdaughter. "Charlotte, what's wrong?"

Charlotte kicked the *Times* under the sofa with her toe then fell into Gennie's outstretched arms. Grandfather pulled a handkerchief from his pocket and offered it to her before making his excuses and fleeing the library.

"Never did like a woman's tears," he muttered as he disappeared into the hall.

Gennie took the handkerchief from Charlotte's clenched fist and dabbed at Charlotte's cheeks. "What in the world has you so upset?"

Glancing down at the corner of the newspaper, barely visible under the sofa, Charlotte sat and made sure her skirts covered the evidence. Gennie would learn of her humiliation soon enough. "I'm fine, truly," she said. "Just being a silly girl. I'm sure you remember those days."

That comment garnered quite a look from Gennie as she handed Charlotte the soggy handkerchief. "I think I recall some of it."

"I wonder if you might give me some advice." Charlotte let the handkerchief drop into her lap and sniffed one last time. "About social things."

Her stepmother looked genuinely surprised. "Of course."

"When one has done something unacceptable..."

"Such as ride on the back of a horse with your skirts flying? I think that's how the gentleman from the *Times* put it." Gennie reached down, pushed Charlotte's skirt aside, and retrieved the paper. "Has your grandfather seen this?"

Charlotte nodded.

"And did he seem upset?"

"A little," Charlotte managed as the lump returned to her throat. "But he also claimed he was relieved not to have as many social obligations."

Now that I've reduced us to pariahs, she didn't say.

"I see." Gennie cast the paper into the fire, and the pages began to smoke. When the embers caught and the fire lit, the *Times* began to curl and turn black at the edges.

"If only you could do that to all the copies," Charlotte said. "But I suppose that's not the solution."

"No." Gennie sighed. "I'm afraid there's no remedy for this except to return to Denver earlier than expected."

"And miss the palace garden party? Your tea with the empress? We can't." Charlotte rose and began to pace. "Surely it was obvious to those in attendance that none of what happened yesterday was planned. The colonel does these things all the time. Why back home he..." She stopped and turned to face Gennie. "I promise it wasn't planned. We were all standing together and Colonel Cody asked me if I'd like to do that trick he taught me last winter when he visited the ranch and I knew you'd not be pleased but we had just argued and I was still somewhat upset so I..."

"Did it anyway?" Gennie offered.

"Yes," Charlotte whispered.

"For one so rushed to become a woman, you certainly excel at behaving like a child." Gennie's sharp expression softened. "However, there's nothing to be done for it."

Much as Charlotte hated to admit it, Gennie spoke the truth. She constantly complained about being treated like a child only to prove everyone right.

Until now.

"Maybe there is something that can be done." Charlotte paused to consider an idea. "Do you recall that when you chastised me after the Hambly party, you said you could only hope that stargazing became all the rage?"

Gennie's mouth set in a firm line. If she had a response, it likely was not a positive one.

Charlotte pressed on. "As I recall, Colonel Cody was quite well received at the Hambly event."

"Well, yes, I suppose he was. But then, he's caused quite the sensation here in London, especially since the queen came out to view the performance last month." Their gazes met. "Why?" Gennie asked.

"Just thinking aloud." Charlotte grinned as the idea became the beginnings of a scheme that just might work. "Would you say the Hamblys are well thought of in London society?"

"Very well thought of. Charlotte," Gennie said slowly, "what are you planning?"

"Nothing at all." The truth, at least for now. The actual plan would come together somewhere between here and Grosvenor Square. Of this Charlotte was completely certain.

6

Social protocol requires a lady to know when she
is welcome and when to claim she is otherwise
indisposed and unable to venture forth.

—MISS PENCE

June 11, 1887
Royal Observatory, Greenwich

"Did you see this?"

Alex looked up from his notes to see Will Pembroke, the family solicitor, at his office door, a folded copy of the *London Times* tucked under his arm. The events of the week combined with the conundrum brought by Jacob's Comet's appearance had him too befuddled to care about whatever goings-on his friend had found interesting. With so much at stake, he had little time to socialize. His paper on the comet was due the next morning, and he'd not yet managed to catch a free moment to finish it.

"What brings you out to the observatory on a Friday afternoon, Pembroke?"

Pembroke helped himself to the chair across from Alex, then spread the paper out between them. "I repeat, did you see this?" He leaned back and cradled his head in his hands.

"See what?" Alex asked without truly caring about the answer.

"That girl. The one who caused you the trouble."

He turned the paper his direction and found a headline that referred to the American heiress whose name would forever be associated with a night he longed to forget.

"Miss Beck," he said under his breath as he rubbed his sore eye. "Indeed I recall her. But what's this? She performed a stunt at the Wild West show?" Alex chuckled. "Interesting girl, I'll give her that much."

"Interesting's not the half of it." Will snatched the paper away and gave Alex a spirited reading of the article, pausing only twice to show photographs of the event. Finally, he looked up and shook his head. "The Earl of Framingham's granddaughter? Can you believe it?"

"She's a Beck," Alex said with the appropriate measure of sarcasm as he went back to his numbers. The mantel clock struck three times, a signal that the day was slipping quickly away. Tomorrow morning would arrive whether Alex had a paper to present to the committee or not.

"Beck or not, she's caused quite the scandal. 'It's one thing to play at riding in a coach and quite another to ride behind a galloping Indian brave with your skirts flying.'" Will paused. "A direct quote from a well-placed bystander, according to the *Times*." He lowered the paper and shrugged. "Anyway, I actually came here to offer a proposition. A business proposition. In America."

Alex pushed his chair back and moved around the desk to stand in front of Will. "My presentation before the committee is due tomorrow morning at precisely nine whether it's done or not. And it's not." He swiped at his forehead. "Then there is the multitude of things I'm facing at home. At any moment I could be called upon to find money to pay a bill or to impersonate a brother. There could not be a worse time to travel."

Pembroke shook his head. "Never have I known a man who needed to get away from things more than you." He grinned. "I've taken the liberty of speaking with a colleague of mine who would love to discuss your idea of researching that meteorite of yours."

"Comet," Alex corrected, "and who exactly is this colleague?"

"It would take all the fun out of it if I told you." He nudged Alex. "But I'll give you a hint. Perhaps you've heard of the Goodsell Observatory."

"In Minnesota? Excellent facility." Alex paused. "Why? Is there a delegation visiting London? Perhaps you could set up a meeting for sometime next week."

"Not exactly, but have you heard of Roeschlaub?"

"The architect?" Alex's temper began to spike. He returned to his chair and attempted a glare. "I gave up riddles when I left the nursery, Pembroke, and I thought you had as well. Just say it."

Will's excited expression did not diminish. "All right, but this is completely off the record." He closed the door, then returned his attention to Alex. "It's possible that a donation will soon be made to secure an observatory in one of the Western states that will rival Goodsell."

"Interesting," Alex said as he retrieved his papers. "But I fail to see what that has to do with you or me or anything else we've discussed since you arrived."

"Leadville."

"Colorado?" Alex shook his head. "I don't follow."

Pembroke returned to the chair across from Alex. "I don't suppose you follow the production reports on the Hambly mining properties in Leadville." When Alex shook his head, Will continued. "Not worth the paper they're written on, though I doubt your father's aware of it. That mine's done for. Summit Hill is, however, on one of the highest elevations in Leadville, and thus a much better location for an observatory than the one now being considered in Denver."

"I see." Alex gave the matter a moment's consideration. "You'd like me in attendance to execute the documents before the investor changes his mind."

"Actually," Will said slowly, "there hasn't been a formal offer to purchase. Yet."

"Then I don't understand."

"You're a personable enough fellow with a string of titles, and—"

"All of them worthless when compared to what my brother will inherit. Why not bring him?" Alex interjected.

"All joking aside," Will continued, "you know how the Americans love nobility. Perhaps a meeting with a few of the key investors would sway the decision in our favor."

"And to do that I would have to…"

"Take a trip out West, my friend. Where the buffalo roam and the skies are not cloudy all day."

Alex shook his head. "You're mad."

"That's partially true, but there's more." Will leaned his elbows on the desk. "The family's in trouble. Financial trouble."

Alex's heart sank. "I'm sorry. How can I help?"

"Not my family. Yours."

"How bad is it?" Alex said, bitterness but not surprise lacing his tone.

Will paused and seemed to be considering his words. "Bad. And getting worse. If you think about it, the only one capable of reversing this is you. Given his uncertain state, Martin certainly can't. Neither your father nor your mother can make the trip either. Thus, it falls to you to save the Hambly dynasty."

Again. Several responses occurred to him, but Alex remained silent.

"There is another way." Will crossed his arms over his chest. "I am reluctant to bring it up, but there is a way to manage the dual purposes of salvaging the family fortune and keeping you in telescopes and stargazing equipment."

Alex paused. "What is it?" he asked wearily.

"Marry a wealthy American. You wouldn't be the first, you know. Worked out beautifully for the Churchills."

Alex only stared a moment at Pembroke before laughter erupted. "That's wonderful," he said. "Why didn't I think of that? Just offer myself up to some insipid daughter of a Yank with bulging coffers and not much in the way of good sense."

"Some are quite lovely." Will pointed to the *Times*. "With decent pedigrees. Such as Charlotte Beck."

"The hellion? Oh no. You've had some odd ideas before, but—"

"Just hear me out," Will said. "A merger of the Beck and Hambly families would be quite the coup. Romeo and Juliet unite a dynasty." At Alex's scowl, Will shook his head. "All right, then, think logically. She's of marriageable age."

"Too young for me, Pembroke. I prefer a woman not fresh from the nursery."

"Let me present my case, for argument's sake."

Alex leaned back against his chair. "Do make it brief, solicitor."

"Like it or not, you shall marry. Sooner rather than later because, again, Martin certainly cannot. You said yourself that you're far too busy to find a suitable wife, so—"

"I said I was busy. No mention was made of wife-hunting."

"Nonetheless, family finances and your conscience dictate that at some point you will cease your work here and take on the responsibility of keeping the countess and the others from being thrown into the street. If you want to dedicate your life to the study of the stars and comets, then why not let me help you arrange a suitable solution to these problems now, before they keep you from that study?"

"You're exaggerating."

"Only slightly." Will's expression sobered. "If nothing is done to change the situation, there will be nothing left in the bank."

"Then start selling properties." Alex rested his palms on the carefully stacked pages of research before him. "Raise as much cash as you can to pay whatever debts are the most pressing. That should do the trick, shouldn't it?"

Will tilted his head. "People will talk."

"Let them," Alex snapped.

A nod. "Done. That should buy a few years of ease."

"Good," Alex said. "Now might I return to my work? I've got a year's worth of research to present tomorrow, and I'd like to avoid looking the fool."

"Yes, of course. There's just one more thing."

"What?" Alex said, the word coming out on a long breath. "And do be brief."

"Miss Beck? Shall I make inquiries as to her father's interest in joining families? I understand the older Mr. Beck is quite levelheaded and decent in comparison to his brother. Though," Will said, with the beginnings of a grin, "I cannot vouch for his ability to connect with a decent left-handed jab like his brother can."

"Out."

"Do find your humor," Will said. "Remember, all you have to do is get the Beck woman to marry you. Then what's hers is yours. What formerly belonged to the Becks will be in control of the Hamblys."

"Will, I've no desire to—"

"I would be breaking a confidence to tell you exactly what she's inheriting upon the earl's death, but you'd be shocked to know the value that's been settled on her head."

"I've no time to be shocked," Alex said, "so your secret's safe. Nor do I have time to entertain potential buyers on the other side of the ocean, be they seeking to purchase family mines or the family name. Thus, I believe our discussion is over."

Alex went back to his notes, settling the massive stack into three smaller and more manageable piles. If only he had actual data on the comet. The data on hand would have to suffice for now.

Someday, however, if he could convince the Astronomer Royal of the value of the project, perhaps he'd find the comet.

"So you won't mind that I've made discreet inquiries as to the cost of a mention in the next issue of *The Titled American*?" Will asked. "I understand it's required reading for the Dollar Princesses."

"Out. Now."

Will steepled his hands and leaned forward. "Understand that while I am paid to see to the Hambly family's interests, the fact that you are my best friend makes me partial to your interests over the rest."

The sharp retort Alex had planned died in his throat. "I appreciate that, friend. Truly, I do."

"Then receive my advice with an open heart. Seek out a bride, preferably Miss Beck, and settle the question of finances once and for all. Then you can live happily with your work, and you'll never have to worry about selling off parts of the Hambly empire to keep the family from ruin." He reached for the documents on the desk between them and Alex's heart lurched. "With nothing to do but compile pages and pages of this stargazing material while your family leaves you blissfully alone."

"Please." Alex reached for the precious documents. "Put those back." When Will complied, Alex breathed a sigh of relief. If anything were to happen to his notes…

"Am I allowed to make discreet inquiries?"

"As to meeting with potential buyers of the Leadville mine, yes. As to an arrangement of marriage? No." Alex held up his hand to silence Will's protest. "As to Miss Beck in particular, I prefer not to be saddled with a woman who can shoot better than me."

"Consider it, Alex."

Alex let out a long sigh. Rarely did his friend prove so persistent. "After my presentation tomorrow and not a moment before." He gave Will a direct look. "Not one minute before. And not another word about the Beck woman. She's completely…" Words escaped him.

"Unsuitable?" Will supplied.

"Indeed. As is the idea of marriage at all. Not when there are other options."

"Understood." The chair creaked as Will rose.

Alex's office door flew open, and words tumbled toward him. "A word with you, Mr. Hambly."

"Miss Beck." Will Pembroke gave the disgraced heiress his most dignified bow then moved to stand between her and Alex. "I don't suppose you'd believe me if I told you the viscount and I were just speaking of you."

7

A lady does not spartle about nor wear a grinagog's
expression when crossing a room.

—*Miss Pence*

Charlotte held her head high as she regarded the green-eyed gatekeeper.
"Apparently you and everyone else in London are speaking of me." She
looked past him to the man she'd come to confront. His right eye was
still bruised and swollen, courtesy of Uncle Edwin and, by association,
her. The urge to apologize again for her childish behavior prodded her,
but Charlotte kept silent. Better, she decided, not to mention the topic
at all. She turned her attention back to the gatekeeper. "Might I have a
moment with Viscount Hambly alone?"

"Yes, of course," the fellow said with far too much enthusiasm.
"Though as his solicitor, I must inquire as to whether the matter you
wish to discuss is business or personal."

Charlotte leveled an even stare at him. "Neither."

"Well then." His smile broadened. "The viscount and I were just
concluding our business. For *today*," he added.

"Then my timing is perfect." Just as she'd practiced, Charlotte took
a deep breath and swept into the room as if she owned the place.

A trio of long windows on the opposite wall had been thrown open
to the sea breeze, filling the room with a heady mixture of sunshine and
salt air. With Miss Pence's instructions foremost in her mind, Charlotte

affixed the imaginary egg to her head and completed her journey across the room.

Helping herself to the empty chair, she settled in and smoothed her skirts before regarding the obviously shocked astronomer with her most casual expression. Only when the door closed behind Hambly's friend did she allow a smile.

Miss Pence would have given her high marks for not only the execution of her walk across the room but also for the effort required to keep the imaginary egg balanced atop her head when her knees were about to buckle.

A lady does not spartle about nor wear a grinagog's expression when crossing a room, Miss Pence was fond of saying. Charlotte had gone to three of Grandfather's dictionaries before translating the statement. Thus, she walked as demurely as she looked, which was without grin or expression.

It wasn't easy.

"Good afternoon," she said pleasantly.

"Not particularly," Viscount Hambly muttered as he sank back against his chair. He seemed to gather his wits and his manners at the same time. "To what do I owe the honor of this visit, Miss Beck?" He shook his head. "No, first, how did you find me?" A pause. "Did Pembroke send for you?"

"Pembroke? Who is that?"

"Never mind," Alex said with a sigh. "Go on with your answer, and do make it brief."

"Interesting story, actually." And one she hoped never to admit to in its entirety. "Your houseman Franz is most helpful."

"So he told you where to find me, did he?"

"I'm afraid he extracted a promise for me not to tell."

Hambly smiled, a welcome change to his rather grouchy personality. "And yet you just did."

Ignoring his comment, she spied a folded copy of the *Times* in the trash bin and retrieved it. "I see you've read today's paper."

"No, actually I've been quite busy. My solicitor, however, was kind enough to bring a copy."

He glanced toward the window and Charlotte followed his gaze. A lovely view of a park beckoned—a scene begging to be painted—but she ignored it to return her attention to the viscount.

"If you've been informed of what the *Times* has printed today, then you understand my predicament," she said. "Our predicament, actually."

The nobleman's laughter held no amusement. "I fail to see how the two of us are bound together in anything resembling a predicament. There was no mention of me in any of the glorious descriptions of your recent performance."

Charlotte lifted a gloved hand to adjust a well-placed curl. "Then you've not spoken to your mother. Because you and I were recently associated in that unfortunate incident—"

"Unfortunate incident?" He shifted positions to offer a look that told her nothing and yet spoke of strong feelings. Slowly, he brushed his knuckle against the purple smear beneath his eye. "Would that be your unfortunate tumble from the heavens or the unfortunate demise of your fan? Or perhaps you're speaking of the unfortunate way your uncle called me out in front of several hundred of my mother's closest friends and then offered up a souvenir of the moment?"

"As I recall, Viscount Hambly, it was your brother Martin who suffered the indignity. At least that is the man to whom my friend Colonel Cody claims he was introduced." She paused to revel in his obvious discomfort. "Never mind. It's none of my business which Hambly twin is which." Another pause. "Though you are Alexander, aren't you?"

This time he responded with a glare. Charlotte suppressed a grin.

"In any case," she continued, "your mother appears to be doing everything in her power to see that the Beck family is shunned from polite society."

"Funny," Viscount Hambly said. "It appears you're doing fine in that endeavor without my mother's assistance."

"Fair enough." Charlotte shrugged. "At least where it concerns the events that occurred at the Wild West show. But I assure you it was all a big misunderstanding."

"Is that so?"

"Yes." She studied her nails then lifted her gaze to meet his stare. "You see, the colonel and my father are old friends, so I'm quite comfortable in his presence, and many of his associates have been visitors to Papa's ranch. When it was suggested that I might perform a postscript to the performance, the timing was most unfortunate. I'd just exchanged words with Gennie, you see."

"Truly, Miss Beck, none of this is my concern." He reached for a stack of papers, but she beat him to them.

Charlotte held the pages against her chest. "Do humor me a moment longer."

His panicked expression was almost amusing. "Please," he said slowly. "You're holding my career in your hands. Quite literally."

She suppressed a laugh and concentrated on her purpose. "Then I can safely assume I have your full attention."

"You do, but I would appreciate it if you gave my notes back."

"Of course," Charlotte said sweetly. "Just as soon as you see to giving my family their reputation back. Starting with telling your mother to cease and desist with her insistence on cutting Gennie and Papa. Not that Papa's here in London, but he'll be furious when he finds out I am the cause of his banishment from proper society."

"Banishment, is it?" the astronomer echoed. "I refuse to discuss anything with you until I am given my property back."

He made a grab for the pages, but Charlotte moved too fast for him. "Viscount Hambly, do control yourself," she said as she scrambled to her feet. "I mean you and your scribbling no harm. I merely wish to be heard."

"Indeed, I've heard you." He rose slowly. "What is it you'd like? Shall I arrange an appointment with my mother?"

Her eyes widened. "Do you think that will help?"

"Miss Beck, I know very little about what might work to persuade my mother to do anything."

This she hadn't expected. "But you're her son. Surely you can persuade the countess of certain facts."

"The countess prefers to consider only such facts as support her current position." With catlike grace, the astronomer moved around the desk. "So unfortunately, you've come all the way to Greenwich for nothing."

Charlotte took a step backward and collided with the chair, but she held tight to the papers the viscount seemed intent to retrieve. "I would just like some measure of justice for my family."

"Starting with absolution from the countess and her well-placed friends for any sins you or your kin might have committed?"

Charlotte grasped the pages tighter. "Yes."

"And this would be for what purpose? To enhance your standing in society?" he asked in a bitter, almost mocking tone as he moved toward her. "Perhaps to secure a marriage to some poor peer of the realm?"

"Honestly, Viscount Hambly, I couldn't care one whit for standing in society. And as for marriage, I've no interest in hurrying the inevitable, be it to a peer of the realm or someone else."

"And yet you're quite anxious to see that your family's standing is secure. Interesting."

He made a quick move toward her, but Charlotte was faster, ducking under his arm before he could catch her. "Do control yourself," she told him, her back to the door.

"I assure you control is no issue of mine." His gaze swept the length of her. "Nor am I swayed by children posing as adults."

His next lunge just missed her as she scooted between the desk and long wall of books. "Really, sir. You're being quite difficult. And I'll have you know I'm well removed from the nursery."

"Hence the maturity displayed in holding hostage valuable research materials."

"I'm going to ignore that." She attempted a cursory glance at the too-handsome nobleman. "You do not appear to be advanced in years either."

"Shall we compare?" he said as if daring her to respond. "I'll soon celebrate my twenty-sixth birthday." He paused. "And you?"

He appeared ready to vault over the desk, so Charlotte clutched the papers tighter. "I prefer to discuss a mutually agreeable arrangement." At the lift of his brow, she hurried to explain. "I've a plan whereby the mess I made will be repaired and, in the process, your mother will be the envy of her friends. You see, I've no small measure of influence with Colonel

Cody. The proprietor of the Wild West show whose acquaintance you recently made?"

"I'm no idiot, Miss Beck, though I confess interacting with you leaves me feeling like one. You didn't come all the way to Greenwich to talk about a Wild West performer." Fists clenched, his attention fell to the pages. "Time is a precious commodity today, so please return my property and state your business so that I may go about mine."

"All right." She cleared her throat and prepared to sound as formal as possible. "On behalf of Colonel Cody and the Beck family, I wish to extend an invitation for the countess to perform a stunt especially devised for her at an upcoming Wild West show performance."

Alex Hambly leaned forward to rest both palms on the desk. And then he laughed.

Charlotte felt heat climbing into her cheeks. "I find nothing funny in that statement, Viscount Hambly. Nothing at all."

"Is that so?" He chuckled again. "Then you know nothing of the countess. My mother astride a racing pony? Or perhaps aiming a weapon at some unfortunate man's hat? I think not."

Of all the nerve. The man hadn't given her idea so much as a decent consideration before scoffing at it.

"I prefer to hear this from the countess," she said, "so if you'll be so kind as to make that introduction, I'll—"

The astronomer made a grab for the pages and came up with half of them. The left half, while she still held what hadn't torn off. When he realized what he'd done, the viscount reached for the remaining pages. Charlotte turned her back to hold the research between herself and the wall.

"Now that was completely uncalled for," she said.

"Miss Beck," he said through clenched jaw. "You've ruined my research notes, caused me bodily harm in my own home, and stolen my grandfather's pocket watch."

She peered over her shoulder. "I returned that watch."

"Nonetheless," he said as he spread the ruined pages on the desk, "you'd do me a great favor if you left." He met her stare and she quickly turned away. "Please, just leave."

For the second time that day, tears threatened. This was not at all going as planned.

Behind her, the shuffling of papers stopped. "Turn around," he demanded.

She complied, wiping her eyes with her free hand.

"You're crying." He sighed and pulled a handkerchief from his pocket then thrust it toward her. "Go on. Take it." When she didn't immediately comply, he added, "It's clean."

Charlotte almost smiled.

"Dribble on yourself then." The viscount muttered something about stubborn women then dropped the handkerchief on the desk between them and went back to his work.

Well, that did it. Charlotte grabbed the handkerchief and dabbed at her eyes then tossed the remains of Alex Hambly's precious scribbling onto the desk and pointed the soggy handkerchief at him. "Yes, I am stubborn," she said. "But I'd much rather be stubborn in pursuit of righting a wrong I caused than stubbornly selfish for my own sake."

He froze, and the page fell from his hand. Charlotte watched it flutter to the floor, some sort of diagram with a string of gibberish beneath it, and land upside down under the spindly legs of an old brass telescope.

Papa always said she would catch more flies with honey, and this was a fly that begged to be caught. Charlotte tucked the handkerchief into her sleeve, bent down, and grasped the torn edge of the paper.

"Miss Beck! Mind the—"

"What?" Charlotte rose abruptly and collided with something sharp that sent her stumbling backward. She landed in a tangle of skirts as a pair of hands reached around her to catch a tumbling telescope.

The earl and his treasure clattered to the ground beside her, and the tripod followed, slamming against Charlotte's foot with a painful thud. The astronomer sat with the telescope cradled in his arms.

Her foot and her backside throbbed, but the viscount appeared to have emerged from the fracas unscathed. His stargazer, however, wasn't as lucky.

"Is it bent?" she asked as she pushed the contraption off her.

Alex Hambly ran his hand through his hair then looked away. "Miss Beck," he said in a tight string of words, "I am a gentleman and thus I must inquire as to whether you've been injured."

She did a quick inventory of her condition and shook her head. "Nothing permanent."

He muttered something that sounded like "a pity," then gently set the telescope aside and climbed to his knees to move closer. "Miss Beck, has anyone ever told you that you're a menace?"

The question should have stung, but Charlotte put it off to the combined indignities of a black eye and a broken telescope, both directly caused by her. "No," she said as sweetly as she could manage, "you're the first."

Viscount Hambly dipped his head then lifted it again to regard her with an even stare. Goodness, he was handsome, even with the black eye. If he weren't so *very* old at five and twenty…

And yet he was, and completely wrong for her in so many ways. Worse still, she became a complete embarrassment every time she came near him.

Out of the corner of her eye, Charlotte spied the item she'd bent to retrieve. Leaning away from the nobleman, she grabbed the torn paper and offered it to him. When he merely stared at it, she let the page drop between them.

The enormity of her situation hit Charlotte harder than the telescope. Humiliation, her all-too-constant companion, delivered the next blow, and her lower lip began to quiver.

"Miss Beck."

Viscount Hambly's image swam before her through the tears. "What?"

"Shall we strike a bargain?"

Charlotte swiped at her damp cheeks with her sleeve and tried to sniffle delicately. "What sort of bargain?"

He climbed to his feet, then removed the remains of the tripod and offered her his hand. The viscount's grip was firm, his expression impassive as he hauled her to her feet then set her hat to rights.

"The bargain is this." He turned her toward the door then ushered her forward with his palm against the small of her back. "I shall do as you ask and see that my mother is present at…" He paused to step over an errant page from his notes. "To which performance shall I deliver her?"

Charlotte stopped short. She hadn't thought that far. A trip to Earls Court was in order, for the colonel certainly had to be informed of the plan.

"Perhaps I should collect that information and send a note," she said. The viscount pressed her forward toward the door, and she complied as she tried to think. "I'm sure Colonel Cody will wish for her to practice at least once. Maybe more."

"Fine, yes, anything you say."

"Wait." Once again she stopped. This time, she turned to face him, and his hand slid against her waist in a most disconcerting fashion. "I—um, that is—you'll not forget that there is a greater purpose behind this bargain."

He looked away, and Charlotte took the opportunity to stare. His lashes were long and dark, and his chin quite well-shaped. Once the injured eye healed, his features would be impossibly perfect.

"The greater purpose," he echoed, "is for me to see that I am no longer plagued by your presence."

Now that really was uncalled for. "I beg your pardon," she said with the appropriate balance between indignity and propriety.

He gestured to the remains of the telescope. "A fine instrument has been irreparably damaged at your hands, Miss Beck."

"Fine, *Viscount* Hambly." All thoughts of Miss Pence went out the window as she pointed her finger at the arrogant nobleman. "Send me a bill and I'll be happy to pay for it." She paused. "Or any other damages, with interest. I will, however, hold you to our bargain."

The nobleman gave her a weary glance. "Did we reach terms?"

"We did. Your mother's cooperation in returning the Beck family to society's good graces in exchange for…" The rest of the bargain escaped her. "I'm sorry, what is my part of this?"

Again, he pointed her to the door, now only a few paces away. "You will go from this place and leave me, never to return. And we shall vow that this conversation is never to be repeated."

Charlotte crossed the threshold into the hall, then turned to shake his hand. "Agreed. And lest you think I will be tempted to go back on our bargain, you should know my time in London grows short. I've made arrangements to attend Wellesley College once my duties in New York and at court are satisfied."

There. She'd said it.

Strange that she'd chosen the irritating Hambly fellow to be the first to know her plans.

"Wellesley?" His gaze showed more than a small measure of skepticism. "Dare I ask what you shall be studying?"

"I'm quite interested in several fields of study. Perhaps something that will allow me to assume a role in Father's company." Charlotte worked to keep a smug expression off her face as she allowed her gaze to land on the broken telescope. "If ever you decide reimbursement is required—"

"I won't." And Alex Hambly closed the door in her face.

8

A lady's social calendar must be filled at all times,
even when it isn't.

—*MISS PENCE*

June 14
Beck House, London

"An invitation?" Charlotte slid down the banister and landed beside
Grandfather's houseman in a most inelegant fashion. But Grandfather
was napping and Gennie had gone to the milliners for a fitting, so what
happened unobserved did not have to be admitted.

She snatched the note off the tray and slipped into Grandfather's
library. It was the one she'd hoped for, the queen's garden party on the castle grounds. And she'd been included along with Gennie and Grandfather.

Charlotte danced in circles across the carpet then fell onto the settee, the invitation clutched to her chest. The viscount had proven
himself a man of his word.

Even if he was a grump.

Were he more agreeable, Charlotte might have asked Viscount
Hambly how he managed to convince his refined mother to don an
Indian headdress and allow herself to be transported across the arena
sidesaddle behind one of Red Shirt's warriors. Charlotte had heard from

the colonel that persons of high character were now lining up to take their turn in the show. Which meant she could stop fretting about losing not only her social standing but also her freedom. Surely Papa would not hold against her what had been so artfully and cleverly repaired.

A sound at the door alerted her to the houseman's presence. "Miss Beck, there are others."

She grinned. "Put them on Grandfather's desk, and I'll sort through them."

The servant returned with a basket filled nearly to the top with calling cards and notes, then hastened to answer the doorbell. The queen's invitation tucked safely aside, Charlotte upended the basket and watched as its contents landed in a pile.

"What have we here?"

Charlotte swiveled to see Uncle Edwin watching her.

"Aren't you popular?" he said as he moved to the window. Curtains green as the baize on the gaming table Grandfather hid behind the folding screen blocked all but a sliver of the morning light.

As Edwin lifted the heavy fabric to peer out, Charlotte noticed the lines of his face made her miss Papa all the more. But while Papa wore his handsome features as if he had no idea he possessed them, Uncle Edwin seemed very aware of the Beck charm.

"Are you unwell, Uncle?"

"Unwell?" He stepped away and allowed the curtain to fall back into place. "Nothing of the sort. Though I am a bit confused by something."

She dropped Lady Stanton's invitation for tea back onto the pile. "What is that?"

His stare was even, his face expressionless. And yet something about his posture made Charlotte sit a little straighter in her chair.

"How is it that you've gone from social pariah to London's darling, Charlotte?" He moved toward Grandfather's chair then chose the settee, where he sprawled across the length of it. "Just this morning I read in the *Times* that your shameless Wild West performance is now the behavior to be copied. And I must wonder, is it a coincidence that the first to imitate you was Hambly's mother? Who did you influence? I guess it was either the heir or his spare." He lifted his head to look at her. "Your charms are considerable, though you're a bit young to begin using them to your benefit. Especially when it involves possible control of our companies being handed over to a Hambly."

Her eyes narrowed. "Uncle Edwin!"

He shifted positions to stare at the painting above the mantel, a decently done oil of the Beck ancestral home Charlotte had painted on her last visit. It was a much better piece than her image of the night sky over Denver that Grandfather insisted on hanging in his bedchamber. Strangely, she'd always been drawn to capturing the constellations in paint but as yet had never quite managed to satisfy herself that she'd done them proper justice.

"Never mind," Uncle Edwin said. "But you did something. Paid someone off."

"I paid no one. I promise."

"And yet you got exactly what you wanted and without lifting a finger to achieve it."

Charlotte pretended to study the gilt edge of the nearest invitation as her mind sorted through several possible responses to the statement. Before she could settle on one, Uncle Edwin began to laugh.

"What's so funny?" she managed as she attempted not to look relieved.

He sobered but continued to stare at the painting. "I was just thinking how like the father the child has become."

"Thank you," she said sweetly, "but I wonder how much like my mother I am." Charlotte held her uncle's gaze, praying her direct request for information might actually gain her some insight into the mysterious mother she barely remembered. "No one seems to want to talk about Georgiana Beck. Do you know why, uncle?"

When he merely returned her stare, Charlotte warmed to the topic. "When I was very small, I thought that perhaps Papa was trying to deflect me from my grief by refusing to discuss my mother. As I grew older, I suspected perhaps it was his own grief he'd been deflecting."

Uncle Edwin gently tugged at his collar.

"But you and Grandfather…" She shrugged. "What possible reason could—"

"Enough, Charlotte," he snapped. "Let it go."

Silence hung heavy between them. Retorts Charlotte longed to say mingled with the petitions she sent heavenward to form a jumble of words and thoughts that made little sense. All she could manage was a sigh as she pretended to sort the invitations that now swam beneath a shimmering of tears.

After a few minutes, Uncle Edwin sat up and rested his elbows on his knees. "How old are you?"

Charlotte glanced up sharply at the odd question. "I'll be eighteen soon."

He nodded. "Older already than your mother was when you were born."

She froze. "I didn't know that."

"Sixteen, she was, or possibly no more than seventeen. At least that's what I recall." His brows rose. "Pretty thing, too. Common of birth but *most* uncommon of countenance." Uncle Edwin paused. "You resemble her. Still, you're a Beck through and through."

And then her uncle's interest in the taboo topic waned, or perhaps his mind had wandered to memories he'd rather not discuss. Whatever the reason for his silence, Uncle Edwin appeared to know Mama quite well. Charlotte sat very still, hoping he would continue.

Unfortunately, the far away expression dissipated, and Uncle Edwin's normal mocking scowl returned. He gestured to the bookcase. "I see how you devour Father's books on business. I fear Mr. Smith's theories are mostly beyond my comprehension, though there are a few concepts I find intriguing."

"Such as?" she asked, hoping to engage him in this conversation in order to somehow turn back to the former one.

He easily warmed to the topic of the systems of political economy, pausing only when she smiled. "Ah, so you did not believe me?"

"Forgive me," she said. "It's just that very few find my interest in…never mind."

"No," he said. "I am interested in what you think."

She shook her head. "Honestly?"

"Yes. For instance, what is your opinion on the consequences of the individual's pursuit of his own gain? Smith has his opinion, which of course you know."

Charlotte shrugged. "Yes, well, I tend to agree with Mr. Smith that the self-interest of individuals can cause certain biases."

"Indeed. And would you also agree that it can blind a good businessman"—he paused to nod in her direction—"or business woman, causing them to make mistakes?"

"Yes, I suppose."

"As do I. Take, for example, Father's friend the Earl of Fensworth." Her uncle paused only a moment. "The Hambly family has made no secret of wanting ownership of our Northumberland mines. Their properties to the north and south of the mine aren't producing as well as ours, and the earl doesn't take that sort of loss in competition well. Then there's the Leadville issue."

"Leadville issue?"

"The earl, your friend Hambly's father, got to Summit Hill before your papa did. He snatched up what he thought was prime property and went to work mining it. Daniel saw the value in that location and bought a piece of land adjacent to it."

"And?" Charlotte said.

"And ever since, the old man's had nothing but trouble and Daniel's had to fend off numerous claims that he's somehow taken the silver off Hambly land. Not sure how he might have done that, but the claim's been made. Trouble is, now neither plot's worth much. Seems a little pointless to squabble over something that's got no value, doesn't it? Especially since the issue came between Hambly and Father. They were close friends once, but your grandfather doesn't take kindly to outsiders who pose a threat to his family."

Interesting, especially given the fact she'd been told all the nonsense between the families had been over some racing bet. As much as she did not want to believe Uncle Edwin, a business issue seemed more logical than trouble over gambling. And it certainly explained Grandfather's adamant refusal to attend the Hambly event.

"I fail to see what that has to do with me." She shrugged. "I've no interest in such things."

"You should develop one," Uncle Edwin snapped. "What belongs to you will, upon your marriage, be under the control of your husband." He shook his head and rose. "Just stay away from Hambly and his sons."

Charlotte went back to her work. "No reason for concern. I'll not be seeking out either of them. Any association will be purely social and only when unavoidable." She set two invitations aside. "You have my word. Now I wonder if I might extract a promise from you." Charlotte continued to shift the letters around on the desk though her thoughts were no longer on them. "Promise me someday you'll tell me more about my mother."

Uncle Edwin looked down at her. "I know very little."

"That's more than I know." Charlotte pushed away from the desk and stood, fortifying her courage and squaring her shoulders. "No, that's not true. I have memories. Nonsensical thoughts about things that might have happened."

"I'm the last person you should ask about Georgiana." Uncle Edwin moved toward the door. "That woman cost me my inheritance." He stomped out of the library.

"Edwin," Grandfather snapped from a distance. "A moment of your time. Upstairs, please."

When her uncle's footsteps ceased and a door closed somewhere on the second level, Charlotte crept up the stairs, avoiding the third step. Finding the room where the men had gone was easy. She merely followed the sound of angry but unintelligible voices. Pressing her ear against the door, Charlotte tried to understand some of what was being said, but the words carried no meaning when filtered through the heavy wood. Uncle Edwin's voice was the louder of the two, but Grandfather seemed to speak more.

Then came a crash.

Charlotte yanked on the knob, but the door refused to budge. "Let me in," she called, her heart racing.

When Uncle Edwin finally opened the door, she pressed past him to see her grandfather sprawled on the floor beside his bed. Contents of a breakfast tray lay in a broken mess beside him, and shards of a ruined plate littered the carpet. One of the curtains surrounding the ancient canopied bed had been torn loose and hung in uneven crimson folds.

"What happened?" she asked, but neither man answered. Heedless of the broken china, Charlotte ran to her grandfather and fell to her knees beside him. "Get help," she shouted to her uncle as she cradled Grandfather's head in her lap. When she turned around, Uncle Edwin was gone.

"Fensworth," Grandfather said as his eyes fluttered open. "Bring him to me."

"The earl?"

He managed a nod then closed his eyes. Charlotte took a deep breath to calm her racing heart. "Don't be silly," she said, smoothing his silver hair back from a nasty knot rising on his temple. "Uncle Edwin is fetching your physician."

At least she hoped he was.

Her grandfather wrapped his fingers around her arm. "Fensworth must come. Tell him that."

She regarded her grandfather in silence. Mama had taken to speaking in circles and making nonsensical requests just before the sickness took her. That much Charlotte did remember, though through the filter of the understanding of a five-year-old.

Pressing her ear to Grandfather's chest, she heard the strong, even beat of his heart. *Don't take him, Lord. Please.*

Her name rumbled against her cheek as Grandfather tugged on her arm. "Charlotte," he repeated when she did not immediately respond. "Look at me when I speak."

Now that was the grandfather she knew. Charlotte lifted her head to see him regarding her with the beginnings of a smile. Though the color in his cheeks did not resemble his normal appearance, neither did he seem to be heading for the grave.

"Darling," he said slowly, "I assure you I'll not be making my amends before Jesus just yet."

Charlotte swallowed hard then affected what she hoped would be a convincing smile. "Good," she said lightly, "then you'll not mind helping me clean up this mess. You've been quite naughty."

"Indeed I have." He attempted to rise to his elbows but only succeeded with Charlotte's help. "Though I warrant you are the only one in my household to use the banister to shortcut the stairs today, which puts us at an even standing on the naughty list."

Her face flushed. "I'll neither admit nor deny this."

"Spoken like a true Beck." He struggled into a sitting position. "Now, about this request of mine. Shall I send a servant to do what I'd prefer my granddaughter would?"

The clock on the mantel ticked loudly, while a street vendor's call from the road below drifted through the curtained window. Charlotte shifted positions and felt broken china crunch under her skirts.

"But Grandfather," she said gently, "might I inquire as to why?"

His brows gathered. "You may not."

"But you and he haven't spoken in years," she offered. "Why—"

"Charlotte, I've no patience for questions. If Fensworth's unable, bring his son. Alexander, not Martin. Wouldn't give you one whit for Martin." Grandfather leaned back against the edge of the bed and wiped a speck of his breakfast from his trouser leg. "That Martin, he's unwell. More unwell than even Fensworth knows. But then a father likes to believe his son's not…"

A door's slam and a commotion on the stairs alerted Charlotte that someone, perhaps the physician, had finally been summoned.

"Ignore my ramblings." Grandfather looked past her to the door, then shook his head. "Before they come to fuss over me, I need to know your answer. Will you take my message to Fensworth?"

"Yes, of course." She leaned back on her heels to rise, mindful of her recent promise to the aforementioned Hambly. "Perhaps a note is in order. Shall I fetch writing paper for you?"

He shook his head. "He will come."

"And if he is reluctant?"

Grandfather smiled and once again reached for her. She knelt again, allowing herself only the slightest wince as a sliver of Grandmother's best breakfast service jabbed her.

"You're a Beck, Charlotte, and you've a better head for figuring than even I do." He winked. "I'm sure you'll manage to convince him. Just promise me you'll not return alone."

She bit her lip, then nodded. "I promise."

9

When making the attempt to sway the attention of
a man of good quality, a lady must use good sense,
witty but sparse banter, and a healthy dose of femi-
nine wiles. Of course, the man must never be aware
of the attempt.

— *Miss Pence*

"You again." Alex Hambly might have closed the door except the Beck
woman already stood inside rather than out. "Franz told me it was
important, but he did *not* tell me..." He glanced over his shoulder at
the obviously amused servant then returned his attention to his unwanted guest. "As I recall, you and I had a bargain."

A hard-earned bargain. No one but he would know how difficult it
had been to convince his mother to make a spectacle of herself. A por-
tion of the credit went to Colonel Cody, who somehow bewitched the
countess into agreement. But he alone had accomplished the seemingly
unachievable feat of actually delivering her to Earls Court in the first
place.

"Technically our agreement is still intact." Charlotte Beck blinked
her impossibly green eyes, and for a moment Alex believed she was as
innocent as she appeared. "I am here to see your father, not you."

"Franz," Alex said to the grinning butler, "did you not tell our guest
that Father is at our home on the Heath?"

"I did not, M'Lord," Franz said.

"Well, he is." He turned back to Miss Beck, crossed his arms over his chest, and affected an authoritative look. "Thus I must ask you to return at a more convenient time."

Her smile disarmed him. "I would prefer that, Viscount Hambly," she said in her peculiar American accent, "or, better yet, not to return at all, but I've no choice. You must accompany me back to my grand-father's home immediately."

"I must?"

"Yes, immediately. Grandfather requires it."

"Is that so?" Alex's temper flashed. "Tell *Grandfather* that Alex Hambly refuses him."

A single brow lifted above her green eyes. "And what assurance do I have that you are Alex and not Martin once again playing at switching roles?"

"Simple. I've a birthmark in a rather delicate place." He did not, but watching the momentary surprise on Miss Beck's face was worth the jest. "Do you wish me to show it to you?"

"Delicate?" Again the perfectly arched brow rose. "Could you be more specific?"

"For goodness' sakes, woman. Do you not see the black eye your uncle gave me?"

Her lips turned up in a smile. "Of course I see it, sir, though as I recall, the person I witnessed in conversation with Colonel Cody was identified to me as Martin. Before I could be properly introduced that evening, the man in question fled the room."

"Martin is no astronomer, Miss Beck, and I am, as you learned when you stole my reason for being in the garden and offered it as your own."

She remained infuriatingly silent. Alex pressed on.

"Then you imposed yourself on my office at Greenwich and reduced a year's worth of research on that very same comet into ruins in a matter of seconds."

"Ruins?" Charlotte shook her head. "Such an exaggeration of an innocent—"

"The more I come to know you, Miss Beck, the more I am certain there is nothing innocent or harmless about you. Now, hear me when I tell you that I *am* Alexander Hambly. That being determined as fact, I will repeat my refusal to accompany you. And thus, do have a good day."

He looked past the Beck woman to Franz. "Get the door for her," he demanded, then turned his back on the both of them and started up the stairs.

Unfortunately, Charlotte Beck followed him.

He allowed her a few more steps and then, when he reached the first floor landing, stopped short. This time rather than colliding with him, the Beck woman nimbly slipped past Alex to stand between him and the upper floor.

"Now perhaps you'll listen to reason," she said.

Her position on the stairs put them eye-to-eye, giving Alex even more than his anger to consider. The American wore an expression of determination that, under other circumstances, he might have found attractive. On her, however, it only drove him to further resist her challenge.

"I've made a promise and I shall keep it," she said.

He shouldered past her and continued his walk upstairs but once again, she bested his pace and halted just ahead of him.

"I've just as little interest in spending more time with you as you have with me," she said.

"Obviously not," he snapped, accidentally inhaling the heady scent of her lilac perfume.

"Do not flatter yourself, sir." She peered around him toward the servant standing beside the partially open door. "Perhaps another bargain is in order."

"For what possible reason would I enter into an agreement with a woman whose sole purpose in life appears to be irritating me and ignoring the terms of any bargain she strikes?"

"I understand how it may appear that I…" She pursed her lips, and Alex had to look away.

Why of all the women in London did this one have to stand so close? He took a step backward and, had she not reached out to steady him, might have plummeted down the steps.

"Do take care, Viscount Hambly," she said. "Now as to this additional arrangement. I propose we suspend my vow to leave you alone only for such time as it takes for you to pay my grandfather his requested visit." She released her grip and lifted her gloved hand to cover her heart. "After that, we shall be back to our original terms."

He pretended to think a moment while he allowed his gaze to travel from her fingertips up the curve of her jaw to her lips and finally, to those green eyes. "No."

He turned his back on her. To his surprise, however, the brazen American snagged him by the arm.

"Truly," she said, "I shall never understand the stubbornness of men, even if I live to be thirty."

"Thirty, is it?" Alex resisted the temptation to remind Miss Beck he'd see thirty far too soon for comfort.

"Viscount Hambly, are you a man prone to wagers?"

"Never."

"I see." Her fingers tightened. "Just a friendly competition, then? One I'm likely to lose, I'm afraid."

Alex could only chuckle. What the woman lacked in good sense, she made up in tenacity. "All right, what's the wager? Not that I'm agreeing to it, mind you."

Wide eyes looked into his and then, slowly, she blinked. "A simple foot race."

His laughter echoed around the grand foyer and was joined, he thought, by Franz's chuckle. "You may go, Franz," he said, then waited until he heard the door shut and the butler's footsteps fade away. "Have you lost your mind?" he asked Miss Beck.

"I told you the results were heavily weighted in your favor." She affected a look he suspected was anything but innocent. "But I owe it to my grandfather to try to do as he asked."

"You're mad." She pursed her lips into the most delicious pout, and Alex was sunk. "All right then," he said. "Are there rules to this foot race?"

Miss Beck pointed to the front door below. "There are always rules." She leaned close. "And perhaps this time I shall even follow them." While he was laughing, she pressed past him. "Touch the doorknob and win."

Idiot that he was, Alex began to take the steps two at a time and easily passed her. Three steps from the bottom, Miss Beck slid past him on the banister and catapulted toward the door.

She reached out to touch the proposed finish line a millisecond before him then looked up into his eyes, beaming.

"I'll be waiting in the carriage, Viscount Hambly. I trust you want as badly as I to get this over with. Any stalling on your part would speak to the contrary." She gave him a sweeping glance. "And mark you as a man who does not place value on his honor."

Miss Beck then slid under his arm to open the door and step outside. A light rain had begun, and she walked through the mist as if impervious to it.

With a nudge, Franz, who had somehow returned undetected, offered Alex his hat and gloves.

"I don't suppose there's any way around this. She did best me in an almost fair contest," Alex said.

Franz leaned forward to peer at Miss Beck's retreating back. Alex joined Franz in his appreciation of the earl's granddaughter as she paused to look over her shoulder, and then allowed the driver to help her into the carriage. He caught sight of a slender ankle as it disappeared inside.

"M'Lord, were I to be so forward as to offer an opinion, which of course I am not..."

"No, of course not," Alex said, amused despite himself.

"I might consider any man a fool who opted not to do as that young lady requested," Franz continued.

"Would you now?" Alex snatched the proffered gloves and hat and stepped out the door. By the time he reached the carriage, the hat was on his head, both hands were covered with gloves, and Charlotte Beck was waiting.

He settled in across from her, and the carriage lurched into motion. "You cheated," Alex said as he adjusted his hat.

Miss Beck began to laugh. "You were bested by a girl." She bit her lip as if to stop further mirth. "But your secret is safe with me."

Alex's temper flashed. "I assure you I've no need for you to keep my secrets."

She rolled her eyes. "Aren't we the grumpy one? Don't you know you can catch more flies with honey?"

The carriage rolled over a bone-crushing spot in the road, rendering a quick response impossible. "What sort of odd American proverb is that?" he asked when he could manage it.

"It means—"

"No explanation necessary." Shifting positions, Alex looked at the wet, green expanse of Hyde Park rolling past. "I know what it means, Miss Beck. What I don't know is why your grandfather insists on an audience with a Hambly."

"You'll have to ask Grandfather." With another jolt, the carriage made a turn at the edge of the park. "Though I warn you not to get him overly excited. He collapsed while speaking with Uncle Edwin, and I'm very concerned it could happen again if he became angry."

"I see."

They rode the remainder of the way in silence, Charlotte obviously caught up in her thoughts, and Alex caught up in a dance of warring emotions: his mind on his conversation with Pembroke regarding the family's finances and his eyes watching Charlotte Beck.

Were she not completely unsuitable for him, both in intellect and age, considering a match with her might have held his interest. As it was, he merely observed her beauty; the way the gray London light slid across her high cheekbones and cast her face in an ever-changing pattern of shadows. Had he not seen ample evidence to the contrary, he might have thought her quite a lady. And when she'd pursed her lips on the stairs, it was all he could do not to kiss her right then and there.

Perhaps a decent kiss might improve her attitude.

"What?" she said when she caught him looking.

"Just thinking about your attitude," he said, "and how it might best be improved."

"Well, I never." She looked away, giving Alex a lovely view of her profile.

"A pity," he whispered.

When the carriage halted and the driver opened the door, Alex bounded out first, just for the opportunity to help Charlotte exit. His hands easily spanned her waist, and her head just reached his chin as her feet touched the ground.

"Thank you," she said and gestured for him to follow. Once inside, a liveried servant took over, and Charlotte Beck slipped into a room that appeared to be a library. "Remember my warning," she said over her shoulder. "I shall hold you responsible should any further harm come to Grandfather."

"And I shall hold *you* responsible for keeping to our bargain, Miss Beck. Remember I am here at your insistence," he called as she shut the library door.

Alex followed the servant up the stairs, to the door at the end of the hall. Two knocks and he was ushered into a room not unlike his own father's chambers. The Earl of Framingham sat in a chair near the window.

"I wondered which of you would come," the earl said. "Is your father unwell?"

"He is at the Heath," Alex said, "with no plans to return to London at this time."

"I see. Well, forgive me for not rising to greet you, but perhaps my granddaughter has told you some of the events of this morning." When Alex nodded, the earl shrugged. "A pity, this old age. I don't recommend it. Do come and sit."

Alex stepped into the room, noting immediately the incongruity of the painting over the fireplace. While the rest of the room could have belonged to any century prior to the current one, the depiction of the night sky over a collection of buildings—hung without benefit of a frame—was as fresh and modern as if it had been hung last week.

On closer inspection, Alex found the colors vivid, the brush strokes bold, and yet the effect subtle. The placement of stars, with Orion at its center, showed not only thought, but also great attention to detail. Though he did not recognize the work, this was obviously a painter of great talent.

"Nice, isn't it?" the earl said.

"Indeed."

"Charlotte painted it."

Alex shook his head. "Your Charlotte?" He struggled to match the woman he'd come to know with the work of art before him. "*That* Charlotte?" he finally managed.

The old man chuckled. "My granddaughter thinks it is abominable. She gave me great trouble about hanging it at all, so I gave in and hung it in here. She's persistent, that one." Beck regarded him with what appeared to be amusement. "So, how'd she get you here, Alex?" He steepled his hands. "You *are* Alex, aren't you?"

"I am, sir. As to your granddaughter's method of coercion…" Alex paused. "Suffice it to say it involved a foot race and a questionable means of emerging victorious."

The earl laughed. "Indeed, that would be my Charlotte. A pity she and the others will be leaving me soon for that debutante nonsense in New York. Never did think much of the idea of trolling for husbands by dressing girls in pretty clothes and parading them across a ballroom. That one's too smart to play at domestic bliss. I intend to see her educated." He lifted his hand as if to wave away the topic. "So, how is your brother?"

"My brother?" Alex studied the old man's face. "Martin is well, sir."

"Don't lie to me, son." The earl gripped the arms of his chair and regarded Alex with an even stare. "My family thinks me a doddering old man, and so long as that suits my purposes, I allow it. But make no mistake; I am by no means disconnected from things of importance in this city. Even those that are neither common knowledge nor spoken about."

Alex let out a long breath. "I see. Well, then, Martin is alive, but his well-being changes from moment to moment."

"That Martin is still alive is answer enough. Some die at war, while others merely lose their lives. Your brother was a good chap, as I recall. I warrant you still care for him well."

Without a fitting answer, Alex could only stare.

"Though I wish I could have spoken with your father, I confess I am glad you're here, Alex. You see, I know things," the earl continued. "Despite current circumstances, I know your father well. He loves both of you, but while his pride is strengthened by your accomplishments, his heart is softened by Martin's failures."

Alex leaned forward and rested his elbows on his knees. "Sir, might I inquire as to why you've summoned me?"

"As I said, I'd hoped for your father," Framingham said almost wistfully. "He'd understand. You cannot know the whole of it. You can, however, offer an absolution of sorts."

"I'm afraid I don't understand, sir."

"No, I'm sure you do not, but your father would." He eyed Alex curiously. "Hambly's in trouble, isn't he? Money in the coffers running low?"

"Sir," Alex said through clenched jaw, "I find your questions insulting."

"Yes," the old man said with a half-grin that Alex would have knocked off of anyone younger, "I suppose you would." The Earl of Framingham leaned back against the cushions and seemed to be considering what to say next. After a moment, he returned his attention to Alex. "Many years ago, your father was invaluable in handling an issue for me. With my demise bearing hard on my mind and my heart, I must make amends for the fracture I've allowed in our friendship."

"With all due respect, sir, I don't think a gambling loss between my brother and your son is worth all the fuss it's been given over the years."

The earl looked away, then slowly returned his gaze to Alex. "Is that what you think this is about? Some foolish wager over ponies?"

The question took Alex aback. "Well, sir, I had heard—"

"Forget what you've heard." The earl slammed his palms against his knees. "There was a time when pride ruled my decisions, and I kept things from innocents who should have been told the full truth. Your father called me a fool for what I did, and I'm here before you now to say he was right."

Alex shook his head. "I'm terribly sorry, but I don't follow."

"No, I don't suppose you would. Suffice it to say that I wish you to take a message to your father. An apology." He rose and went to a bedside table to retrieve a letter. "In the event your father did not come, I prepared this."

Alex extended his hand to take the letter, then met the old man's stare. "I'll see that he gets it."

"Beg his forgiveness for the hasty manner in which it was written and presented," the earl said. "But with age comes clarity, and I wish not to allow another moment to go by with these words unsaid."

"I see."

As the earl rose to say his good-byes, he added, "Thank you, young man, for allowing me to deliver this letter." He shrugged. "It does not make up for the one that should have been received, but I'll have to find another way to repair that." He chuckled wryly. "Perhaps Edwin will assist me in that endeavor, without his knowledge."

"Of course." Alex tried to decide whether the old man had lost his mind or was merely being extremely crafty.

He left not knowing which.

A lady's posture should be such that an egg balanced
on her head might stay in place no matter what her
activity. Keeping this in mind should prevent all
manner of bad posture.

—*MISS PENCE*

In his haste to leave the Beck home, Alex took the stairs two at a time
until he heard what sounded like crying. Curiosity bested his instinct to
run, and Alex slowed his descent. With each step lower, the sound
increased until he was fairly certain it came from behind the door Miss
Beck had recently slammed.

Interesting. Then he landed on the third step from the bottom and
the sound of protesting wood drowned out the whimpering.

Alex quickly moved past the broken step, but the damage was done.
Silence reigned, punctuated by a series of soft sniffles. Ignoring good
sense, he tucked the envelope into his pocket and rapped on the closed
door.

"Miss Beck?" When no response came, he knocked again. "Miss
Beck, are you unwell?"

He glanced around, hoping he might catch the attention of a servant, but saw no one. He heard another sniffle followed by a stifled sob
and reached for the knob.

Silence. Slowly he drew back his hand. The emergency must have passed. Alex backed away from the door and headed for the exit.

With one foot outside, he heard the wail.

"Oh, for the love of…" Alex reached the library door in long strides and, rather than knock, turned the knob and walked in without invitation.

He found Charlotte Beck with her back to him beside the fireplace, tossing bits of torn paper into a roaring fire. In between tosses, she let out soft sobs.

She obviously hadn't noticed his presence, so backing silently out of the room was an option. And yet as Alex let his eyes slide slowly down the length of the infuriating woman, he found it impossible to flee.

Miss Beck's hair had come loose from its pinnings and hung in waves down her back, shimmering with golden highlights. As she moved to throw more paper into the fire, loose curls teased the oversized bow at her waist.

Alex watched the slips of paper float from her fingers into the flames and thought of the report he'd stayed up most of the night rewriting because of her.

And the dented telescope.

And the black eye that was fading far too slowly for comfort.

The Beck woman paused in her efforts and seemed to be gazing at the flames. Slowly she knelt to retrieve a pale blue scroll of rolled fabric and held it at arm's length. From where he stood, Alex could see a bit of lace and a tangle of ribbons wrapped around it.

"Stupid corset." Miss Beck lifted the frilly item over her head and threw it into the fire. "Burn," she said as she reached for the poker and stoked the flames. "Figures the awful thing would be fireproof."

With a cry akin to a cat being skinned, the earl's granddaughter raised the poker and speared the burning corset with the skill of an Olympian. In an instant, the heat in the room became unbearable.

If he needed any proof for calling Charlotte Beck scandalous, it lay before him. In her agitated state, the American was likely to do anything. Someone should intervene. Find a servant or the earl himself to see to her. Failing that, perhaps move her gently away from the inferno and see her resting on the pillow-filled settee until help could be summoned.

Unfortunately, all Alex could do was laugh.

Miss Beck whirled around, an expression of surprise on her tear-stained face. "You!" Her eyes narrowed as Alex continued to chuckle. "How long have you been spying on me, Viscount Hambly?"

"Long enough," he managed through the laughter. "Are you done roasting corsets or do you have other items to burn?"

"If I had my Worth trousseau, I might throw it all in as well, seeing as how I'll not have need of it. Not that I was in any hurry to use it."

"I had no idea you were betrothed," he said with equal amounts of interest and disappointment.

"Heavens no." She swiped at her forehead then gave Alex what he figured was her version of an angry glare. "Now if you will do the gentlemanly thing and leave, I would be most appreciative."

Behind her, a wisp of smoke trailed toward the ceiling. Then came the scent of something other than logs—or a corset—burning.

"Miss Beck," Alex said, craning his neck to get a better view of the fire, "might a spark have landed on the rug?"

"A spark?" Her angry expression relaxed as she returned her attention to the fireplace.

As soon as Miss Beck presented her back to him, Alex found the source of the smoke—a small but quickly growing fire in the general area of her bustle and the oversized bow that covered it.

Alex hurdled over two ottomans and a tasseled stool to snag a pillow from the settee. Reaching Miss Beck just as the flames began in earnest, he gripped the pillow tightly and took aim at the fire.

Green eyes widened as the first swing made contact. "What *are* you doing?" she demanded as she scooted out of his reach.

Alex easily caught her. "You're on fire," he attempted to say, but the words were muzzled by the smoke. "Be still." He held her with one hand and swatted at the bustle with the other.

Rather than recognize his rescue attempt for what it was, Miss Beck shrieked, attempted to wriggle from his grasp, and finally grabbed the nearest object—thankfully another pillow from the settee—to fend off his blows.

Despite the American's efforts to the contrary, after three more swats, the emergency was over. Miss Beck's dress bow would never again see use, but the rest of the feisty female appeared to have emerged from the flames unscathed. Alex dropped the pillow and leaned forward to catch his breath.

"Are you insane?" Miss Beck shouted as she took aim once more with the cushion.

Alex dodged her poor attempt at retribution then wrested the pillow from her and tossed it aside. "Are *you*?" he countered.

"You hit me!" She pointed to her posterior. "On my...well, never mind where, but you accosted me!"

"I did no such thing! Your..." He pointed to the edges of her blackened bow. "That is, you were on fire."

She sat a moment and stared toward the fire, which still burned far too brightly for a June afternoon. "I'm ruined," she whispered.

And then the tears fell again.

Alex groaned. Why hadn't he made good on his exit when he could?

He reached into his pocket and once again offered the sniffling Miss Beck a clean handkerchief. This time she accepted it without comment.

He sat very still, hands in his lap, hoping her waterworks might dry up so he could leave. Instead, her soft crying increased until Miss Beck was sobbing uncontrollably.

"Miss Beck," he said above the wails. "I do not know how to comfort you."

"Just go." She blew her nose on his handkerchief then offered it back to him.

"No, keep it." Alex moved to the edge of the settee and leaned forward. Before he could stand, the American let out a stifled sob. "All right," he said as he turned to face her. "What's wrong? And do not blame your troubles on me. You were crying before you attempted to make a bonfire of your frock."

Miss Beck reached for the pillow wedged behind her back and held it against her chest. In the golden glow of the fire, her face seemed almost luminescent—all but her nose, which was bright red. Her lip trembled, and once again Alex felt his heart lurch. When she turned her green eyes—thick lashes wet with tears—on him, it was all he could do not to look away.

"You're right," she said softly, her voice trembling. "This time you've no part in my misery."

"This time?" He shook his head. "Miss Beck, were you not recently on fire, I might point out the error of your statement. However, I am here, albeit briefly, if you wish to tell me what's set you off. Should you choose to remain silent and allow me to leave blissfully ignorant of your troubles, I can accommodate that as well."

"Good." She crossed her arms over the pillow. "Go ahead and leave."

"Very well, then." Alex rose. "Good-bye, Miss Beck. It's doubtful we'll see each other again, as I understand you'll be traveling to New York soon and I shall be off to attend to family business in Leadville in a few weeks, so—"

Charlotte Beck's wail interrupted his exit and his good wishes for a safe voyage. As he watched the earl's granddaughter dissolve once again into a fit of sobbing, Alex knew he must either run while he could or sit back down and be a gentleman.

Biting back a complaint, Alex returned to his place on the settee. "All right, Miss Beck. I'll hear your troubles and offer comfort if I can. Do be brief."

"Brief?" She shook her head. "What sort of comfort is that?"

Alex shrugged. "Considering our past history…"

Miss Beck sighed. "Well," she said slowly, "I suppose you *are* partly to blame."

"I never said—"

Her lip stuck out in what he assumed was some sort of protest, and all words ceased.

"Do continue," he finally said.

The Beck woman let out a long breath and toyed with the tassels on the pillow for a moment. Then her attention turned to Alex. "I won't be going to New York after all. Worse, any chance of going to Wellesley in the fall is completely lost."

"I'm sure your grandfather will be pleased that you've chosen to lengthen your stay," Alex said. He didn't think he could manage anything more under the steady gaze of those impossibly green eyes.

"Actually," she said slowly, "my father has called me home."

"I see." He paused to think of an appropriate response. "And this has you upset."

"Upset?" Her voice rose. "Upset? Yes, I'm upset. I studied for weeks with that awful Miss Pence. I walked across rooms with an imaginary egg on my head and wore that torturous contraption, and for what?"

She looked at Alex as if he might actually know the answer. Or, for that matter, understand the question.

"Does he not know the lengths I went to bring this family back into the good graces of London society? Why, I alone made performing in the Wild West show a trend that all the fashionable set is now following."

Alex nodded. Bringing up his role in her social resurrection seemed imprudent.

"And all Papa can say is that I've once again behaved badly and need to come home." She gave him a sideways glance. "Home? After spending weeks in Paris enduring fittings for a half-dozen trunks full of clothing for my debut that I will now have no reason to wear? And if he's angry about this, imagine how he will feel when I tell him I wish to choose Wellesley over a husband. Can you feature it?"

This time he shook his head. "No," he bravely added.

"Exactly." Miss Beck tossed the pillow in the air, then watched it land on the carpet beside her feet. "Apparently he feels I am in need of greater supervision than I am receiving in London. According to my father, I am to remain with him until he feels I have grown beyond the stage where I will be an embarrassment to the family name. An embarrassment. He actually wrote those words. About me."

"I see." The words slipped out, and Alex cringed. "Did he indicate how long that might be?"

"Yes, actually," she said. "I'm free to leave when I'm either old or married. Not educated, mind you. Oh, no. Given his belief that I am nothing but trouble, he will likely forgo any discussion of my attending

Wellesley and consider nothing but a wedding. At least then I will be someone else's problem." Miss Beck eyed him directly. "Have you ever heard of something so awful? Using marriage as a means to an end?"

Again she fell into a bout of tears. Rather than speak, Alex kept his silence as her question plagued his conscience. What was the difference between Miss Beck's father betrothing his daughter to rid himself of the responsibility of her care and his own possible consideration of trading a well-placed marriage for a fresh infusion of money into dwindling Hambly coffers?

"Miss Beck," he said over the noise of her wails, "do listen a moment." When she quieted slightly, he continued. "You wish to attend university?" At her nod, he asked, "For what course of study?"

"I'm quite handy with numbers," she said with a sniffle. "I'm sure you'll think it quite humorous, but I wish to pursue a course of study in mathematics.

Mathematics? Not what he'd expected.

"I wished to be of some help to Papa or Grandfather in their businesses," Miss Beck continued, "but it appears the only course to freedom now is marriage. Though there's a risk even then that I might be wed to some fellow who feels I belong in the bedroom and not the boardroom."

"Ah." Alex tried not to think about that statement. "Then it's unlikely you'll spend much time away from your adventures. A pretty girl like you could be betrothed before sundown if she put her mind to it."

Miss Beck swiped at an errant tear then tucked the handkerchief into her pocket. "You're right. I could, couldn't I?" She paused. "But what if I marry a man only to discover he's more intent on keeping me home than my father?"

"Perhaps you could find a man whose interests are only financial. An

agreement for a quick marriage and hasty annulment could solve both
your problems."

"Annulment?"

"Yes, it's done all the time." He warmed to the topic. Anything to
keep her from bursting into tears again. "As long as the husband and
wife do not..." He paused to rethink the statement for propriety's sake.
"That is, should the marriage remain unconsummated, then the union
could be annulled. Or, at least that is my understanding."

"I see." She sat very still, her gaze steady and her nose still pink as
the evening sky at sunset. "So if my father does not come to his senses,
I could find a man and marry him..." She leaned forward and rested
her hands on her knees. "Thank you, Viscount Hambly," she said
abruptly. "You've given me much to consider."

"You're welcome." He inched to the edge of the settee. "If my serv-
ices are no longer needed then..." He cast a sideways glance at the earl's
granddaughter and found her deep in thought. "Yes, well, do have a safe
voyage home."

"Thank you," she said absently, "you do the same."

He started to stand, but her voice stopped him.

"Viscount Hambly?"

His momentary hope for escape plummeted. "Yes?"

"You mentioned Leadville. I've spent quite a lot of time there over
the years. Will you be traveling for business or pleasure?"

Alex exhaled slowly. "Business, I'm afraid."

She worried with the blackened end of her ribbon then flicked away
the burnt pieces littering her skirt, a frown on her face. "Leadville isn't
as awful as all that. It's not London or even Denver by any stretch, but
this time of year it's quite lovely."

Lovely or not, Colorado was just another stop on the campaign to see that his family remained solvent and his future remained clear of any further encumbrances. "I'll be meeting with a group of investors."

Her gaze collided with his. "Are your investors buying or selling?"

The question surprised him, as did the interest with which it appeared to be asked. "Buying."

"I follow mining stocks, as well as a few others, and things are going well as far as..." Charlotte shook her head. "I'm sorry. I rarely mention my silly interest in the stock market to anyone."

"Yes, well, stocks are one thing and actual profits on a mine another. And it's the mine we're considering selling." Alex straightened his cuff. "Production is down while expenses are going up, but the elevation of the property... Sorry. I'm sure you're not the least bit interested in all this."

"Go on," she said.

He slid the ingénue a sideways glance. Had he less sense, Alex might have thought Charlotte Beck was prying him for information. However, what possible use of these facts could she make, her statement regarding the stock market notwithstanding? Besides, an interest in their current conversation meant Charlotte Beck might not revert back to the prior one. And that meant he could make his escape.

"My interest in astronomy is no secret. Thus, I would like nothing better than to offer our property to the consortium of investors considering a location for a new, and quite impressive, observatory."

"An observatory in Leadville?" She looked away. "That's nothing I'd expect."

"Indeed." He ignored the urge to steer the conversation into safer waters. "The combined elevation and accessibility by railroad, along with the base of commerce that is already well established, makes the city an easy choice over any other locations in the west."

"How so?"

Giving to his excitement over the project, Alex told Miss Beck just how well suited the view of the heavens was from the remote mine and even mentioned the possible connection to Roeschlaub and the Goodsell Observatory. After a few minutes, he realized that he appeared to have lost his audience. Only when he ceased speaking did Miss Beck return her attention to him.

"Do continue, Viscount Hambly," she said.

"No, I've kept you long enough. I should be going."

She looked away, and he froze. Now what?

"Miss Beck?"

Then he heard the sniffle, and his heart sank.

"I should go," Alex said, knowing he couldn't leave the woman like this.

"Yes," she responded softly.

He willed his feet to move, but they refused. Instead, he returned to his place beside her. To his surprise, she turned to him and melted into his arms as her tears once again flowed. "There, there," he said, trying to deduce exactly what to do next. Awkwardly, he placed his hand on her shoulder and then slid it to the middle of her back to pat her softly. "It can't possibly be as bad as all that."

Miss Beck looked up, her long lashes wet and her eyes wide. "You don't know the half of it," she managed. "Everything's ruined."

"Miss Beck," he said as she rested her forehead on his shoulder, "the only thing I can see that's ruined is your bustle and ribbons." When her soft giggle reached his ears, Alex continued. "And if not being allowed to parade across a ballroom in hopes of snaring a man is your version of the worst thing that can happen, then you're sorely mistaken."

She peered up at him, her face still half-hidden by his coat. "There's much more to my plan than all that, so I must disagree."

"Well, of course you disagree. You're trained to believe this silliness is important. Why, I warrant there are plenty of men who don't care one whit for all of that nonsense. I certainly don't."

This seemed to take her by surprise. "You don't?"

"No. And neither should you. As I said before, a woman as lovely as you…" He leaned back to lift her head with his forefinger. Somehow his palm slid to cup her jaw. "Should…"

She blinked slowly. "Should?"

His thumb brushed away a tear then rested for a moment on her lips. Insanity beckoned in the form of a strong need to kiss some sense into the weeping female.

"Miss Beck…" He made a valiant attempt—and failed—to look away from her wide green eyes. "I've forgotten what I was going to say," he admitted.

She reached for his lapel. "Something about a woman as lovely as me, I believe."

Another tear slid down her cheek, and all measure of caution was lost. "Miss Beck," he said as his palm moved to rest against the nape of her neck, "are you truly asking me to admit that I believe you're lovely?"

"A lady would never ask such a thing," she said in a husky whisper.

"Agreed," he said, "though were you to ask, you *are* quite lovely."

The corner of her lips turned up in the beginning of a smile. "I am?"

"You know you are." He curled a tendril of honey-colored hair around his finger. "Though if I were to admit this, I would have to add that you're also the most irritating,"—he paused and lifted the curl to

touch his cheek—"aggravating,"—the strand fell from his hand to settle back against her shoulder—"impossible,"—Alex moved close
enough to inhale the sweet scent of lilacs mixed with the acrid smell of
burned fabric—"frustrating woman I've ever had the disadvantage of
meeting."

He was close enough to kiss her.

So he did.

Only after he kissed her a second time did he come to his senses.

"I—that is, well…I should be going." Alex rose, then looked down
on the lovely but impossible Miss Beck. "Avoid any further conflagra-
tions, please, for I shall not be present to put them out."

Thoughts of the kiss they'd just shared followed him out the door
and settled somewhere between his addled brain and his heart. A dan-
gerous woman, Miss Beck. Or she would be, if she lived long enough to
see adulthood.

Not that Alex intended to find out. He'd just proved that standing
too close to the flame, even when it was no longer smoldering, could get
a man burned.

11

Finding one's way in the world is simple: just follow
the most fortunate unmarried fellow in the room.
He's obviously going in the right direction, and so
will the lady who chooses him.

—*MISS PENCE*

As his boots found the front steps, Alex breathed a sigh of relief. Even
so, he caught himself glancing back over his shoulder at the room on the
southernmost corner of the first floor.

A golden glow still danced across the window panes and silhouetted
the figure of the green-eyed girl who watched him leave.

He turned away and stepped into the carriage. As much as he might
enjoy getting lost in the starry gaze of those green eyes, Charlotte Beck
was the last woman in the world he'd ever wed.

With each turn of the carriage wheel, his vow strengthened and his
thoughts turned to safer topics. He and Pembroke would make their
way to Colorado in less than one week. The timing was excellent, as
Alex had projected another passing of Jacob's Comet during their week
in Leadville.

With his paper on the subject receiving much positive attention in
the scientific community, Alex hoped to find additional proof for his
theories on the comet before the next international gathering of
astronomers in Zurich. The Astronomer Royal had already added him

to the delegation, allowing him to give a presentation that would seal his career with the observatory.

No minor feat for someone his age. Alex grinned. Though the Beck woman thought him old, his colleagues tended to dismiss him for the opposite reason.

"Thank you," Alex said when the carriage rolled through the gates.

He made quick work of retrieving his papers, stuffing them into his satchel, and then stepped out into the upstairs hall. A servant met him, tears streaming down her face.

"Did you hear the news, sir?" she asked.

"News?" He shook his head and shifted the satchel to his other hand. "No, what news?"

"Your father," she sobbed. "He's dead, sir."

"Dead?" His mouth barely wrapped around the word as he struggled to let it into his heart. As far back as Alex could remember, he'd thought of his father as an old man. With his thick patch of gray hair and the wrinkled features of the ancestors who decorated the walls of the ancestral home at Hampstead Heath, he had always appeared older than the other lads' fathers. Alex had learned early on to cease comparison and merely think of Father as one who neither aged nor would ever die.

It was folly. And now he was gone.

"What happened?" he managed, but the maid had already fled, leaving him to his questions.

Alex made his way to his mother's chambers, where he found the countess seated in the chair beside the window. At his entrance, she looked up with a weary expression.

"You've heard."

"So it's true," Alex said. "What happened?"

"A quiet end. He took his evening meal at the Spaniards Inn with great gusto then went home and slept soundly. The maid found him mid-morning. He was already…" She paused to wipe away her tears. "Yes, well, I'm glad he had his night at the Spaniards Inn. It's fitting."

"Indeed." Of all the dining establishments and pubs near the Hambly home, the old pub was indeed his father's favorite spot to dine. Between those in his employ and those who called him neighbor, Father rarely had to dine alone at the Inn. He was a different man in Hampstead Heath than he was in London, as if he wore the clothes of nobility looser the closer he got to home.

"Do you think he enjoyed himself at the Inn?" his mother asked. "I wonder whether the meal was a good one."

A ludicrous question to be sure, but grief knew no logic. And for all their differences, no one could claim his mother did not love his father.

"I'm sure it was a fine last meal among friends," he managed.

Her gaze lifted to meet his stare. "The responsibility as head of the family is now yours."

The truth, and Alex knew it. Yet he needed his mother to admit the situation. "But I am the spare. Look to your elder son for leadership. Isn't that what he's been bred for?"

"No," she said softly. "But *you* have."

Her admission took him aback, as did the lack of guile in her expression. When he looked into her eyes, he saw only fear. Her expression softened. "You always were the one who looked to the stars. Your father, he despaired of Martin's place in the world, but you he never doubted."

"He might have mentioned that, don't you think? Perhaps one of those times he asked me to impersonate my brother. I grew used to the idea that Father thought there was only one of us," Alex shot back, bitterness lacing his tone.

"Martin is the heir but you—" She paused. "You were always your father's—"

"I am the spare. Leave me to it. I never wanted Martin's place or his responsibility." He took three steps toward the door, then thought better of his actions and turned around. "Forgive me."

"There is nothing to forgive, darling. I know the responsibility for the family was not meant for your shoulders." She clasped her hands, eyes downcast. "And yet it appears the Lord has chosen you for it all the same."

That his mother mentioned the Almighty at all stunned Alex. While he could not look at the heavens and not think of their Maker, the countess had never professed such a belief.

"Alexander," she said softly. "Your father is lost to the grave and Martin is lost to his nightmares. You're all I have." Her fingers strayed to his sleeve, but stopped shy of grasping his arm. Instead, her gaze captured his. "Please do not leave me penniless. I'll accept any terms."

How easy it would have been to turn and walk away, leaving his mother and, by default, Martin, to their own devices. But Alex knew his conscience would never allow it.

"Very well. I shall have Pembroke draw up something that bypasses Martin's authority on any business transaction." He offered his mother a curt bow. "Upon your signature, I shall do all in my power to keep this family from ruin. I only ask in return that you do the same for Martin and keep the seventh Earl of Fensworth safe in my absence. I can no longer fetch him from wherever he's run if I am busy seeing to the family's interests. I'm sure Pembroke can recommend a minder for him. Someone with the authority to see to Martin's best interests and overrule any poor decisions he might make while I am away. Someone who will be kind even when Martin is not."

Her nod was slow as a lone tear slid down her cheek. "As you wish," she whispered.

"Fine." He paused. "There are things I will need to attend to outside of London. Visiting the Leadville property is one of them. It may require my extended absence, but I give you my word I will return."

She swiped at her damp cheek with her sleeve. "I see."

"My departure will be rescheduled for after the funeral, of course."

"Of course." Her gaze fell to the carpet. "I am not heartless, Alex," she said. "I hope someday you will forgive your father for his inability to show his love equally to his sons. Perhaps when you have sons of your own, you will understand."

Several responses bit at his tongue, but out of respect, Alex spoke none of them aloud. He turned his back and walked out. At the first opportunity, he retrieved the letter and crumpled it in his hand. Whatever the elder Beck wished to say, it was far too late now.

Alex stepped outside to find his carriage waiting. "Heading to Greenwich now, sir? Shall I deliver you to the train station?" the driver asked as Alex tossed his satchel into the carriage and climbed in after it.

"Pembroke's office."

The driver tipped his cap. "Bond Street, then?" He reached for the reins.

At Alex's nod, the carriage lurched into motion. And as they rolled out the gates, he couldn't help looking back to see his mother watching from the first floor window. When she lifted her hand to press her palm against the pane, he turned away.

A short time later, he walked into Will Pembroke's office unannounced, the solicitor's assistant trailing in his wake. Pembroke waved away the harried help.

"Been expecting you." Will set aside his work to give Alex his full attention. "My condolences on your father's passing. I assume you wish to postpone our trip."

"I'm afraid so. At least until certain arrangements can be made." Alex repeated the substance of his conversation with his mother.

"I can have those papers drawn up immediately."

Alex settled across from Will. "With the Leadville property disposed of, I can return to London without the burden of requiring a return visit. Correct?"

"Correct." Pembroke leaned forward to rest his elbows on the desk, then steepled his hands. "And the other matter?" At Alex's confused expression, Will said, "The heiress."

"You know my feelings on that."

Will bowed his head briefly as if contemplating something. "I do. However with this turn of events, there will be an even greater burden on the estate. Inheritance taxes and the like."

"I hadn't thought of that." Alex let out a long breath. "How much will be needed to handle these costs?"

Will reached for a file and opened it. "I've been working on that, actually."

"You're fast," Alex said with a lifted brow.

"Just thorough," Will responded. "I would be remiss in my duties if I had not planned for this eventuality."

The barrister read from the pages before him, and with each moment that passed, Alex's hopes for covering the Hambly debts dimmed. He waved his hand.

"No need to go on. I get the idea. The Hamblys are well and truly penniless."

"Not exactly penniless," Will said gently. "There are certain assets of value."

"Then get rid of them."

Will shook his head. "Not all are so easily liquidated."

"I understand the ancestral lands cannot be sold," Alex said, "but surely other things can."

"Yes, of course." Will lifted a page from the file and slid it across the polished surface of his desk toward Alex. "As we'd already spoken of this option, I've taken the liberty of making a list. Some of the items, of course, will likely be exempt for sentimental reasons."

Alex handed the paper back to Will. "Sell them all."

"But you haven't even looked at—"

"All," he repeated firmly.

"But surely the countess will complain about losing some of her prize possessions. Why, the rubies were a gift from—"

"The countess will complain much louder should she be forced to spend an English winter without heat or endure a roof that leaks. Or, worse, being cast off on some of her lesser titled relatives abroad. Imagine her reaction to that."

"Duly noted." Will tucked the paper back into the file. "Now, as to the matter of a wife. Might I reopen the topic for just a moment?"

Alex removed his watch from his pocket and immediately thought of Charlotte Beck. He wrangled the image into submission and tossed it away. "You've got sixty seconds, friend, and not a second more."

"I could proceed with expedience and an abundance of caution. No public announcements of our plans or adverts in *The Titled American.* And once a suitable wife is under the roof at the Heath, your responsibility to the family is done. You can go back to your astral charts and telescopes without concern of any sort."

"Except the sort that comes from marriage, be it for love or want of funds."

Will gave him a stern look. "I demand extra time on the clock for your interruption."

"No need. I'm taking the matter under advisement, though were I required to respond at this moment, the answer would still be a resounding no. Especially given the amount of funds available once those items are liquidated." Alex slid the watch back into his pocket and regarded his old friend with gratitude. "What of the Leadville mine? Any closer to a sale?"

"Not yet, though I feel we have a strong position in the negotiations," the solicitor said. "Things are being kept quiet, as speculators know the property values will increase once the observatory plans get out."

Alex leaned forward and rested his palms on the table. "Then why sell to investors? Why not cut out the middleman and sell directly to the ones doing the building? Wouldn't the profits be greater?"

"They would, but the certainty of having the land purchased would decrease. What if the builders go with another location? Or what if there is a delay in the plans to build the observatory? There would be little need to secure the land if there is doubt about whether the building will go forward." He paused to shake his head. "My advice is to take what we can get now and be done with the property. To hold out ownership might cause you to be without any buyer at all," Will said. "Though even if the sale goes through, what we gain will only provide for your family's needs for the short term."

"How short?"

"Depending on the cost of settling your father's estate, you might be buying the family a decade of comfort. That is, if the countess cooperates and holds her spending to a minimum."

"She won't."

Will leaned back in his chair. "In that case, I'd say you will be looking at an empty bank account in two years. Three, if the Lord works a miracle."

"But if He works a miracle, my friend, I won't need to worry at all, will I?"

Alex moved toward the door with the question hanging unanswered between them.

12

The only interest a lady should take in business is to determine before marriage the number of zeros in a potential husband's bank account. The minimum for a happy life is seven; for a modicum of contentment six might be permissible. More, however, is preferable to fewer, which is not to be considered.

—*MISS PENCE*

Long after the viscount left, Charlotte remained on the settee, the scent of burned ribbons still in the air. What was it about that man that attracted trouble?

Charlotte touched her lips. And what in the world had possessed her to kiss him?

Twice?

"A moment of temporary insanity," she whispered. "Brought on by extreme upset."

And likely to happen again, should she allow it.

Charlotte realized she needed to return to Colorado at once—both to right the wrong committed against her by a loving but misguided father *and* to keep her distance from the viscount.

Who would also be traveling to Colorado. Charlotte groaned.

But Colorado was a big state, and the odds of seeing Alex Hambly were small. While she would be in Denver or at her father's ranch outside Fort Collins, the viscount would be conducting his business in Leadville.

"Leadville."

She released her grip on the ribbons as a thought took hold. If the Hambly family was sending a member of their own all the way to Leadville, this observatory must mean a transaction of some importance. What had Uncle Edwin said about the trouble between the Hamblys and the Becks? Something about a dispute regarding a place called Summit Hill.

A smile dawned as Charlotte recalled the reason. "The properties are side-by-side."

Which meant, of course, that if Hambly property was considered a good spot for the observatory, there was nothing keeping Beck property from the same designation. Papa constantly threatened to sell the mines and be done with the trouble of the mining business, and unless she was mistaken, this particular piece of land—situated too far up Summit Hill for easy travel in most months—wasn't profitable at all. Not like the other mines Papa had purchased.

She rose and kicked a cushion out of her way as she began to pace. What would Papa do given this kind of information? Likely he would contact Mr. Sanders, the Pinkerton agent who'd married dear Anna Finch from next door, to see what facts could be unearthed.

Then what?

Of course. Charlotte hurdled over the remaining pillows to make her way into the entrance hall.

"Gennie!" she called as she ran up the stairs. "Where are you? I've an urgent—"

"Charlotte, must you shout?" Gennie stepped from her chambers into the upstairs hall. "It's quite unbecoming." Her eyes widened. "Is that smoke I smell? Is the house on fire?"

"I was, but only briefly, and the viscount…" Charlotte made a valiant attempt at not blushing. "Never mind. Everything's fine. However, I need to return to Denver." She paused to slow her racing heart. "Immediately."

"Immediately?" Gennie gave her a confused look. "But we've plans that cannot be changed. The palace garden party is still a week away. And there are fittings and a very important—"

"You may stay," Charlotte said. "I only wish to return home." She paused. "To Papa."

Gennie crossed her arms. "Whatever is the rush? You've had your heart set on attending Jubilee Week for ages. Now I'm to believe you've suddenly changed your mind?"

What to say? Charlotte sorted through several possible responses. "Though I shall be terribly disappointed to miss seeing the queen and the empress, I wish to prove myself worthy to Papa and I cannot do that from London."

"Go on," Gennie urged as she leaned against the railing. "And tell me the whole truth, Charlotte."

"The whole truth is…" Charlotte paused to gather her thoughts and, in the process, an idea of impossible brilliance occurred to her, "I wish to become full partners with Papa in the business and I must return to tell him immediately. And to earn the right."

Gennie affected a look of disbelief.

Irritation tugged at Charlotte, but excitement kept the feeling at bay. "I've made no secret of my interest in such things, and I've written to Papa with a plea to send me to Wellesley."

"And his answer was no, Charlotte." Gennie sighed. "And for good reason."

Charlotte considered her words carefully, then put on her most repentant expression. "I know I've shown little to recommend my maturity in the past, and I am truly sorry. But working alongside Papa—and eventually Danny—at Beck Enterprises is what I was meant to do. After a proper education, of course. And this time I know Papa will say yes. Only I must get to him without delay."

"Don't be ridiculous." Gennie swept past her and started downstairs.

"You wouldn't say that if it were your son asking."

Gennie's glare told Charlotte she'd gone too far. Ignoring the urge to slide down the banister and beat her stepmother to the ground floor, Charlotte gripped the rail and moved quickly to catch up.

"Look, I'm not being ridiculous. I'm being smart. And no matter what else you might say of me, you must admit I am quite clever when I put my mind to it."

"True enough." Gennie stopped and regarded Charlotte with interest. "So what is it that you've suddenly discovered that will change your father's mind?"

Charlotte continued as if Gennie hadn't spoken. "If I were to send a cable to Papa, who knows who might see it and beat him to the deal? And a letter could get lost. The only possible solution is to return to Denver immediately so that Papa and I might take advantage of a once-in-a-lifetime opportunity."

Again Gennie looked at her askance. "Once-in-a-lifetime, Charlotte? Truly?"

"Truly. I've got information, Gennie. Given to me at a most vulnerable moment by a source in a position to know. And if Papa were to act on this information…" Charlotte stood a little straighter. "Not only would he make a fortune on the deal, but he just might best a rival at the same time."

"Details," Gennie demanded.

"I've learned an observatory may be coming to Leadville." Charlotte paused. "Right now the property being considered is at Summit Hill, but it's not Papa's land they're looking at." She paused again and couldn't contain a laugh. "Not yet, anyway. And as much as I would love to join you at tea with the empress, beating the Hamblys at a business deal holds much more appeal."

Gennie shifted positions on the stairs, her expression thoughtful. "I had hoped to introduce you at Court. I suppose that can be done at another time."

"Of course it could."

"Still…"

Charlotte pressed her advantage. "Papa's talked about selling that mine for years. Can you imagine how upset he will be when he learns he missed an opportunity not only to sell it but for a profit? And surely he's ready for his family to return."

"He did mention how very much he longed for us in his last letter," Gennie said softly. "I suppose I could send a note to the jeweler and that lovely man who makes the gloves. And the milliner can surely ship our hats when they're finished. And of course we will send our regrets to the queen's social secretary." Gennie seemed to warm to the idea. "I'll have someone from the staff change our tickets. There's much to do."

Charlotte stifled a smile. "Yes. Much."

A door at the top of the stairs opened, and Grandfather stepped out. "You ladies sound as if you're having a grand time."

"We're just making plans for our return," Gennie said. "I'm terribly sorry we interrupted you."

"Not at all. I enjoy the sound of family in the halls."

"Will you excuse me," Gennie asked.

"Of course. Now Charlotte," Grandfather said when Gennie had disappeared upstairs, "thank you for seeing to the viscount's visit. He mentioned your persuasive nature made it impossible to say no. Well done. You're a true Beck, dear. When we put our minds to something, it gets done."

Charlotte saw her chance and seized it as she closed the distance between them to embrace her grandfather. "Thank you. I was just telling Gennie how much I wish to join Papa in the family business. I think I have quite a head for it."

"Mining?" Grandfather shook his head. "Hardly think you've had enough experience to know the field."

"No," she said. "Not mining specifically. I'm more interested in Beck Enterprises, though I intend to get an education first."

"I'm very glad to hear it," Grandfather said, "but what might you do at Beck Enterprises?"

"There are more ways to make money in this modern economy than the mining business," Charlotte said. "I can help Papa explore new avenues."

"Such as?"

"Oh, I've an idea or two. Stocks being one of them." She winked. "Then there's our mutual friend Viscount Hambly. He was a wealth of information today."

"Was he now?" Grandfather held her at arm's length. "Did he realize he was imparting valuable information to someone who might actually be listening?"

"I think he was a bit flustered by the fire." At her grandfather's confused expression, Charlotte continued. "An accident, I promise." She touched the burnt ends of her ribbon.

"I thought I smelled smoke." He shook his head. "Are you certain you've got the stomach for this, Charlotte? The business world is not for the faint of heart."

She squared her shoulders, then kissed her grandfather on the cheek. "Of course I am sure. As for being faint of heart, just ask Colonel Cody. He'll tell you I've never once showed any—"

"All right, all right." Grandfather chuckled then quickly sobered. "You've made your point. Now let me make mine. While I commend you for your decision to seek an education and become more involved in your father's company, I must caution you on crossing a Hambly."

Charlotte smiled. "Perhaps it is the Hamblys who should be cautioned not to speak so freely in the presence of a Beck."

13

A lady must wait to be introduced so as to avoid entering a room where she is neither known nor expected.

—MISS PENCE

July 1, 1887
Leadville, Colorado

"Finally!"

Charlotte stepped off the train in Leadville and inhaled the bracing air. The trip had seemingly taken forever, what with delays and other such bothersome things, but finally she was home in Colorado. Only a return to Denver instead of Leadville might have made her happier, for she still had not seen her friend Gussie, but she could not wait to see Papa's face when she told him her plan. While those assigned to her care handled mundane things such as luggage, Charlotte set off toward Papa's office with her news.

Keeping to a ladylike pace, Charlotte tucked the telegram from Mr. Sanders into her reticule and swept into the Beck building with only the briefest of nods to the assistant perched at the desk in front. Voices low and deep hummed through the space between Charlotte and her father's office, and she picked up her skirts and ran.

"Papa," she said as she burst through the door, "I've such great news that I hurried home to tell you all about—"

"Charlotte Beck," said Papa from behind his massive desk. The room was full of strangers, and they all stared at her.

She dropped her skirt and adjusted the hat that had gone askew in transit. "I'm terribly sorry," she said as she felt heat rise in her cheeks. "I fear I've interrupted something important."

Papa crossed the room and enveloped her in his arms. "Buttercup, you always did know how to make an entrance." He planted a kiss atop her head then turned her to face the others. "Gentlemen, meet my favorite daughter, Miss Charlotte Beck. Newly and unexpectedly returned from abroad."

In deference to Miss Pence's teaching, she offered a nod and smile. "How do you—"

And then she saw the green-eyed man from Viscount Hambly's office at the Royal Observatory. Upon her discovery of him, the fellow rose.

"I believe we've met," he said. "William Pembroke at your service, Miss Beck."

"Yes, hello," Charlotte said, her voice wavering only slightly. "How do you do?"

"You two are acquainted?" Papa skewered the Briton with his best fatherly glare. "And how might you have made my daughter's acquaintance, Mr. Pembroke?"

"Papa, really," Charlotte said. "In London one meets so many people. I doubt our meeting made much of an impression on Mr. Pembroke." She turned her attention to her father. "I know you're terribly busy, but might I borrow you for one tiny second?"

"Of course. Would you all excuse me?" He cast a glance at Hiram Nettles, his right-hand man. "Continue without me."

Charlotte linked arms with her father and walked with him down the hall, past the fellow at the front desk, and finally out into the bright Colorado sunshine. She sneezed twice. "Figured to outgrow that one day," she said, smiling.

"Perhaps when you're actually grown up," Papa said with a sideways look that offered more than a little humor.

She patted her father's hand. "Shall we forever be embroiled in the debate as to when I'm grown, Papa?"

"Perhaps not," he said, "though I warrant the discussion will continue for some time. But surely you didn't come here to try to win that argument."

"There's no argument," she said, "but no. I've got such exciting news I couldn't bear to wait. So exciting that I wish to table our upcoming discussion on your claim that I am an embarrassment to you."

"About that," he began, "have you any idea what it's like to read such a—"

"Truly now, I've much better things to discuss, or we might not have hurried back. Convincing Gennie to forego tea with the empress was no simple feat."

"We?" Her father's brows rose. "Are my bride and son also in Leadville?"

"They are, though Gennie begged a nap for the two of them before they could be considered presentable."

Papa's smile was quick and warm, a testament to the woman who had brought much happiness to both of them. "So what is this exciting news?"

Charlotte stopped to look around. Satisfied she and Papa could continue without curious ears listening, she took a deep breath and let it out slowly. A prayer went up for just the right words, and she began. "Papa, I wish to join you at Beck Enterprises."

"Do you now?" To his credit, her father did not laugh. Neither, it appeared, did he take her seriously.

"In a position of some responsibility," she clarified.

"Responsibility. I see." His expression gave no hint of his thoughts on the matter. "Might I inquire as to what position within the firm you'd be taking?"

"Yours, eventually. At least until Danny is old enough to join me in managing the company."

When Papa laughed, she remained silent.

"For now," she continued, once he'd quieted, "I would like you to change your mind about allowing me to attend Wellesley in the coming term." She held her hand up to stop his protest. "After achieving stellar marks on my coursework and receiving my diploma, which of course I will do with honors, I wish to return to Denver to work with Hiram on learning the business. He's the best employee you've got, am I correct?"

"You are," he said with a skeptical look. "But I've already told you my opinion on Wellesley."

"Opinions change, but facts do not. I've got a head for business, which I will prove beyond a doubt in just a moment. As for Hiram, it would be wonderful to learn the ins and outs of Beck Enterprises from you, but our father-daughter relationship might get in the way of a fair and accurate assessment of my skills. Correct?"

Papa sobered. "You're serious."

"I am."

"Buttercup, you know I adore you." He grasped her hands in his.

"It's a proven fact that if you asked for the world, I'd wrap it up and place it in your palm."

She focused on her father's face. "But?"

"You're a beautiful girl who should be looking for a husband, not a place at the boardroom table." This time he held up his hand to stop her protest. "And a brilliant, talented artist who should be devoting her time to that pursuit and not getting her lovely French-made dresses dusty here in Leadville."

Disappointment threatened with tears, but Charlotte pressed it aside. "I've plenty of dresses and years to paint or find a husband," she said. "What if I could prove you wrong? About my head for business?"

"Charlotte, honestly, you've been trying to prove me wrong since you were five. What possible—"

"Roeschlaub."

Her father shook his head. "Roeschlaub?"

"He's an architect, Papa. He built the Goodsell Observatory in Minnesota. Mr. Sanders checked into him for me, so I can verify this is a fact." she paused. "You're wondering what that has to do with Beck Enterprises?"

Her father crossed his arms and regarded her curiously. "I am, actually, though I am also curious why you took the initiative to contact Jeb. Impressed, but curious."

"The men in your office. Might they be a group of investors looking to include you in a business transaction?" She only paused for a second. "Maybe one that involves selling off the abandoned mine site adjacent to the Hambly property?"

Papa's eyes widened but he said nothing.

"My guess is you and Hiram have been baffled at the sudden interest in a worthless property but thrilled at getting the old mine off the books. This also begs the question of why Hambly would want more property, since their mine has been losing money for the better part of two years. I credit Mr. Sanders and the Pinkertons in his employ for that bit of information as well." She reached into her reticule to retrieve the telegram and thrust it toward her father. "Perhaps you'd like to see the telegram he sent."

"A summary is sufficient," Papa said, but he looked impressed.

"Of course." Charlotte folded the telegram and returned it to her reticule then took a deep breath. "Mr. Pembroke is Viscount Hambly's barrister. Or is it solicitor? I never can remember the difference. Anyway, my best guess is they are looking to add to the property already in their possession so as to sweeten the deal they're making."

"It's solicitor." Papa shook his head. "What deal? Far as Hiram and I can tell, it's merely a speculative transaction with one miner offering another a chance at digging a little deeper to make a profit. It doesn't hurt that this would finally put to rest the ridiculous accusations that Beck Mining has somehow extracted silver from Hambly properties."

"Perhaps," she said slowly, "but I have inside information that the Hambly family plans to sell their mines to a consortium of investors actively looking to build an observatory. My source tells me it's all but a done deal."

"Your source?" he said.

Charlotte linked arms with her father. "Truly, Papa, are you still skeptical?"

"No, but I am curious. How did you come by this information?"

She pursed her lips as she recalled the two kisses. "There was a small fire. Nothing intentional, mind you. But Viscount Hambly happened to be in the vicinity and, well, as you can imagine, I was upset at having my ribbons singed."

"Of course."

"And he was quite helpful in…" Charlotte paused. "He was quite helpful. And quite willing to speak without considering that I, a mere woman, might actually be listening and taking note of the topic. So, Papa, what do you think of my proposition?"

"You made a proposition?" He shook his head. "Remind me what it was."

"I'm going to run your company someday, Papa." She grinned. "But today, just promise I'll be attending Wellesley when the new term begins."

Papa raised a brow. "Are you sure about this?"

"I am, and I'll not change my mind," she said. "I want you to be proud of me."

The truth, she realized, and the whole reason for everything else.

"Then you must promise not to give up on your painting," he said. "Colonel Cody will have my head if he learns I've kept his favorite artist from her craft. And I enjoy your work. You've quite the talent."

"Of course," she said, her hopes rising. "If it makes you feel any better, I've got four canvases rolled and ready to send to him. Once we finally set sail, the return voyage was quite uneventful, so I was able to paint every day."

"Excellent." Her father gathered Charlotte into an embrace. "I expected you to be furious with me for refusing to allow your New York debut. I thought you might never forgive me for that."

Charlotte affected a demure look that would have made Miss Pence proud. "Oh, Papa," she said sweetly, "Not forgive you? Perish the thought!"

"Very funny," he said, releasing her. "Now go tell my wife I'll be around to fetch her to the railcar in a few hours."

Charlotte shook her head. "Whatever for?"

"We're going home to the ranch. I've no need to continue meetings here, do I? Not when I've been given important information that completely changes the face of the negotiations."

Charlotte smiled. "No, I suppose not."

"That's right." Papa gave her a kiss on the cheek. "Not when I can speak to that architect personally. What was his name?" He waved away her response. "Never mind. Sanders will know."

She turned in the direction of the hotel with a broad smile. Were she not of better and more refined stock, Charlotte might have added a whoop of joy. Instead, she vowed to wait until she reached her chambers.

"Charlotte?"

She turned at the sound of her father's voice. "Yes?"

"Good job, Buttercup." He paused. "I'll have Hiram alert the admissions office at Wellesley that you'll be accepting their offer of admission after all."

"Wellesley," she said under her breath. And then, despite her best intentions, Charlotte let out a whoop that would have made the Wild West show participants proud.

14

When meeting nobility, a lady should show proper
deference while expecting the royal in question to
be far more impressed with her.

—*Miss Pence*

Alex paced his corner room at the Tabor Grand Hotel like a caged tiger.
Three floors below on Harrison Street, the citizens of Leadville went
about the business of building and losing fortunes, oblivious to the fact
that he was about to lose his mind.

As much as Alex trusted Will Pembroke, his preference had been to
attend the meeting with the investors himself rather than send his solicitor in his stead. But Pembroke insisted he make the men wait to meet
such esteemed nobility, and so, reluctantly, he had.

His project, while he waited, was to reconsider his reluctance to
marry some local heiress. Pembroke had not only put together a list of
possible candidates, he'd had the audacity to discreetly contact their
fathers. One in particular had expressed swift and strong interest in an
alliance.

A marriage brokered under such circumstances could not be called
anything else.

But whenever Alex tried to think about marrying anyone, his brain
refused to allow it. Worse, when pressed, the only face he could imagine
on the pillow beside him belonged to the one frustrating female he could

never imagine being betrothed to. Ever since he'd had the bad sense to kiss her, Charlotte Beck had plagued his thoughts and tortured his dreams.

And yet, given the same opportunity, Alex knew he'd kiss her again.

He spied Pembroke crossing Harrison. "Finally," he muttered. Alex continued pacing until the door finally opened and Will stormed inside.

"You were right." Will shrugged out of his coat and threw it toward the nearest chair, then tossed his hat after it. Neither reached their destination, but Pembroke didn't seem to care.

"Right about what?" Alex watched his friend walk to the window then turn and lean against the sill.

"The Becks." Will spit out the name as if it left a bad taste in his mouth.

"He didn't sell?"

"No." Pembroke took a deep breath and let it out slowly. "We were making great headway too. Had the man just about to sign a bill of sale for the mine at a price that was dirt-cheap. Pardon the pun."

"But he changed his mind," Alex said.

Pembroke yanked off his collar, and it landed atop his jacket. "Apparently he was persuaded to do so after a conversation with his daughter."

"His daughter?"

"She said something that caused her father to change his mind." Will shook his head. "It was like night and day. One minute he was ready to sign and the next he came storming back into the office and sent us all away. Said he had second thoughts and wasn't selling."

Alex went to the window and looked down at Harrison Street. From his vantage point he could see most of Leadville and the mines beyond. A dreary sight at best on this cloudy summer day. "And what exactly caused this change?"

"You'd have to ask Miss Beck. Her father offered no reason." Pembroke went to the writing desk and sat down. "So, have you finished your letter to Mr. Miller regarding a meeting about marriage negotiations once we arrive in Denver? I'd hoped to post it today."

"About that. I've despaired of it. Perhaps you could lend a hand."

Alex spied a familiar figure some distance down Harrison. Charlotte Beck was making her way toward the corner of Seventh and Harrison. She paused at the corner, then crossed the street, picking her steps with care as she waited for traffic to slow. All the while, the large blue feather adorning her hat bounced up and down as it matched paces with her.

"You want me to write a letter to the father of the woman you're in negotiations to marry?" Will asked. "In your stead?"

"What?" Alex tore his attention from Charlotte Beck. "Yes, would you? After all, you're the one negotiating. I'm merely the prize bull up for auction. Or is she the...well, never mind. Just write it, would you?"

"Fine." Will craned his neck and rose slightly from the chair in order to see what Alex found so interesting. "Is that who I think it is?"

"It is."

"Are you going to do what I think you are?"

"Probably." Alex reached for his hat and coat.

He walked out the front door of the Tabor Grand just a moment after Charlotte Beck strolled past. As crowded as Harrison Street was, she seemed to have no trouble navigating around stalled persons and vehicles. He almost lost her twice, but finally three blocks past the hotel, Alex fell into step beside her.

"Good afternoon, Miss Beck," he said in his most formal voice. "Lovely afternoon, isn't it?" Owing to the thin air, his greeting lacked enthusiasm. Still, he managed to stop the Beck woman in her tracks.

"Viscount Hambly." A distinct shade of pink climbed into her cheeks. "I did not expect to find you here in Leadville."

"No?" He allowed his gaze to slide over the features he'd already memorized. "I have a vague recollection of telling you I would be here." He met her wide-eyed stare. "I believe it was either before or after our kiss."

"Kisses," she corrected without evidence of embarrassment. "As I recall, there were two."

Not the response he'd expected.

"Well, then," Miss Beck continued. "Good day, Viscount Hambly."

And off she went, her blue feather bobbing as she continued down the sidewalk.

"Wait," he called, heedless that it was the height of impropriety to shout at a woman. Fortunately, none of Leadville's finest seemed to notice.

She'd already turned onto Chestnut Street when Alex caught her, his lungs burning from the thin air. "Truly, Miss Beck," he gasped. "You're not one to stand still for long, are you?"

Miss Beck neither slowed nor offered any recognition that he now walked beside her. The woman was insufferable.

The man was insufferable. Charlotte picked up her pace, determined not to let on that her lungs burned for air. While she'd practically grown up in Leadville, it had been quite some time since she'd been at this elevation.

It would come back to her, she knew, but for now just forcing an even breath took effort. But given the expression on the viscount's face, the effort was worth it.

Her plan to visit the dressmaker changed as she realized this man would likely follow her inside, and everyone knew gossip started at Trudy's Hats and Finery. She bypassed her intended destination and set her sites on the livery next door, where Papa kept a buggy and horses. Perhaps she could send Viscount Hambly scurrying back to where he came from by offering to deliver him herself.

"Welcome back, Miss Beck," the livery boy said.

"Charles." She gave the boy a wide smile then opened her reticule to offer him a handful of coins. "Might I trouble you to ready Papa's buggy?"

"Already done it, Miss Beck," he said as the coins dropped into his pocket. "Standing rule 'round here is t'keep Mr. Beck's buggy ready to go whenever he's in town."

"I see." She pressed past the viscount without acknowledging him and followed the lad to an open area outside where her father's main means of transportation waited.

"Might you need someone t'drive you, miss?" the boy asked.

"No need for that," said the deep voice behind her. "Miss Beck will be perfectly safe with me."

Before she could form a decent protest, the viscount had climbed into the buggy and taken hold of the reins.

"Well, I never," she said, but she allowed the lad to help her up beside the Englishman.

Viscount Hambly leaned toward her and grinned. "Not true, Miss Beck," he said just loud enough for her to hear. "You have. Twice."

She might have swatted him with her fan for his impudence had she not admired his gumption. Charlotte turned away to hide her smile.

By the time the buggy lurched forward, she'd replaced her grin with a sour expression. "Might I inquire as to where we are going?"

Viscount Hambly slid her a sideways look. "Did you not have a destination in mind when you raced over here?"

"I...well...actually, I thought I might just enjoy the weather." A glance up at the sky exposed the lack of truth in that statement, for ominous clouds bore hard on the western horizon.

"I see." He nodded. "In that case, I've a place I would like you to see. I think you'll enjoy the weather just fine from there."

She gripped the edge of the seat as the Englishman whipped the buggy around the corner and blended into the mix of people, wagons, and livestock on Chestnut Street. At Harrison Street, he nearly toppled a street vendor's handcart when he took the turn too sharply.

"Careful." Charlotte offered the cursing vendor an apologetic look. Turning to her companion, she added, "You're a menace, Viscount Hambly."

His laughter caught her by surprise. "That makes two of us then, Miss Beck."

Soon the people and wagons were left behind and nothing but the mountains lay ahead, and Charlotte relaxed. The beauty of the landscape—as long as one ignored the blight of the mines—was breathtaking. And though she'd seen the view a thousand times since her first trip to the city, Charlotte never tired of leaning as far as she could over the edge of the buggy to peer down at what lay so far below.

Trees, people, and ramshackle buildings all seemed insignificant when viewed from this height. Only the church steeple, the needle upon which the compass of Leadville balanced, seemed the same.

"You're quite taken with this city," the viscount said.

Charlotte straightened, assuming a more proper demeanor, as the buggy bounced over deep ruts in what had become more trail than road. "Yes, I suppose I am."

He gave her an appraising look. "It suits you."

"Does it?" Charlotte shrugged. "Perhaps. It didn't always, though. When I was ten, I got into some serious trouble here."

"You?" The viscount's dark brows rose as he affected a poor version of a surprised expression. "I find that hard to believe."

"Sarcasm is unbecoming," she quoted. "Miss Pence."

"Miss Pence?" He gripped the reins to slow the horses as they approached the summit. "I don't follow."

"My etiquette teacher. She does not approve of sarcasm. But then, she'd be horrified to know her prize student was once a pie thief. Oh, and I was threatened at gunpoint by the most awful..." Charlotte forced the memory away and put on a smile. "Anyway, it turns out Gennie is pretty handy with a gun."

"That's the story? I doubt that's all of it." Viscount Hambly halted the buggy, then swiveled to face her. "Enlighten me, Miss Beck."

"There's nothing to tell beyond the fact that I angered the wrong man."

"Is that so?"

"And then there was the time I convinced my friend Gussie to..." She looked at him and blushed. "Never mind."

Despite the curiosity and confusion evident on Alex Hambly's face, Charlotte kept her mouth closed, and eventually he returned his attention to the horses.

While the Englishman was otherwise occupied, Charlotte took the opportunity to study him. He had a fine profile, she decided, one that begged to be recalled over and again. His hair was dark, not black as night but rather that shade that turned from the color of deepest evening to the golden hue of dawn's first light when the sunlight danced across it.

Papa would say his features were pleasant. Gennie would call him easy on the eye. Charlotte thought him far too handsome for his own good.

Not that she would ever tell him so.

He caught Charlotte staring. "With your permission, I'd like to show you something."

"Yes, of course," she managed before looking away.

He urged the horses forward, and they headed back down the trail off the summit. Then, without warning, he swung the buggy to the left, and Charlotte tumbled toward the edge of the seat.

The viscount hauled her back against him, leaving her breathless. "Careful, there," he said practically against her ear.

"Careful?" Had Charlotte not been shaking like a leaf in the wind, she would have told the man exactly what she thought of his ridiculous warning. "Slow down," she said instead. "And release me at once."

Hambly appeared surprised at her statement, as if he were unaware of holding her against him. "Yes, right," he said as he removed his arm from her waist.

The buggy still flew across the ruts and poorly cut out roads, but the viscount took more care making the hairpin turns that characterized the remainder of their trip. He gestured to the rise and the steep trail that seemingly went straight up to disappear between a rocky outcropping. "I've only traveled this way on horseback. Might be rough, but I'm the adventurous sort. Shall we give it a go?"

She only gave the idea a second of thought. "Of course. Just let me tighten the ribbons on my hat. Wouldn't want to lose it."

He chuckled as her fingers, sore and cramped from holding onto the buggy seat, fumbled with the ties. Finally he handed her the reins. "Here, let me do it. Just don't let go."

"Truly, Viscount Hambly, I—"

"Please," he interrupted as his fingers toyed with the ribbons, "call me Alex."

She watched the silk slide across his hands and noticed a scar that spanned the space between his thumb and forefinger. "This is most improper."

He tightened the knot, and his knuckles grazed her chin. "Improper?" He lifted one dark brow. "Interesting how you define propriety."

Charlotte closed her eyes to avoid staring directly into his. "How so?"

Something brushed her face. She opened her eyes to see the Englishman tucking a strand of her hair back under her hat.

"Wouldn't want to be improper," he said as he patted the ribbon back into place atop her curls. "I think that will do nicely. Do hold on."

He turned and took the reins. With a slap of leather and a shout of encouragement to the horses, the buggy jerked into motion. They moved fast at first and then, by degrees, slowed as they climbed, until Charlotte knew for sure they'd begin rolling backward at any moment.

And then, just as she'd given up hope, the trail leveled out and all of Leadville lay before her. The sun shone around clouds that portended rain, covering the town in a patchwork of light and shade. Squinting, she spied the Clarendon Hotel and, nearby, the Tabor Opera House and Mr. Tabor's Grand Hotel. And, of course, the church spire that anchored the view.

"Breathtaking," she whispered. Charlotte turned to her companion and found him staring not at the view, but at her.

He slowly looked beyond her. "Do you know where you are, Charlotte?"

She looked around. "This appears to be the highest summit in Leadville. Am I correct?"

"You are," he said. "But it's more than that."

The wind picked up, lifting the ribbons the viscount's hands had tied. Charlotte reached for the brim of her hat to steady it against the breeze. The Englishman continued to look out at the valley.

"What else is it, Viscount...Alex?"

At the mention of his name, he glanced up sharply. "Alex, is it?"

"Don't make a fuss about it or I shall go back to calling you Viscount Hambly." She returned her attention to the clouds hovering above them.

"This is Summit Hill. Hambly land." He gestured to the city below. "Purchased by my father before most of that was here."

Charlotte's heart sank. The land where the observatory was to sit. Was it possible he knew she'd told Papa of his intentions?

"I see," she managed. "You know, it appears rain is on the way. Perhaps we should get back to town before we're drenched and the road becomes impassable."

"What did you say to your father?"

A simple question, and yet one she did not intend to answer. "I am uncomfortable remaining here." She gave him a direct look. "A gentleman would not keep me here against my will."

"And a lady," he said slowly, "would not meddle in affairs where she had no business."

"Look here," Charlotte said as her ire rose, "I am neither meddling nor compromising my position as a lady."

"I see." The viscount snatched up the reins. "The fact remains that your father has decided not to allow a purchase of the land directly south of this." He nodded toward a rocky patch some distance away. "See that?"

Charlotte followed his line of vision and found nothing but the crumbled remains of a miner's shack. Not much more than a pile of kindling, really.

"There's nothing a man or a miner could want," he said. "It's been dug to death and there's not a glint of ore under it. No value to anyone anymore, and what little came out of it is possibly from the Hambly side of the property line, though that's a story I've yet to confirm. Your father was eager to get rid of it. Then, suddenly, he was not."

She shook her head. "I have no idea—"

"Spare me." He slapped the reins and turned the buggy. "You told your father of our plans. Beck's a businessman, and he knows when to sell. That's the only explanation."

Her mouth resolutely shut, Charlotte endured the bone-rattling ride over the rise in silence. Finally she could stand it no more. "Look here," she said, holding tightly to the buggy seat to keep from being catapulted out. "Stop at once so I can speak."

The viscount slid her a sideways look, then, with a shake of his head, complied.

When the horses were still, Charlotte released her grip and swiveled to face him. "All right. I admit I told my father about the observatory."

Sunlight slanted over his features, which did not change with her admission of guilt. A muscle worked in his jaw, but otherwise the viscount remained silent.

"But tell the truth, Alex." Charlotte touched his sleeve. "You would have done the same thing."

A lady's behavior must be exemplary at all times.
At least in public.

—*Miss Pence*

You would have done the same thing.

The Beck girl was right. The admission chewed at his conscience. Under the same circumstances with the same information, he would have taken the same steps to secure his family's stake in what could be a lucrative business deal.

As the trail leveled out, so did Alex's temper. After maneuvering around a deep rut, he slowed the horses and stopped the buggy.

"Miss Beck," he said when he had her full attention.

"So it's Miss Beck now," she said with sarcasm.

"Charlotte," he amended wearily. "You and I have been at cross purposes since we met."

"I suppose." Charlotte studied her hands. "Though I never asked you to catch me in the garden. I could have landed quite nicely without your help. And had you not, likely the rest of the things that have transpired would never have happened. Thus it all begins with you." She lifted her gaze to settle on him. "But I forgive you, Alex."

"You forgive me?" Was she mad or merely baiting him? In either case, Alex bit back the rest of his response. "That's quite magnanimous of you."

"I try," she said. "Now, perhaps we should hurry back." She gestured at the gathering clouds. "It appears we're about to be inundated."

"Wouldn't want that." Alex raised the reins, preparing to send the horses hurrying forward, then thought better of it. "Charlotte," he said, "now that you've forgiven me, perhaps we might discuss a little business proposition."

"Business?" She shook her head, and the feather on her hat bobbed in time. "I'm a lady who should not meddle in business affairs, remember?"

"Save it for someone who will believe you. It seems you've a better head for business than I do, though I'd never admit to anyone I've said that aloud." The horses startled at a rumble of thunder, and it took him a moment to quiet them. When he returned his attention to Charlotte, he found her watching him openly. "You're smart, Charlotte Beck. Much smarter than I've given you credit for. And you're more mature than you appear, an image I warrant you both enjoy and cultivate."

Green eyes widened slightly before her mask of indifference returned. A brisk wind caught her silly hat and she yanked it back into place.

"And you," she said, "strike bargains you do not keep."

"I do not."

One hand still on the hat, she pointed at him. Her eyes narrowed. "You do. Remind me of the agreement we made in London."

He shrugged. "I arranged to have your ridiculous behavior become all the rage, and you promised to leave me alone."

"That's not exactly as I would have stated it," she said, "but the fact remains that you and I were to go our separate ways. You, sir, have not allowed this to happen."

"Me?" Again the horses startled, and this time Alex gave them their way and allowed the buggy to jerk into motion.

"Yes, you," she said. "You continually insinuate yourself into my life, Alex Hambly, and then you somehow decide it's all my fault."

"I insinuate *myself*? How do you explain our current situation?"

The buggy tilted dangerously as the horses took a hairpin turn too fast. Alex pulled back on the reins and made sure his passenger still sat beside him. She did, but her hat hung askance and the blue feather bent with the rising breeze.

"We have no situation beyond that which you caused by purloining my father's buggy," she said. She sat straight as a schoolteacher, her fingers toying with the ribbons he had just tied. "Nor should we attempt to continue this conversation."

She had a point, at least in the claim he'd stolen the buggy. Though technically a buggy could not be stolen if the daughter of the owner willingly joined in the journey. Charlotte Beck had made no move to leave once he slid into the driver's seat. For all her bluster, perhaps she was more interested in him than she let on.

After all, she had let him kiss her.

Twice.

Alex gave her a sideways glance. "Leave the ribbons alone or you'll lose your hat."

"Mind your driving," she snapped in response.

The buggy negotiated another turn, this time with much greater success. However, while the road was becoming smoother, the weather was not. A quick calculation gave them less than even odds of returning the buggy to the livery before the clouds burst.

"Hold on, Charlotte," he said, slapping the reins and urging the horses to pick up their pace. "I'm getting us off the mountain before the rain has us sliding."

"But how will you—oh! There went my hat."

The curls that had once been tamed by the silly hat were now free to form a damp halo cascading past Charlotte Beck's shoulders. Despite it all, she looked even lovelier, which only served to irritate Alex further.

"We must go back for my hat," she insisted. "The milliner made it especially for me, and I've no immediate plans to return to Paris."

Lightning darted across the western sky, increasing the need for their quick return. "I told you to stop playing with the ribbons," Alex said.

The light rain made the reins slick, but the road beneath them remained passable. Up ahead, however, darker clouds loomed over Leadville.

"Hold on," he warned. Raindrops continued to pelt them.

She braced herself as the horses responded, remaining blessedly silent until the buggy reached the edge of the city.

"Perhaps a less direct route to the livery might be in order," Charlotte suggested. "I look a fright."

"You're beautiful," Alex said without thinking.

"And your poor eyesight explains the awful driving." She grasped the fabric of his sleeve. "Please stop, Alex."

"Don't be silly, we're almost to—"

"Stop!" Charlotte reached over him to yank back on the reins.

The horses stuttered to a sliding halt, and the buggy careened toward the precipice.

A moment later, the slide ended with the buggy thankfully on solid ground. Alex took a deep breath of the thin mountain air and willed his heart to slow its furious clamor.

Holding tight to the reins, he gave Charlotte a stern look. "*Never* do that again. We could have been... Are you crying?"

"No." She sniffed. "It's the rain."

"It is not the rain." He reached into his pocket and handed her his handkerchief. "Take it."

Charlotte shook her head then wiped her already-damp cheeks with her sleeve. "No."

"This is becoming a habit," he muttered as he leaned over to dab her cheeks. "I've never seen a woman with so many tears to spare."

"I'm not crying." She snatched the handkerchief from his hand then lifted it to her nose and blew. "I just know what will happen when my father sees me looking like this, especially now that he trusts me again and is willing to allow me to go to Wellesley and then to…" Charlotte blew her nose again. "Well, anyway, never mind what my father's allowing me to do."

"No, let's talk about that, Charlotte." He shook his head. "So you're working for your father?" At her weak nod, Alex continued. "Exactly how long have you worked for Beck Enterprises?"

"I don't yet. I merely have a promise of a position once my studies are completed." She tensed. "And this is not a conversation I wish to have with you."

"And yet we shall have it all the same." Alex placed his free hand atop hers. "Did you get your 'promise of a position' because of the information I gave you or did you get information from me because you were working for your father?"

"Papa loves me," she said defiantly. "His wish has always been for me to someday take an active part in the business I will inherit. I'm sure of it."

A not-so-subtle reminder of the disparity in their bank balances. Alex chose to ignore it.

"So why are you crying? The way I see it, you've won, no matter which scenario is true."

She looked up into his eyes. "You wouldn't understand."

"Try me," he said.

"All my life I've tried to make my father take me seriously. Elias says that's why I was so much trouble as a child. I was trying to get my Papa to really notice me."

"Elias?"

"Our, well…he's just Elias." Shaking her head, Charlotte continued. "That's why I took up painting. My mother loved it, and I hoped my father would love that I loved it. And I am good at it." Again her gaze collided with his. "Really good at it. And Papa is proud. Which is why I continue to paint for Colonel Cody even though I prefer the night sky to a stampeding herd."

"Night sky?"

"Yes." A raindrop traced down her cheek, or perhaps it was a tear. "The sky at twilight is lovely, but a night sky is so…"

"Beautiful," he supplied as his knuckle brushed her cheek and swiped away the dampness.

"Yes," she whispered. "There's just something about the light and how the stars…"

"Sparkle." He looked into her eyes.

"Yes," she repeated, softer.

He became aware of the warmth of her hand under his and the chill of the raindrops as they splattered around them. But most of all, aware of the extreme nearness of the soggy, lilac-scented Charlotte Beck.

Without warning, Charlotte slid her hand from under his and bounded from the buggy.

"Where are you going?" Irritation fought with amazement at the lengths the woman went to ignore his wishes.

She gave him a stricken look. "I should never have told you all of that. I don't know what it is about you that makes me lose my good sense." She examined her surroundings. "There's a stream on the other side of that rock. Give me a moment to wash my face and set my hair to rights, and we can return to Leadville."

"You want to freshen up?" He lifted his face to the skies, and rain pelted his cheeks. "Wouldn't that be better done back at your home or your hotel or wherever it is the Becks stay in this town?"

"The Clarendon," she said as she turned her back on him and walked away. "Papa prefers the Clarendon. He and the management have a long history. Something about Papa and Gennie's wedding. They joke about it, but neither will offer details beyond the fact that it involves a nightmare I used to have as a child. Oh, there I go talking too much again. I sound like Anna Finch. She never could stop talking when she was around..." And then her voice was drowned out by the sound of the rain hitting the parched ground.

Alex watched her walk across the damp prairie as if she were crossing a ballroom floor. Head held high, back straight, and curls bouncing despite their soggy condition. She glanced over her shoulder to meet his incredulous stare then disappeared behind a boulder.

"Come back here this moment," he called.

"No!"

"If you don't return to this wagon this instant, I'm coming after you."

"No, you won't," she called.

"And why is that?"

"Because you're a gentleman." The words echoed from some distant place.

He stood and stretched, trying to see her, but found no trace of Charlotte Beck. Returning to his seat, Alex let the rain slide down his neck as he leaned his elbows on his knees and tried not to think of how the moment could be made any worse.

And then he heard the click. He turned his head and looked down the barrel of the sheriff's rifle.

16

Miss Pence's instructions well heeded will result in
a husband well-heeled.

—MISS PENCE

"I'm glad you're here," Alex said to the sheriff. "I wonder if you'd do me
a favor and see if you can find Miss Beck. She's run off in that direction
and I cannot get her to return. Or I can go, and you can see that the
horses don't spook. With the weather such as it is, I'm afraid to leave
them untended while I go after my missing companion."

The sheriff shoved his hat back a notch. "Is that right?"

"Yes, it is." Alex gestured to the path Charlotte had taken. "She's a
stubborn woman and refuses to listen to me at all. I should have used
that hat ribbon of hers to tie her to the wagon instead of allowing her to
wander free."

The older man's eyes narrowed. "Well, I reckon I've heard enough."

The sheriff reached into his pocket and pulled out a pair of handcuffs. Before he could form a decent protest, Alex found himself cuffed
to the wagon and on his way to the Leadville jail.

"Aren't you going to wait for Charlotte?" he asked.

"Charlotte?"

Alex struggled to remain upright as the buggy lurched around a hole
in the road. "Yes, Charlotte Beck."

The sheriff chuckled as the rain splattered off the brim of his hat. "Mr. Beck promised a reward for whoever brought back his buggy. Didn't say anything about bringing back his daughter."

But when the buggy rolled up in front of the jail, Daniel Beck burst out the door and demanded to know where his daughter was. While Charlotte's father argued with the sheriff, Alex sat in the pouring rain and marveled at the fact that once again, associating with Charlotte Beck had caused him nothing but trouble.

Finally, the sheriff tossed Daniel Beck the key to the handcuffs and unhitched his horse from the buggy. With a scowl, the lawman set out back in the direction they'd come, where he'd likely find a mad, wet Charlotte waiting for him.

Once released from his imprisonment, Alex climbed out of the buggy and regarded Charlotte's father with an even stare. Several responses came to mind. *Thank you* was not one of them.

"Alex Hambly," Beck said. A statement, not a question.

Alex shook off the rain. "I am, sir."

"You and I are long overdue for a talk. Let's get out of this weather, shall we?" Beck gestured to the building across the street. "My office."

"Gladly," Alex said as he bit back on his temper.

Mr. Beck adjusted his hat and gave him a sideways look. "Spoken like a man who has something on his mind."

Alex let out a long breath. "Other than false imprisonment? Yes."

"About that." Mr. Beck paused. "There was some confusion when I sent for the buggy. I was told a man had driven off in it. Only after I sent the sheriff looking for it—and you—was I informed that Charlotte went along for the ride. So I owe you an apology."

"Apology accepted." Alex lifted the collar on his coat against the rain pelting his back.

"This way." Mr. Beck paused to allow a wagon to pass then stepped into the street. "I don't understand why Charlotte wasn't in the wagon when the sheriff found you."

"I don't understand that either, sir. We were having a relatively calm conversation, given the limitations your daughter puts on my sanity, and then she took off. Said she had to freshen up. In the rain?" Alex side-stepped a puddle of muddy water and stepped up onto the sidewalk. "I did my best to talk her out of it."

"With no luck, obviously."

"Obviously."

Beck held the building's door open for Alex, then gestured down the hall. "My office is at the end on the left," he said, nodding to the man behind the front desk. "Go on in and make yourself at home. I'll be right there."

Alex did, though nothing in the rustic space felt the least bit like home. From the hand-hewn walls to the animal hide covering the lone settee in the corner, the room belonged in some hunter's cabin rather than as the center of Beck Mining's operations. Only the desk, of regal proportions and provenance, gave hint of the room's purpose. Then there was the oddly elegant white marble fireplace. Strange in such a setting. Above it hung something even more odd: a painting of a meteor shower in the spring sky.

"The Lyrids," Alex said under his breath.

"I believe so. Comes in the spring, around Charlotte's birthday." Daniel Beck closed the door behind him. "I understand you've an affinity for the stars and planets. So does my daughter, though she would not admit it."

Alex's heart lurched at the thought that Charlotte Beck might also enjoy stargazing. "Until recently," he said when his thoughts untangled,

"I was employed by the Royal Observatory at Greenwich. I hope to return to that position once my business here is completed."

"And this business," Beck said as he settled behind the oversized desk, then gestured for Alex to join him, "it is of what nature?"

Alex took the seat across from Beck. "Forgive me, sir, but my business is none of yours."

"Well done, Viscount Hambly. I like a man who stands up to me. There's one problem with your statement, however. Your business here is none of mine, except for the property on Summit Hill." Beck steepled his hands. "That piece of land is of great interest to you, isn't it?"

"Only as it applies to my goal of settling debts and ridding the family of unprofitable property."

"Your Summit Hill property isn't worth the paper the deed is printed on." Beck shrugged. "Neither is the plot I own, for that matter. So you can imagine my interest when I'm confronted with a group of investors keen on taking this worthless property off my hands for what they term a good price."

Alex felt his rain-soaked shirt drying against his skin and tugged at his collar. By degrees, he realized he sat before the father of the woman whose kisses still haunted him. His traitorous mind immediately wandered to smoldering ribbons and the kisses they'd shared. When he realized Daniel Beck was staring at him, Alex cleared his throat and collected his thoughts.

"Yes, well, if there's nothing further you require of me, I'll be going." Alex turned to leave but stopped when Beck called his name.

"Tell me about my daughter, Viscount Hambly."

Alex froze. "What of her, sir?"

"What do you think of her?"

Alex swallowed hard and worked to keep his expression neutral. "I think she's a fine young lady."

"Go on," Beck said slowly and with no small measure of menace.

"A woman of excellent reputation and—"

"Honesty," Mr. Beck said, "is more highly valued in this office than flattery. I am well aware of my daughter's good qualities. However, I also know of a few that are not so good."

What to say?

"She's a beautiful woman, Mr. Beck," Alex said before he could stop himself.

Charlotte's father leaned forward. "But?"

"But…" His thoughts jumbled and the words disappeared faster than Jacob's Comet. Alex let the silence fall between them as he plotted his escape.

"Has she picked your pocket yet?" Beck asked.

Alex hadn't expected that. "Actually, yes. But she returned the watch," he hastened to add. "She said she was merely trying to get my attention."

"And it worked?"

He nodded. "It did."

Mr. Beck's laughter filled the expansive office. "That's my girl. She can be frustrating." He gave Alex a sideways look. "Listens about as well as a doorpost unless she's of a mind to."

Again Alex adjusted his collar. "Indeed. A walking disaster." He glanced quickly at her father, who merely nodded in agreement.

"Break some of your things, did she?"

Alex thought of that afternoon in the observatory. "I've a telescope that's a bit worse for wear because of her. And there was a project I spent all night recreating thanks to her decision to…" He shook his head. "Never mind. What she takes in patience she makes up for in entertainment value."

"Keep going," Mr. Beck said. "I rarely come across another man who understands my daughter as well as I do. And tolerates her."

"I can't say I tolerate her," Alex protested. "It appears fate continues to put us together, though I've no sane reason as to why."

"Perhaps it's not fate at all." Beck paused. "Perhaps it's the Lord who directed your paths to meet."

"If that's true," Alex said, "then the Lord has a greater sense of humor than I do."

"I'm curious," Mr. Beck said. "Those newspaper stories. The *Times* and those others. Were they exaggerated?"

"Exaggerated?"

"Was she truly the star of Bill Cody's show? I just wonder if she's as wayward as the press makes her out to be. I've heard Gennie's opinion. I'd like to hear yours."

"I don't think wayward is quite the term. She's…" Alex shrugged. "I'm sorry, sir, but your daughter defies description."

"But she did ride across the arena behind one of the braves and shoot a hole in Bill's hat?"

"That is something she did confirm. And I heard the story too many times from eyewitnesses who described how spectacular she looked while…" The impropriety of the image in Alex's head hit him full force when he looked at Charlotte's father. "In any case, rest assured your daughter can handle her own with a horse and a weapon."

"And the fact that my brother gave you a black eye for getting too familiar with her." Beck crossed his arms over his chest, revealing the pistol at his waist. "Tell me more about this."

Again, Alex needed a moment to process the change of topic. "Yes, well, I was standing in my garden, looking for Jacob's Comet."

"Jacob's Comet?"

"As I said, I am an astronomer by trade," Alex explained, "and I recently wrote a paper on the comet, which until now has defied calculations on its orbital…" He shook his head. "Anyway, I was standing in my back garden, hoping to catch a glimpse of the elusive comet, when I heard an odd sound, not unlike the protest of a small child."

"I see," Beck said. "And this was my daughter?"

"It was, actually, though I did not know this until I caught her."

"Caught her?" Beck shook his head. "I don't follow."

"Best I can tell, she must have climbed out the window and managed to fall over the balcony."

"During a formal event?" Mr. Beck's eyes narrowed. "Were we speaking of anyone but my Charlotte, I would dispute your claim. In this case, however, please proceed."

"That's it. I was looking up at Orion, which was partially obscured by clouds, when I heard the aforementioned cry. And then your daughter landed in my arms."

"I see."

Alex waited while Charlotte's father sat quietly, either disputing the tale or merely imagining it as it played out.

"So," Mr. Beck finally said, "if you were innocently studying the heavens and Charlotte was merely doing what Charlotte generally does and disobeying all the rules of good and proper behavior, what was it that made my brother angry enough to hit you? Especially right there in your father's ballroom?"

"That I cannot say."

Beck lifted a brow. "Cannot or will not?"

"Cannot," Alex stated with assurance. "I only sought to bring your daughter's missing fan back to her before it was found and an explanation required of her. I did not intend to besmirch anyone's reputation. In fact, I thought I was protecting hers."

Again silence fell between them, punctuated only by the rain tapping against the window. Alex felt the water in his boots as he shifted positions.

"So," Daniel Beck finally said, "how long have you been in love with my daughter?"

A lady does not let love, either the lack of it or its presence, hinder her from considering a proper and well-placed marriage.

—*Miss Pence*

"Love?" Alex gulped. "Sir, I hardly think my passing acquaintance with your daughter constitutes love."

Mr. Beck chuckled. "No?"

"No."

Though the kissing might.

And the way his heart raced when he looked into those green eyes of hers.

But he couldn't possibly love her. He'd have to forget all of her irritating qualities, which he certainly could not.

"You're certain of this, Viscount Hambly?"

"I am," Alex said, though the opposite was more likely true.

Charlotte's father slowly nodded. "I suppose not. Though it does appear you have some strong feelings for her, and the two of you have a shared history."

"I will admit strong feelings. Anyone who has spent much time in Charlotte's presence would. But not as strong as you're suggesting, sir."

"Charlotte, is it?" Beck's expression turned serious. "I've sources, Alex. Good ones. It is an established fact that Charlotte did indeed land in your arms in the garden and stole your watch. Am I to understand there was nothing else?"

Alex considered his words carefully. "There was a dented telescope and a ruined set of notes that almost cost my career. Those I've already mentioned. Oh, and the fire. And the race. She cheated, by the way." He paused. "And the fact that she's ruined our business deal, and then I almost went to jail today when I was merely trying to have a simple conversation with the woman."

And kiss her.

With each incident imparted, Mr. Beck nodded. He didn't seem a bit surprised by any of the audacious things his daughter had done.

"Is that all?" he finally asked.

"Isn't it enough?" Alex answered, exasperated.

"Pies," Mr. Beck said. "Has she stolen any yet?"

"Pies? I don't follow, sir."

"No problem with hanging the staff's unmentionables from the trees or spittoon tipping?" He waved away the odd comment. "Never mind. I suppose there are some things my daughter has outgrown in her slow search for maturity."

Alex shifted positions. "Don't be so certain."

Mr. Beck lifted a brow. "My daughter thinks I find her an embarrassment to the family. She may have mentioned I'm not allowing her to participate in the ridiculous New York season this year."

Alex chuckled. "Indeed, she did. As I recall, she was burning her corset in her grandfather's fireplace at the time."

"Hence the fire?" Beck shook his head.

"It was sparked by flying embers from your daughter's excessive use of a fire poker. She was quite adamant that the undergarment burn."

Mr. Beck began to laugh in earnest. "And it did?"

"Along with the ribbons on the back of her dress. She was already in a mood, so you can imagine how well received my efforts at putting out the fire were."

The businessman's laughter ceased. "And how did you manage this?"

"A pillow," Alex said. "In her state, I dared not douse her with water. She might have turned the poker on me."

Again Mr. Beck dissolved into a fit of laughter. "So you beat out the flames with a pillow?"

"Perhaps not *beat*," Alex corrected, "but yes, I did use some measure of force to halt the fire before it did any further damage."

"And this was not"—he struggled to speak while laughing—"not well received?"

Alex grinned. "It was not."

"And yet you persevered."

"I did, sir."

Daniel Beck shifted positions to regard Alex with a suddenly serious expression. "I like you, Alex." He seemed to be considering his words. "You're a good man."

The unexpected praise left Alex with nothing to say beyond a hasty, "Thank you."

"I am aware of your accomplishments in the field of astronomy. How did you attain your position at the observatory?" He paused. "Did you depend on your father's connections?"

Alex paused to consider how best to state his thoughts to the Earl of Framingham's heir. "With all due respect, sir, I depended on no one other than myself."

"I see." Outside, thunder rolled low and long, and the window-panes shuddered. "Would it surprise you to know I disagree?" Beck waved away Alex's protest. "Oh, it's fine that you get along without any-one's help. I applaud that. You've only just slightly miscalculated."

"Have I?"

"Indeed. The Lord. He knows our plans, but He makes His own, and His ways are not ours."

Not the argument Alex expected. "Yes, well, that is true."

"You a believer in the Almighty, son?"

"I am, sir, though I'm not much for vocalizing the fact."

Beck seemed to be appraising Alex. Before he could speak again, however, the door flew open and a soggy Charlotte Beck stormed in. From the top of her rain-soaked head to the tip of her mud-caked shoes, she looked as if she'd been walking in the weather for days rather than an hour.

"You!" she said, spying Alex.

"You look awfully sour," he said as she slogged toward him, wet skirts trailing in her wake. "Apparently the freshening up didn't work."

Charlotte's eyes narrowed, and she pointed at him. "I told you to wait. Did you? Oh, no, of course not. I just wanted to freshen up. Is that too much to ask? Truly, Alex, I fail to see why—"

"Enough, Charlotte." Alex grasped her wrist just tight enough to still her hand. "Stop talking. This instant."

She froze, her lips half-forming her next words and her green eyes wide. By degrees, Charlotte closed her mouth, and her eyes narrowed.

Then came the laughter and applause.

From Daniel Beck.

"Well done, Viscount Hambly." Mr. Beck walked around the desk, leaned against its edge, and crossed his arms over his chest. He turned to Charlotte. "Sit down, Buttercup. We need to have a conversation."

Alex quickly released her then took a step backward lest she retaliate. "If you'll excuse me then."

"No, stay a moment," Mr. Beck said. "This pertains to both of you." He turned to Charlotte, who stood rooted in place. "Do sit down. You're dripping everywhere."

"I will not. Not until this man explains why he left me out in the wilderness in a rainstorm." She began to lift her hand and point again but obviously thought better of it. "What sort of man does that to a lady?"

"What sort of lady wanders off into the wilderness in a rainstorm?" Alex demanded. "That is the most childish behavior I've ever witnessed. And because of you, I was handcuffed and hauled back into town by the sheriff with the purpose of being locked up in the Leadville jail for stealing your father's buggy."

"I have no idea what you're talking about," she said with slightly less starch in her speech.

"Of course you don't, Charlotte. You arrived mad as a wet hen and assumed things were a certain way. *Your* way." Alex paused to be sure she was looking directly at him. "And you were wrong. Yes, Charlotte. Wrong. You. Imagine that."

"Well, I never."

"Yes, you have, Charlotte. Twice." The words were out before he could stop himself, but Alex refused to look at Daniel Beck, either for apology or clarification. Charlotte knew what he meant, and that was sufficient for making his point.

Slowly, she straightened her shoulders and adjusted the mud-stained cuffs of her dress. Then Charlotte Beck turned her back on him and walked toward the door.

"Where are you going?" Mr. Beck called.

"Back to the Clarendon for dry clothes," she said as she reached for the knob. "You can't possibly expect me to stay in these ruined—"

"Stop right there, Charlotte," her father said. "We're not done, and I know you do not want the embarrassment of Viscount Hambly fetching you back. Be it from across the room or across Harrison Street."

Charlotte looked over at Alex, who fought the urge to grin. "You wouldn't dare," she said.

"Only with your father's permission," Alex responded.

"Which he has," Mr. Beck added.

Never let a man have the upper hand, even if he
already does.

——*Miss Pence*

For all her bluster, Charlotte Beck obviously knew when she was bested,
for she straightened her back, lifted her chin, and slogged across the
room to the chair beside her father, leaving a trail of mud, rainwater, and
leaves in her wake.

"Do not move," Beck said to Charlotte. He walked over to clasp
Alex's shoulder. "Again, well done."

"My pleasure, sir."

Daniel Beck nodded. "I've not seen anyone handle my daughter
that well. I could learn from you, Viscount Hambly."

"I'm right here, Papa," Charlotte said. "I can hear everything you're
saying."

Mr. Beck shook his head as if to dismiss his daughter's statement.
"I've reconsidered my stance on the property sale. If your investors are
still interested in my part of Summit Hill, I'm sure we can come to
mutually agreeable terms."

Alex ducked his head to hide his surprise. "While I appreciate your
offer, sir, I want you to understand that I did not seek out your daughter to try to influence you."

"I have my own theory as to why you sought out my daughter." Mr. Beck paused. "Suffice it to say I will be happy to do business with you. If we can come to terms, that is."

"All right, then." Alex shook Daniel Beck's hand.

"All right, then," Mr. Beck echoed. "Just one more thing. I'd like you to stay a moment and hear what I'm about to tell my daughter."

"Yes, sir, of course."

As her father walked past Charlotte, she turned and made a face at Alex. Alex blew her a kiss.

Mr. Beck turned just in time to see Charlotte's surprised face. "Do try to keep your attention on me, Buttercup."

She swiveled to face her father while Alex affected an innocent expression. Outside, thunder rumbled as rain splashed in torrents against the windowpanes.

"I've asked Viscount Hambly to stay and hear what I have to tell you for a specific reason. As I mentioned to Alex while we were awaiting your arrival, I have excellent sources who keep me informed on certain things related to you, Charlotte." Mr. Beck glanced over at Alex. "And you as well, young man."

Alex met his stare but said nothing.

"Charlotte," her father said, "I want you to understand that I am making an informed decision about your welfare."

She sat a bit straighter. "Truly, Papa, I am well past the age to make decisions regarding my own welfare."

"This is not a debate," he told her.

"Yes, Papa," she said softly.

"I love you, Charlotte, and while I'm not thrilled with some of your antics over the years, you have never been an embarrassment to me. Do you understand? A frustration, yes. Embarrassment, never. I regret my use of the term." When she nodded, Mr. Beck continued. "However, you have reached the point where I must examine your behavior with an eye toward the future."

"I don't follow," Charlotte said. "Have you changed your mind about Wellesley?"

"I haven't decided." He paused. "In light of what's just happened here, I will be taking you back to the ranch. There you will be free to paint or do whatever you ladies enjoy until I figure out what to do with you."

"All because I ran off in a rainstorm? Papa, that's absolutely ridiculous."

Daniel Beck froze and slowly turned toward his daughter. "Care to say that again?"

"I said," Charlotte replied in a tone far less forceful than her previous statement, "that if you are making a fuss because of a little rain…" Her pause seemed less intentional and more a requirement so that she might once again find her voice. "That is, surely you aren't changing your mind about sending me to university." Another pause. "You wouldn't."

"I would," he said, "and I am. And no, it is not simply because of a little rain. For now, at least, you'll be at home on the ranch and nowhere else. Do you understand?"

From where he stood, Alex could see Charlotte's lip quivering. There would be tears before this conversation was over.

"The ranch? But there's nothing there! And what about Wellesley and then working alongside you?" she managed, her voice trembling. "What of those things?"

Rather than acknowledge her question, Mr. Beck turned to Alex. "Leadville is too far from home and hearth, and I prefer other pursuits, so if your investors would like to purchase two mining properties rather than just the one, I am open to offers."

"Duly noted, sir." Alex's mind reeled with the possibilities.

"Now back to things of a more personal nature. Charlotte, there is a second option." Mr. Beck looked at Alex. "This also involves you, Viscount Hambly."

"Oh?"

Mr. Beck returned his attention to his daughter. "You're free to marry, Charlotte. And once married, you would also be free of your restriction to remain on the ranch, though that would preclude any further education at Wellesley."

"Marry?" She shook her head. "I prefer not. Besides, what man could I find while living on the ranch?"

"I've done that for you, Buttercup." He gestured to Alex. "My sources tell me Viscount Hambly is looking to barter his title for fresh funds in the family coffers and some extensive repairs of the family home at the Heath. Well, son, I'm willing to make that offer of my daughter."

Alex's heart seized. A solution and a new problem all at once. "Mr. Beck, I don't know what to—"

"Papa!" Charlotte rose. "You're not serious. You wouldn't dare trade me for some silly title. You've got one of your own. Why add another? Especially his."

"I assure you, Charlotte, my interest in seeing you yoked to the viscount has nothing to do with nobility." Mr. Beck's laugh held little humor. "It is because I've never seen anyone handle you and your outrageous behavior as well as Alex does."

Charlotte's face went red with fury. Thankfully, she appeared temporarily unable to speak.

Alex stepped forward, his fists clenched. Daniel Beck might be a man of power, but Alex would not be treated as if he were a pawn in a chess game.

"While I appreciate your offer, sir, I cannot imagine life saddled with your daughter." Alex shook his head. "Forgive me. That did not sound as I intended. Your daughter is quite lovely." Alex shot her a look and found Charlotte glaring at him, as though this were his fault. "However, I've been party to theft, injury, and property damage at her expense. The mind reels at what she could do with a lifetime ahead of her."

Daniel Beck's chuckle was interrupted by his daughter's cry of outrage.

"So you don't want me? Is that how it is?" she said to Alex. "Well, fine, because I cannot imagine life saddled with you either. And as for you, Papa, would you truly forbid Wellesley in favor of sending me off to be this man's wife?"

Daniel Beck looked at Alex then back to Charlotte. "In a heartbeat, Buttercup."

Her expression might have caused Alex to laugh had the situation not been so grave. "I must add my protest, as well, sir," Alex said. "I wish no disrespect, but if the bride is unwilling…"

"Indeed," Mr. Beck said, "however, I've given the bride options, which is more than it can be argued she deserves, given her behavior." He turned his attention to Charlotte. "In lieu of the option to cloister you at a nunnery until your behavior becomes less outrageous, I have set two choices before you. Which will you take, Charlotte?"

"Marriage or imprisonment?" she said, shaking her head. "Neither." At her father's exasperated expression, Charlotte Beck amended her statement. "Lock me up then, Papa. I'd rather be allowed to roam free at the ranch than be married to him." Her voice trembled, as did her fists.

"Thank you, Miss Beck," Alex said. "I completely agree. Given the options, it's preferable to me that your father keep you under lock and key rather than give you the ability to torment me further." He looked past Charlotte to address her father. "And Mr. Beck, I'd like it to be clear that I abhor the trading of titles for bank deposits. I am considering the path suggested by my solicitor under protest and duress, and only as a last resort to care for my widowed mother and the ancestral lands after years of financial mismanagement by people associated with my father. Marriage is, at this point, one of several choices, nothing more."

"Understood," Mr. Beck said.

"Should the property on Summit Hill sell for a decent price, I will happily return to Greenwich without the burden of a wife, or the need for one." He paused to look at Charlotte. "And should the opposite occur, I already have another candidate in mind."

"You do?" She sounded almost hurt.

"Yes. Now, if our business here is concluded, I will ask you to excuse me, Mr. Beck." And, without a backward glance, Alex walked out of Daniel Beck's office with his head held high and his heart racing.

Beck had offered up both mines. The solution to Alex's troubles was at hand, and it did not involve marriage to a stranger.

Nor to Charlotte Beck.

With deliberate restraint in case either of the Becks was watching, Alex walked slowly across Harrison Street through the downpour. As rainwater sluiced down his back and mud tugged at his boots, he thought about how easy it might have been to accept Daniel Beck's offer of his daughter's hand.

And how difficult.

All hope would have to be lost before he considered it.

He stomped into the hotel lobby then shed his soggy jacket as he made his way upstairs to his room. He found Will studying a stack of telegrams.

The solicitor looked up as the door shut. "You've been gone quite awhile, Alex."

"You wouldn't believe me if I told you all that's happened." He tossed his coat onto the nearest chair then shrugged out of his shirt. "Suffice it to say I have news."

"As do I." Will pushed aside the telegrams and rested his palms on the desktop. "But you first."

"The Summit Hill property is ours if we want it." Alex sat on the side of the bed and removed his boot. "You'll have to negotiate some, but Mr. Beck indicated he is amenable to selling to us." He paused. "He also mentioned selling Beck Mines and seemed interested in dealing with our people on that as well, though a sale on such short notice with our meager capital might be impossible."

"You had a meeting with Beck? And he offered not only the Summit Hill property but also his mining operation to you? How did you manage it?"

Alex tugged on the other boot then set it beside its mate. "It all goes back to his daughter. And he qualified his position by saying he would be willing to entertain offers. Not that he was eager to sell. There's a big difference between the two."

"Yes, of course. But back to Charlotte Beck." Will leaned back and crossed his arms. "She facilitated the meeting? I didn't expect her to be sympathetic to our cause."

"It was not exactly voluntary," Alex said. "She came looking for me and the buggy. The sheriff brought her. By then Mr. Beck had already removed the handcuffs, but we were all soaked and more than a little upset." Alex waved away Pembroke's questioning look. "It's a story for another day."

As was the tale of the offer of a Beck bride.

"Indeed." Will's brows rose. "Unfortunately, I've a story that cannot wait."

"All right." Alex leaned forward to rest his elbows on his knees. "What is it?"

"In lieu of a letter to Mr. Miller of Denver, I sent a telegram." The solicitor reached for the stack of telegrams and sorted through them until he found the one he wanted. "We've had a rather hasty response regarding his daughter Augusta."

"Oh?" Alex closed his eyes and let out a long breath. "What does it say?"

"To paraphrase, Mr. Miller is eager to begin negotiations for Miss Miller's hand in marriage. We are to meet with him in three days. Should negotiations progress, he will require his daughter to return from New York so that you might meet her and a wedding take place."

Alex opened his eyes. "The rest of my life reduced to a business deal."

"Well, yes, I suppose," Will said. "But these business deals happen all the time. You know that. Churchill and Manchester are but two of many." He paused. "I thought we'd agreed. Are you rethinking the plan?"

"This was to be one of several possibilities, not the plan," Alex said, even as he began to rethink the whole thing.

"Look." Will shook his head. "Americans have money, and we have those ridiculous death taxes. What's a man with a crumbling castle to do but find a wife with enough in her dowry to shore up the walls? I say there's no shame in it."

Alex rose and walked to the window, where the rain ran in muddy rivulets down panes that hadn't been washed in quite some time. "I say it's easier commented upon when you're not the sheep being led to slaughter."

"Fair enough."

Will's chair scraped across the floor as he stood. Alex turned to see his best friend regarding him with irritation.

"What?" he asked Will.

"Just wondering whether I should coerce you into this or allow you to ruin your future and the future of the Hamblys with your lofty ideals." Will shrugged. "Your friend would tell you to run, while your solicitor would have you on the first train to Denver."

Alex looked past Pembroke to the desk. "There are other telegrams."

Will sighed. "Yes, you're quite popular. Unfortunately all but two are from your mother, insisting you send money for one dire need or another. Apparently the telegrams had been collecting at the Western Union office for some time."

"And the other two?"

"From the observatory. Wanting to know when you'll be returning."

Alex collected those from Will and turned his back on the others. "Inform the countess I shall be handling her debts as soon as possible, and set up a meeting of our investors for three days hence in Denver. I rather like the Windsor, so perhaps a lunch at their dining room."

"Of course," Will said. "Shall I inform them of the topics to be discussed at this meeting?"

Alex thought a moment. Marriage to the Miller woman would give him leverage not only to repair the family's finances but also to grow them. And with Pembroke handling the business ventures, he could go back to studying the stars.

He tossed the telegrams onto the bed, then sat beside them. "Tell them nothing beyond the fact that the viscount has become aware of an additional investment opportunity and wishes to discuss the possible option of including them. Emphasize possible. I want them to think I don't need them. Any hint of desperation here, and we're sunk. And while I'm speaking with the investors, I'll let you see to Mr. Miller."

Four days later, Alex once again sat across the desk from Daniel Beck, this time in the Beck Enterprises headquarters in Denver. Unlike their last meeting, Alex walked in the door in dry clothes, carrying the promise of a bank draft that would make him a wealthy man. He placed the proposal on the desk between them face down.

Rather than look over the documents, the owner of Beck Enterprises steepled his hands and gave Alex an amused look. "You appear quite sure of yourself, Viscount Hambly. I take it you've come to purchase the Summit Hill property for your observatory."

Alex worked to keep his expression disinterested and gestured to the papers. "I bring an offer to purchase not only Summit Hill but also Beck Mining."

The businessman's brows rose, and he reached for the pages. "I see." Mr. Beck thumbed through the pages but did not appear to read them. "I don't suppose you're asking to sweeten the deal by including my daughter as well?"

"No," Alex replied firmly.

"And these offices?" Mr. Beck said with an amused tone. "Will you have them too?"

Alex glanced around the nicely appointed room, then returned his attention to the man across the desk. "Thank you, but no."

"I see." Mr. Beck returned the papers to the desk then sat back and regarded Alex with an even stare. "I have a counterproposal."

"But you've not yet seen what we are offering."

"I'm sure it is fair. More advantageous to you than to me, which is to be expected, but fair." Daniel Beck shrugged. "But my counterproposal is this: Marry my daughter, and Beck Mining is yours. With all the additional capital needed for expansion and any other miscellaneous needs both here and abroad."

"Thank you, Mr. Beck. Your counteroffer is generous." Alex paused to choose his words carefully. "But I've a potential commitment that prevents me from accepting."

"A potential commitment. Might that be the cause for your attorney's meetings with the esteemed Mr. Miller?"

Alex remained silent.

Mr. Beck waved away any comment. "Of course you wouldn't answer. You're more of a businessman than you let on, son. Your head might be in the stars, but you've the heart of a man interested in commerce."

"Nothing could be further from the truth." Alex rose. "However, I would appreciate a prompt response to our offer. Three days should be sufficient."

"Three days, it is."

It only took two before Alex learned he was the new owner of Beck Mining as well as Beck's Summit Hill mine. All that remained was to finalize the arrangements with Augusta Miller's father for her hand in marriage, and then all accounts with creditors and investors could be settled.

And he could go back to the Royal Observatory and reclaim his position in the astronomy community.

19

A man must never know when a lady has determined he is to be her groom. Better to lead him to the altar unaware than allow him to believe he did not do the choosing.

—MISS PENCE

July 13, 1887
Beck Ranch near Fort Collins, Colorado

Her best friend Gussie Miller was in trouble. The letter had arrived in that morning's mail—mixed in with a half-dozen missives from fellows who begged for Charlotte's attention or her hand in marriage.

Just last week Gussie had sent three lengthy descriptions of her adventures in New York, complete with final fittings for gowns, visits to milliners for just the right hats, and a trip to a lovely place in Newport for an outing with numerous others of their set. Now it appeared that while Gussie was in Newport, her papa had struck a business deal that had nothing to do with his interests in railroads and manufacturing and everything to do with Gussie.

Help me, Charlie. I can't possibly marry a fellow I've never met, even if he does own a castle and hold a string of titles. I just want to have my debut and think of marriage later. To someone I choose, not the man of Papa's choosing.

The words leaped off the page and lodged in Charlotte's heart. How many of their set had done exactly the same thing? Marriages of convenience between girls termed Dollar Princesses by the press and the titled European men who took them and their money away to drafty old houses in need of repair.

Well, it wouldn't happen to her best friend. It couldn't.

A plan most brilliant and only slightly devious kept Charlotte busy most of the morning. Of all the boys who'd begged for attention since her return from London, George Arthur provided the key to her jail cell—and Gussie's.

With a bit of practice, she just might be able to convince Papa he was the one. What Papa mustn't discover was that Mr. Arthur would be the one who got her off the ranch and into Wellesley next term, not the one she would marry.

Today she merely needed to make Papa believe he had a future son-in-law on the hook and that Charlotte must go to Denver to reel him in. While in Denver, she would see to ending the ridiculous arrangement to marry Gussie off, then declare her own engagement off as well. If she played her cards right, Papa would believe that nothing could aid in her recovery from the busted betrothal except attending Wellesley as originally planned.

She went over the finer points of the strategy and found nothing wanting. With enough encouragement from Charlotte, Gussie's Englishman would fall head over heels for her and forget his deal with Mr. Miller. And as for George Arthur, all Gussie had to do was bat her blue eyes a few times and convince him she was the better bride. In the end, neither man would be wed, and both women would get exactly what they wanted.

It was a brilliant plan.

Charlotte put on her most convincing expression and marched to her father's office with three of George's best declarations of undying love in her hand. She paused to stage a crazy-in-love expression then entered the room.

Her father looked up from his reading, and his face filled with concern. "Are you unwell? You look as if you've eaten something disagreeable."

Charlotte frowned. "No, Papa, but I've something of an important nature to discuss with you. I have letters here. Declarations of a certain man's intentions. I wish to pursue this further."

He closed the book and set aside his reading spectacles. "So Viscount Hambly has come to his senses?"

"I fail to see why you're so enamored of the viscount," she snapped. "Any man looking to marry for money cannot possibly be in his right senses."

Papa stared at her for a moment, and then he slowly shook his head. "You truly do not understand, do you? Hambly's a good man who happens to be in an unenviable position right now."

Charlotte shrugged, but couldn't help remembering their kiss. *Kisses,* she corrected.

"A position, I might add," her father continued, "that is not of his own making nor truly his to resolve. That he's taking on the responsibility and doing something honorable for his family is quite impressive."

She turned up her nose at the glowing compliments. "You don't know him as well as I do. If you did, you'd change your mind." She lifted the letters in her hand. "Now, George Arthur, on the other hand, is—"

"Tell me about this painting Bill Cody has requested," Papa interrupted. "Will it be another of those Wild West show posters, or has he requested something for his home?"

Charlotte resisted the temptation to flop against the cushions of the settee and make a scene, for that would merely prove her father's assessment of her maturity correct. Instead, she lowered herself with all the grace and deportment she could manage and then let out a long but dignified breath. "It is a rendering of his favorite horse. I did a sketch while in London."

"I see. Then perhaps you'll finish it soon, with all the time you have on your hands here." Papa reached for his letter opener and opened the topmost envelope on the stack of mail before him, then began to read.

"Father," Charlotte said when she could no longer keep her silence. At her use of the formal title, Papa's brows rose, but he did not look up from the letter. "I wish to dispute your claims."

"Which claim would this be?" he said evenly, still not looking at her.

"The claim that I am a child and not capable of choosing the right path for myself. Were you to admit the truth—"

"Were I to admit the truth, I'd remind you that you've been trying to convince me you were grown since you were still young enough for me to rock you to sleep." He lifted his gaze, but only for a moment. "As yet, there's been very little argument for it, and your behavior only testifies against it."

"That's completely unfair. Perhaps in the past I might have made a few missteps in judgment, but I assure you I have—"

"Missteps?" Her father's inelegant snort was quite out of character. "Darling, I seem to recall a certain incident in London that had you riding around Earls Court like Annie Oakley and shooting holes in Bill's hat."

"I started quite a trend in London."

"Indeed." Papa seemed to be considering something. He leaned forward. "George Arthur, eh?" He shook his head. "He comes from good stock, I'll admit, but you're only entertaining his offer because he doesn't have the starch in his spine to stand up to you."

"George adores me," she protested, her only defense against the truth.

"Adores you," Papa echoed with a shake of his head. "He allows you to lead him around as if he didn't have a thought of his own." He paused. "Am I wrong, Buttercup?"

He wasn't.

"Exactly," he continued. "And though marriage to a docile man might make for smooth sailing on your part, I warrant a man willing to take on the challenge of loving you by standing up to you on occasion will make for a much more interesting and longstanding match."

"But Papa, I—"

"I've said my last word on the subject of George Arthur beyond this question: are you so intent on escaping the ranch that you'd lie to me? Or do you have another plan for poor George?"

Caught. And yet she couldn't possibly tell him about the plan she'd concocted to free Gussie.

As if amused by her discomfort, Papa chuckled. "Take my advice and find your paint box and canvases. That will give you plenty to fill your time." He paused as the mantel clock chimed, then looked down at the page still in his hand. "Bill's last letter reminded me he'd be sending some of his performers again soon."

Charlotte rolled her eyes, grateful for the brief respite from her frustration. "Please, not again. The last time Colonel Cody's friends came to visit, the buffalo got out and trampled Gennie's roses." She sighed. "You're already investing in the show. Must you also provide free room and board to its performers? It's unbearable here with a veritable circus in the house."

Papa gave Charlotte a cross look. "You've just proven my point. Only a child wouldn't see past a bit of inconvenience to provide for a need." He exhaled a long breath. "Are you truly saying I should refuse them?"

"Well," Charlotte managed, "when you put it like that, I suppose not."

"That's my girl. Now, I suggest you get busy on Colonel Cody's commission."

"I've got a good start on it," she said, "but I find the ranch too distracting. I need to go back to Denver. It's the only way I can paint."

Papa looked as if he might respond, but then he shook his head and went back to his reading. He turned his chair to face the opposite direction, dismissing Charlotte.

She clenched her fists, crumpling George's letters. She would find a way to get to Denver. Gussie needed her. She made one more stab at her original plan. "About George."

"The discussion is closed."

"Because I am a child who cannot decide for herself?" Charlotte's anger flared. "So, Papa, were you and my mother children when you—"

She couldn't say it. She wouldn't rattle the dead bones of the mother she barely remembered to make her point.

And yet a quick glance at her father told Charlotte her point had been made. As he leaned back in the well-worn leather chair and closed his eyes, lamplight played over hair that time had woven with strands of gray.

"You're being unreasonable, Papa," she said in what she knew sounded like the whine of a child. "Why, as soon as—"

"Charlotte," he breathed with what was likely the last of his patience.

She'd gone too far. "Not Buttercup?"

Papa's eyes opened, and he met her stare. "No. Not this time."

"Meaning?" she asked, dreading the answer.

"Meaning I'm done humoring you."

"Wonderful." Charlotte kept her tone light, her expression teasing even as her heart slammed a furious rhythm against her chest. "For I wish to be taken seriously, not humored, and as such, I shall be on the next train to Denver to see to a situation with Gussie. And when the new term begins, I shall be at Wellesley."

Her bravery in short supply, Charlotte waited a moment before daring to look at her father. To her relief, all she saw was a curious expression.

"How can you be both married to George Arthur and attending university, Charlotte? And what's going on with Gussie that requires a visit?"

The clock over the mantel ticked at an even pace, and from outside, a horse's whinny drifted in on a fresh breeze.

Her father allowed the letter to drop from his fingers. "My guess is this is some sort of elaborate plot you've hatched. Knowing Augusta Miller, she's only going along with whatever you've decided to do. Same temperament as the Arthur fellow, that one." He appeared ready to continue his argument then let out a long breath. His expression hardened. "A married woman no longer needs her father's money beyond whatever is settled on her before marriage. A single woman, however, belongs at home with her father until she can prove herself trustworthy enough to be allowed to attend university. That's the end of the discussion."

"And should I strike out on my own?" She paused for what she hoped would be dramatic effect. "Would you send me off with nothing?"

"You won't."

"I might." Papa's eyes narrowed, and Charlotte hurried to amend her statement. "That is, I *could*. Would you leave me penniless?"

"Don't try me, Charlotte."

So he would disown her. Or at least divest himself of her care. This knowledge caused Charlotte to see even her pretend flight into George Arthur's arms in a different light.

The idea was unconscionable, as was remaining here amongst the cattle and the odd cast of characters who came and went due to her father's soft heart. But leaving Gussie to a fate she did not deserve was worse by far.

"Do you wish me to waste away to nothing here in this horrible wilderness?" Charlotte rose, unable to contain herself any longer. "What sort of father would allow this when he could easily send me to a suitable university to study mathematics?"

Papa's expression softened. "The sort who would rather have his much-adored daughter safely home rather than in the keeping of someone unworthy of her." He barely paused to take a breath. "I will give my permission for you to marry the first man I feel can truly be a husband to you and not a fool who allows you to carry his pride in your pocketbook. At this juncture, the only man in the running is—"

"Don't say it, please."

As much as she longed to argue the point, Charlotte knew she couldn't. What George lacked in gumption he made up in adoration. It was a decent trade.

Until one considered the issue of finances. Or rather the lack of them.

But at least he didn't frustrate her to distraction like a certain British astronomer.

"And in the meantime?" she asked.

"In the meantime I will continue to petition the Lord that the right man makes himself known."

"I thought you'd already found that man," she quipped.

Now she'd done it. Papa's spine straightened, and he appeared near apoplexy. "I have."

He allowed the silence to stretch between them, broken only by the tick of the mantel clock and little Danny's squeal from somewhere upstairs.

Charlotte knew when Papa would tolerate nothing further from her. She'd get to Denver somehow, and then to Wellesley after that, but prodding an already furious father would serve her no purpose.

"Well, then, I shall go and find my paints." Charlotte offered Papa a smile worthy of Miss Pence's best instruction, balanced the imaginary egg on her head, and moved across the carpet.

"Excellent idea," he snapped. "If only I'd thought of that. Try to keep out of trouble while you're at it."

"Don't be silly," Charlotte responded with as much sarcasm as she could manage. "You know I've never given you a moment's worry."

The comment carried her almost to the door before Papa's chair squeaked, indicating he now stood. "Buttercup," he called. "Come back here."

She complied, albeit slowly.

"I am furious with you," he said. "Absolutely beyond understanding why you must be so difficult." He paused to take a deep breath. "And yet, it's true. You do have quite a head for business. What if I gave you a chance to make your first deal as a junior member of the firm?"

"You're inviting me into the firm?" Hope rose inside her, as did suspicion.

"Pending your agreement to my terms, yes."

She reached for the door frame and held on tight. Had she misheard or was her father actually giving in? "And what might that be?"

He returned to his chair and regarded her for a moment. "You know my feelings about Viscount Hambly."

"Oh, Papa, no. Must you continue to bring up that man? I know you hold him in the highest esteem, but truly—"

"First lesson in business, Charlotte. A smart businessman—or woman—listens more than speaks." The chair creaked as Papa leaned back and looked at her, shaking his head. "Never judge the worthiness of the deal until it has been presented in its entirety."

"All right," she managed with the proper amount of contrition. "Please continue and I'll not interrupt."

Whatever the deal, she'd likely agree to it if it meant she got what she wanted. Her only prayer was that the irritating viscount was not part of the arrangement.

"Sit down."

She did. Quickly and quietly.

"You wish to attend Wellesley," Papa said after a moment. "And I will allow it."

Charlotte kept her smile in check, but inside, she jumped with glee. "Thank you, Papa."

"Don't thank me yet." He reached for his pen and studied it a moment before setting it aside. "The remainder of the bargain is this: To secure a position as a junior partner upon your graduation from Wellesley, you will have nothing further to do with your Mr. Arthur. And I mean nothing. No flirtations, manipulations, or communications of any sort. Do you understand?" When she nodded, he continued. "Now for your friend Gussie. She will be spared the arranged marriage the two of you are so keen to prevent."

"Oh, thank you," Charlotte said as she jumped to her feet. "I couldn't have agreed to Wellesley in good conscience without helping Gussie too. But how did you know? About Gussie, I mean?"

Papa's brows rose but he said nothing. Likely whatever he knew of Gussie and the mystery royal came from his friend Mr. Sanders at the Pinkerton Agency. Papa did have his connections, after all.

"I'm sorry," Charlotte returned to her seat. "Do continue."

Her father took a deep breath and let it out slowly. "Please understand that though you are hearing this for the first time, I have been thinking very seriously about this arrangement since I returned from Leadville. Also, you must know I wish only the best for you." He paused. "You do know how very much I love you, don't you?"

"Yes," she whispered. As much as she and Papa butted heads over just about everything lately, the fact that he adored her was never in dispute.

"All that remains, then, is for you to agree to the final terms of the bargain." Papa's gaze swept the length of her. "Upon graduation from Wellesley, you will return to Denver to take a position as full partner on the board of Beck Enterprises. And you will marry Alexander Hambly."

Had she heard correctly? "Marry…"

"Yes, Charlotte," he said in his sternest voice. "Marry. After a four-year engagement, during which you will complete your education."

"But, Papa, I…" She couldn't find the words. "He will never agree to it," she finally managed.

"Leave that to me. I wish to know whether you agree."

Four years was an eternity. Anything could happen.

"And you're certain Gussie will not be forced to marry whatever duke or earl her father's found for her?" she asked.

"I'm certain of it," Papa said. "And for the record, the fellow is a viscount and a rather likeable one, at that."

"So let me be clear," Charlotte said in her most businesslike voice. "What happens if, theoretically, the engagement is called off? By Mr. Hambly, of course," she hastened to add.

"It won't be. Hambly's a man of his word. But in any case, you cannot be held responsible for a broken engagement unless..." He shook his head. "Oh, no, I'll not be offering any sort of opportunity for you to get out of this. The deal is a marriage to Hambly four years from now in exchange for a place on my board, and that's final."

"Even if Alex does not cooperate?"

"Buttercup," her father said, "have you ever met a man who refused to cooperate with you?"

The truth, and they both knew it. And then she remembered something. Hadn't the viscount told her in great length about the ways a marriage could be annulled? Surely she could strike a bargain of her own with the awful man.

Four years from now, of course.

Charlotte jumped to her feet and launched herself into her father's arms. "Yes, Papa, I agree."

He tucked her head under his chin and enveloped her in an embrace. "You're certain?"

"I am. Very certain."

Certain that four years was long enough to figure out a solution that did not involve a lifelong marriage to Alex Hambly, no matter what Papa said.

20

A lady should know two things: how to make an
entrance and when to make an exit.
—MISS PENCE

July 20, 1887
Leadville, Colorado

"Impossible. The investors cannot possibly be asking for more time."
Alex slammed his fist against the wall of the newly leased Leadville office
of Hambly Mining Ltd., then turned to face Will Pembroke. "Negotiations are complete."

Will shrugged. "I've no explanation for it. This morning things were
fine. A half-hour ago this came."

He handed Alex a telegram. *Funding on hold until further notice.*

"That's it?" Alex demanded. "What does this mean?"

"It means that should you wish to go forward with your purchase
of the Leadville properties, your funding options have now become
limited."

"Limited."

Alex moved to the window to look down at Harrison Street, then
lifted his gaze to the sky, where smoke from the smelting operations
threatened to choke out the sun. For all the wealth that flowed from the
Leadville mines, so did an equal or greater measure of ugliness. Even the

stars were obscured on all but the rarest of nights by the smoke. The odds were that tonight, even with no moon, the comet he'd hoped to see would not be visible.

And yet an observatory was to be built here?

He'd considering bringing up the matter with Will or perhaps even with those who would build the observatory. As an astronomer in the employ of the royal offices at Greenwich, Alex had an obligation to bring up such concerns. But as a Hambly bent on shoring up his family's crumbling fortune, to offer up anything but silence on the matter was unthinkable.

So he'd kept his opinions to himself, even as his conscience became harder to quiet.

"There are other ways to do this," Will said, interrupting Alex's thoughts. "Or we can abandon the deal altogether."

Again, Alex's conscience complained. Still, what he owed to his family took precedence.

"The deal's already been done and the documents signed." He crumpled the telegram and threw it. "All that remains is to write the check."

Will said nothing.

"Yes, I know. From a bank account that has little in it." Again the temptation to slam his fist against the wall beckoned. "They're stalling. What do you make of it?"

"Could be any number of reasons for the delay," Pembroke said. "Men with money tend to be skittish."

"Yes, well, I wouldn't know."

The truth in that statement stung. Unlike these Americans he found himself surrounded by, he felt wealth was to be used but not flaunted. He was a Hambly from a long line of well-connected and regal Hamblys, and as such, money had rarely held any value beyond the fact that it kept the land in the family and prevented boredom or empty bellies.

Until he had to, Alex hadn't given money or the lack of it any consideration.

"Look," Will said, "You're a man of means. At present, your means just happen to be on hold."

"Until the investors come to their senses," Alex said. "And depending on the reason for this delay…"

He couldn't continue. The idea of walking away from a deal so close to being done was beyond consideration. As was failing.

"Or until your upcoming marriage to the lovely Miss Miller," Will supplied.

A reminder Alex didn't need. "I suppose."

Will shifted positions to affect a casual pose. "Might I remind you that your wife's father holds no small amount of influence in this state and beyond?"

"Miss Miller is not yet my wife," Alex said. "And what assurance have I that the issue would be settled in a timely manner? My understanding is that Americans make a fuss and drag these things out for months. Why, I haven't even met the woman I'm to share a name with, Will. Don't you find that a bit odd?"

"Many things these Americans do strike me as odd." Will grinned. "But what matters is that there is to be a marriage, Alex, likely by the end of next week, and with it a substantial deposit into your bank account."

"Of course."

"That should be in plenty of time to appease anyone looking to dip into the Hambly coffers."

"And if it is not?"

"It must," Will said. "And then you're free to return to your work at Greenwich while your wife goes about the business of whatever it is wealthy American women do once they've been wed to a royal." He joined Alex at the window. "Say, isn't that Beck's right-hand man there?"

Alex followed the direction of Will's gaze and spied Hiram Nettles crossing the street toward them. A moment later, Nettles disappeared inside the building.

"Wonder who he's come to see," Will said.

A moment later, the door opened, and Alex turned to see Beck's man standing in the entryway. "Guess that answers your question," Alex said to Will. "Do come in, Mr. Nettles."

"A moment of your time is all I need," Nettles said. "Mr. Beck wishes a meeting with Viscount Hambly."

He thrust an envelope toward Alex. When Will stepped between them to retrieve it, Nettles allowed it with a sigh.

"It appears our presence is requested on the evening train bound for Denver." Pembroke met Alex's stare. "Which leaves at a quarter to four."

Alex reached for his watch, an action that never failed to bring thoughts of a certain green-eyed pickpocket. "It's half past two already," he said as he snapped the cover shut and replaced the watch in his vest pocket. "Surely Mr. Beck's not so interested in seeing me that he'd require me to miss my dinner plans."

Not that he had any.

"I assure you great concern has been given to your comfort, sir," Nettles said. "Mr. Beck sent his rail car for the occasion, and his private chef will see to your evening meal. Elias makes a delicious mutton."

"Mutton," Pembroke echoed. "I always enjoy a delicious mutton."

"What is the nature of this meeting, Mr. Nettles?" Alex crossed his arms over his chest. "And please do not expect me to believe you're ignorant of the facts."

"I believe it concerns a business proposition that Mr. Beck wishes to make." Nettles shrugged. "He mentioned you would be likely to agree once you were told he could repair any delays in your current situation."

"Any delays," Pembroke echoed. "So Beck's behind this."

Nettles put on a look of complete confusion that was either genuine or extremely good acting. "The truth, sirs, is that this time all I know is what I've told you." He paused. "I'm to let Mr. Beck know immediately whether the three of us are going to be on that train. He will want to see you as soon as you arrive. What say you?"

Beck appeared to be going to a lot of trouble for this mystery meeting. It might be worth seeing what he wanted. That Alex might catch a glimpse of Beck's daughter was both a reason to say no and a cause to hurry.

"There's certainly nothing keeping us here. Not today, at least. Yes, why not?" Alex said as he once again went to the window.

"Excellent," Nettles said. "I'll inform Mr. Beck. In the meantime, you're welcome to board the rail car at your earliest convenience."

When Nettles had gone, Will joined Alex at the window. "What do you figure this is about?"

"Could be anything." Alex reached for his coat and hat. "There's only one way to find out."

"I'm still holding him responsible for our issues with the investors," Pembroke said. "No matter how good the chef's mutton is."

While Pembroke declared the mutton quite tasty, Alex had no stomach for it. For any of it. Between the issue of the observatory and the irritation of marrying an American stranger for money, nothing from the kitchens of the Beck rail car could tempt him to eat. By the time the train reached Denver, Pembroke and Nettles appeared to be fast friends, while Alex had sat in sullen silence the entire trip.

Thus, his mood upon greeting Daniel Beck was not the best, though he was slightly less irritated than the first time he stepped inside an office owned by the man.

Of course, this time he wasn't soaked to the bone and just released from a pair of handcuffs.

Unlike his Leadville office, the Denver headquarters of Beck Enterprises were palatial in size and grand in décor. The quality of artwork defied anything Alex had seen in the Louvre or the Tate, though he was unsure of the provenance of all but a few pieces.

"Welcome," Mr. Beck said. "Forgive the lateness of the hour, but I'm sure you understand that some matters are far too important to delay."

"About that—" Pembroke started.

"Mr. Nettles," Beck interrupted, "would you and Mr. Pembroke excuse us? I've a private matter to discuss with the viscount." He turned his attention to Will, who seemed perturbed. "I'm sure you understand, sir."

To his credit, Pembroke looked to Alex for his answer. When Alex nodded, Will did the same. "Agree to nothing," he said as he allowed Hiram Nettles to escort him out.

When the door shut behind the pair, Mr. Beck gestured to a chair then settled behind his desk. "Thank you for coming so quickly."

"I was assured this was a matter of some urgency," Alex said in response.

"And it is." Mr. Beck paused to adjust his spectacles. "For you, that is."

"I don't understand."

"You've received disappointing news."

A statement, not a question. But did Mr. Beck refer to the situation with the investors or did he have information regarding Miss Miller and her father that had not yet reached Leadville?

Alex let his gaze fall from Beck to the contents of his desk. Papers and folders were stacked in neat piles on one corner of the marble top, and half a dozen books had been situated on the other. In between sat a humidor that likely held cigars of excellent quality. When Alex looked back at Mr. Beck, he found the man studying him.

"Why am I here, sir?" he asked Beck.

To Alex's surprise, the older man grinned. "Well done, son," he said. "I appreciate a man who isn't afraid to get right to the heart of the matter." He paused. "I will do the same. I've a bargain to strike with you. A good one."

His tone came across as a bit too patronizing for Alex's liking. "And why would you wish to strike a bargain with me?"

Beck let out a long breath, then nodded. "I like you, Hambly. You and I, we take care of our own." He waved away any possible response from Alex. "I'll get right to the point." He opened his desk drawer, pulled out a file, and set it on the desk between them. "Read it."

With equal measures of curiosity and reluctance, Alex opened the file and began to read. Though his knowledge of contracts lacked in comparison to Pembroke's, Alex could easily ascertain that this offer would not only fill the Hambly family coffers but also provide ample monies to replace the funding now on hold with the current investors.

He closed the file and set it back on the desk, then shook his head. "This is a generous proposition, Mr. Beck."

"It is."

"What's the catch?"

Mr. Beck leaned back in his chair and gave Alex an appraising look. "My sources tell me your solicitor has not yet struck an agreement with the Miller family for Augusta's hand."

Alex's first thought was to protest. While nothing had been signed, Pembroke had assured him the wedding date was set for next week. And yet Daniel Beck was no man to be trifled with.

"That is true," Alex said. "At least not formally."

"I can assure you that you won't." He paused just long enough to allow Alex to consider the implications. "However, I wish to offer a substitute. My daughter."

"But, sir I couldn't possibly—"

"Save your protests, Hambly," Mr. Beck said. "Charlotte was no happier about this than you. However, she agreed, and I believe you will as well. You see, all I require from you is four years of engagement while Charlotte is at Wellesley and then a marriage upon her graduation."

"A marriage?" It took a moment for the idea to register. "With me?"

"Yes, with you." Again Beck waved away protest. "Lest you think I'll leave my future son-in-law wanting for funds during the betrothal period, please consult the papers in front of you. Not only will you see that I'll provide enough to satisfy your current needs, including paying those blasted inheritance taxes the queen's so fond of, but I've also allowed for a generous allowance while you're waiting to claim Charlotte as your bride."

Most of this Alex heard from far away. The distance between the opposite side of the desk and the chair where he sat suddenly widened with the thought of spending the rest of his life with the green-eyed menace who possibly detested him.

The woman who found it perfectly acceptable to burn her corset, to best him in a race by cheating, and to ruin not only a year's worth of research but also a perfectly good telescope.

The woman whose kisses still seared his mind and haunted his dreams.

"Hambly?"

At the sound of his name, Alex's attention returned to Mr. Beck. "Yes, sorry."

"I need an answer."

Alex rose. "I'd like my solicitor to look these papers over before I sign them."

Daniel Beck barely blinked, nor did his face give away what he might be thinking. "So you're accepting the offer? Pending Mr. Pembroke's review, that is."

Alex swallowed hard and willed himself to say anything but yes. Unfortunately, that was the only word that would come out.

An hour later, as he left the offices of Beck Enterprises with Will happily chattering about celebrating beside him, all Alex could think about was that four years was a very long time.

Anything could happen.

Part II

To the Victor the Spoils

Four Years Later

21

When seeking a suitable mate, a lady must first look to the future and then to the bank account. Failing that, a title is always preferable to a simple Mrs.

—*Miss Pence*

June 8, 1891
Denver, Colorado

The eighth day of June dawned gloriously clear with only the slightest bit of chill to the thin Colorado air. Charlotte stretched, half-expecting to feel Papa's rail car rocking beneath her as she turned away from the sunlight and buried her head in her pillows.

With her college days behind her, there was no need to stumble from bed for a predawn meeting of the Crew Club. No more endless afternoons working on the editorial boards of the *Legenda* or the *Prelude*. No more classes in Greek or philosophy. And no more lunchroom chores.

Charlotte yawned, her fingers curling around the edges of her blanket as her gaze landed on the stack of trunks that held her things from Wellesley. Where had the last four years gone?

Of all that had been left behind when she boarded the train for home, Charlotte would miss Professor Harris's mathematics lectures most. Though many of her classmates groaned at the thought of the courses, Charlotte reveled in every moment.

Now she could take what she'd learned in pursuit of her diploma to her desk at Beck Enterprises. Her first day in her new position would begin that afternoon, as Papa had indicated last night that he would be spending the morning otherwise occupied and wished no interruption from his newest employee.

Charlotte snuggled into the comfort of her bed and allowed her eyes to drift shut. Only then did she allow the thought that had been whispering through her mind since the beginning of her senior term: would Papa recall the ridiculous bargain she'd made all those years ago?

Thus far he hadn't mentioned a thing, and neither had Gennie. In four years, not a single reminder that upon graduation she would be obligated to marry Alex Hambly. This she took as Papa's way of coming to his senses without admitting he'd been wrong.

It was an answer to the prayers she'd spoken each night and repeated each morning for most of her first two years at Wellesley. By the third year, the prayer had become a whisper on the winds when Charlotte felt the need, and by her senior year the only wedding she would admit to thinking of was her friend Ava's, and then only in terms of what she might wear and what sort of parties would be held in celebration.

It seemed that the only thing her father required was her attention at board meetings and a full and thorough application of her education to the benefit of Beck Enterprises. And today was the day she began doing just that.

"Thank You, Lord, for this day," she whispered as sleep once again overtook her.

"Charlotte Beck, are you still abed?"

Gennie's voice jolted Charlotte from her slumber. As her wits and her vision cleared, she found her stepmother standing over her, illuminated by the sun pouring in the window.

"Papa said I wasn't needed at the office until after lunch," Charlotte protested as she pulled the covers over her head.

"Your father can have you when I'm done with you." The blankets gave way to Gennie. "And I need you downstairs in twenty minutes."

"Twenty minutes? Surely you're joking." Charlotte struggled into a sitting position.

"I assure you I'm quite serious." Frowning, Gennie released her grip on the blankets and summoned the maid. "I do not wish to make important decisions without you."

While Charlotte sat open-mouthed, Gennie turned and walked out the door.

"What sort of important decisions?" Charlotte called, but her stepmother did not respond. "Gennie? What—"

"Excuse me, Miss Beck." A maid appeared at the door, her arms filled with a simple day dress that apparently comprised Charlotte's ensemble for the morning. "Mrs. Beck asked that I bring these to you." She paused. "We're to hurry. Only a simple hairstyle for now. That's what the missus would like."

Charlotte bit back a sharp retort concerning what she would like and allowed herself to be dressed, styled, and released to find her way downstairs with three minutes to spare. She found Gennie in her favorite spot, the back parlor, deep in conversation with her dressmaker. While most rooms in their Denver home reflected Papa's love of dark woods and masculine appointments, the back parlor was Eugenia Cooper Beck's domain.

Today that domain had been invaded by bolts of fabric in shades of yellow, soft sage green, deepest red, and a lovely shade of blue, among other colors. Several handfuls of ribbons and lace coiled in a pile in the velvet chair nearest the marble hearth. Baskets of trim and other dressmaking paraphernalia had been deposited atop the table under the eastern-facing window, where the sun glinted down on scissors shaped like an odd little bird.

Gennie and the dressmaker looked up from a book of patterns.

"Oh, I'm sorry," Charlotte said. "Am I early?"

"Not at all." Gennie gestured to the chair beside her. "Join us. I'm just showing Molly the latest copy of *La Mode Pratique*."

Curiosity propelled Charlotte forward. "What are they showing for winter?"

Gennie pushed the magazine of French fashions out of Charlotte's reach. "There will be time for that later. For now, we've some decisions to make regarding your wardrobe." She turned to Molly. "Go ahead and measure her. She's a bit thinner than when she went off to university, but there should be little to do other than the alterations we've discussed."

Charlotte submitted to Molly's measurement tape. When the seamstress finished, she hastened away, taking the new French magazine with her. In her place came a maid bearing a breakfast tray.

"What is the hurry with having a fitting this morning?" Charlotte asked as she bit into her favorite morning treat, a warm croissant slathered with butter. "And why did she take the *La Mode Pratique* but leave all her fabrics and trims?"

"So you can choose which you prefer." Gennie shrugged. "Am I wrong to assume that as long as the dress is the latest fashion, you will wear it?"

Charlotte frowned. "I suppose, though it might have been nice to see…" She shook her head. "I'm sorry. Ignore me. I'm just a little anxious about seeing Papa today."

Gennie reached for her teacup and took a sip. "I see."

After one more bite of croissant, Charlotte shoved the plate away. It wouldn't do to indulge in too many of these, lest Molly be required to let out her dresses before she'd had a chance to wear them.

"So, shall we make some choices for you?" Gennie gestured to the treasure trove of cloth and trims, her expression animated.

Too animated.

Charlotte set her napkin beside the plate and gave Gennie a sideways look. "You seem nervous."

"Nervous?" Gennie shook her head then reached for the basket of trims. "Don't be silly. I'm just glad you're home. And now that you're no longer at Wellesley, you will need a new wardrobe." Her fingers worried with a length of tatted lace before she met Charlotte's gaze. "For all those social events you have coming up."

"Social events?" Charlotte took a deep breath and let it out slowly. *Please don't let her be thinking of the wedding that will never happen.*

As soon as the idea occurred to Charlotte, she tucked it away. Nothing had been mentioned, so nothing was planned. Gennie loved to plan, and a wedding would have been the topic of conversation for months, possibly years. That Gennie had said nothing gave even more credence to Charlotte's belief that there would be no joining of the houses of Beck and Hambly.

Gennie set the basket aside then moved to the settee, seating herself between the mounds of fabric. "Christmas will be here before we're ready, and you know how busy we always are during the holidays. With all the parties and receptions and the other events taking place during that time, you'll be glad I planned ahead."

"But it's only June," Charlotte protested.

Gennie's eyes widened as she looked away. "But the holidays will be upon us."

Charlotte leveled a look at Gennie. "So Christmas is the only reason for all this hurry?"

"Well, no." Gennie looked away then hurriedly returned her attention to Charlotte. "I'd hoped to spare you this on your first day back in Denver," she said softly, "but there's to be a wedding soon."

"Oh, no, there is not," Charlotte snapped. "I absolutely refuse to be held to something I agreed to when I was just a child."

Gennie's brows rose, and then she began to laugh. When she composed herself, Charlotte's stepmother returned to her seat at the table. Gently, she placed her hand atop Charlotte's.

"Darling, it's not your wedding I'm thinking of." She worried with the edge of the napkin with her free hand, then gave Charlotte's fingers a squeeze. "I know that once you left for Wellesley, you and Gussie Miller grew apart."

A tinge of regret seized Charlotte. As much as she might blame their varying interests for the gap in her communication with Gussie in recent years, Charlotte knew the fault lay squarely with her. She was the one who lagged in responding to Gussie's letters, who begged off from holidays at the Miller home in Newport, and who ultimately allowed their friendship to die from inattention.

"Gussie is getting married?" she asked meekly. "I didn't know."

Gennie appeared ready to issue a reproof but must have thought better of it, for she shook her head. "Just last week at church, Gussie asked about you. She mentioned that she had not yet received a response from you."

"A response?" Charlotte winced.

"Yes," Gennie said. "To her letter asking whether you knew she would be marrying George Arthur. She's concerned you'll be upset."

"George Arthur?" Charlotte couldn't help laughing. "Really? Oh, Gennie, he was never anything other than a sweet fellow who followed me around like a lovesick puppy. I had no feelings for him."

Gennie frowned. "So her worries were unfounded. It might have been nice to let her know."

"I'm sorry." And she was. "Perhaps we should invite them to tea."

"Perhaps you should go see her," Gennie countered. "Make amends for your absence. What about this afternoon? Unless you irritate me terribly, I'll go with you."

"I can't." Charlotte rose and straightened the wrinkles in her skirt. "I'm joining Beck Enterprises today as Papa's new vice president."

One blond brow rose. "Is that so?"

"Yes. Didn't he tell you?"

"He did mention he would be speaking to you today regarding a matter of some importance," Gennie said slowly.

"This is definitely a matter of some importance. Papa promised I would join the firm upon my graduation from Wellesley. He gave me his word." She paused at the door to look back over her shoulder at Gennie. "Well, I've graduated. So, as much as I'd like to visit with the Millers, duty calls."

"Duty," Gennie echoed. "Yes, your father's always felt duty was important. As is keeping your word. I'm sure you'll make a wonderful employee, dear."

"Thank you. I'm going to do my best."

"I'm sure you will," Gennie called. "No matter what your father asks of you."

Charlotte hurried up to her room. With the whole day ahead of her, there was no reason to stay home. If Papa didn't need her until later, she could surely busy herself doing something of value until the time came to begin her official duties.

She would start with a letter of congratulations to Gussie. And perhaps an invitation to tea.

When she arrived at Beck Enterprises, Charlotte went directly to Hiram Nettles's office. She found Papa's second-in-command partially hidden behind a stack of ledgers, his complete attention on his work. He scrambled to his feet when she cleared her throat.

"Is it noon already?" he asked, straightening his spectacles.

Charlotte shook her head. "No. Just a quarter past eleven. I'd hoped to settle in to my new office before meeting with Papa. If you'd be so kind as to tell me where it is, I'll not bother you any further."

Footsteps sounded behind her, and Charlotte turned to see her father walking toward them, his head down as he read a page held at arm's length.

He looked up. "Hiram, are the…Charlotte? You weren't supposed to arrive until later."

His expression bore surprise along with something akin to annoyance. Not exactly the greeting she'd hoped to receive.

"I thought I'd be early." She smoothed the front of her skirt and met her father's stare with a smile. The smile went unreturned.

Papa looked past her to Hiram. "I trust the papers are in order."

"They are," he said. "All signed and…" He gave Charlotte a nervous glance before returning his gaze to the page he'd been studying. "Signed and awaiting completion of the...umm, well...the transaction."

"And those arrangements have been made?"

"They have, sir."

Papa spared Hiram only a quick nod before linking arms with Charlotte. "Come this way, Buttercup."

She followed her father across the wide expanse of hallway to his office. "Shouldn't you take me to *my* office?" she asked as he ushered her inside and closed the door.

Her father walked past her to stand at the window. Silhouetted against the expansive view of the snow-capped Rockies, Papa still looked large and imposing. But it was a lovely day in Denver. The sunshine. The birdsong. And Charlotte Beck was about to join her father's company. She reminded herself of this as a niggle of concern snaked up her spine.

"Sit down, Buttercup," Papa said without turning around.

Something in his voice caused Charlotte's heart to sink. "You've changed your mind," she said. Then her anger rose. "Papa, you made a promise, and I wish to see you make good on it."

"I plan to." He turned her direction, his face obscured by the brilliant sunshine streaming around him. He gestured toward a lovely black leather case positioned in the center of his desk. "For you."

"Me?" She rose at his nod and retrieved the satchel. As she lifted it, she noticed the monogram engraved in gold letters just above the clasp. She looked at her father, who regarded her with arms crossed. "CBH?"

"Charlotte Beck Hambly." He stepped away from the window and the lamplight caught his gentle but firm expression. "Immediately after your wedding, you'll take a position in your grandfather's London office."

Charlotte sank back into her seat, her hands gripping the leather case, and closed her eyes. "I thought—hoped—you'd forgotten about that." She took a shaky breath. "Papa, I…"

She what? Did not wish to hold up her end of the bargain? Would refuse a position if it meant marrying against her will?

"I simply can't agree to it, Papa."

He lifted one brow. "You already have, Charlotte."

"I was only a child!" She shook her head. "Surely you'd not hold a grown woman to promises made in her youth."

"And yet you assured me on many occasions that you were, in fact, a grown woman. What am I to think?"

He had her there. Still, she'd not go down without a fight.

"But there must be another way. I simply cannot…" Words failed her. Of course, Papa was right, even if what he had required of her four years ago was not.

She ran her hands across the initials, then let out a long breath. Slowly, refusing to allow the tears to fall, she lifted her gaze to meet Papa's stare. As much as she wanted to argue or, failing that, flat out refuse, Charlotte knew when to pick her battles. And right now was not the time to argue. Not when she was so ill prepared for a debate with such huge consequences.

She affected a neutral expression and managed to ask, "What does my intended say about this?"

"Your intended realizes his good fortune in being wed to the heir of not one Beck fortune but two. You see, Charlotte, when my father dies, as long as you are a married woman, everything he owns goes directly to you."

This she had not expected. "But what about you? And Uncle Edwin? And Danny?"

"Your uncle is well set. Your brother will someday take over for me, and he will become the earl upon my death, which means he will inherit the ancestral home and lands. But the Beck companies are yours." He took the chair behind his desk, then folded his hands. "Provided you have a husband."

"I see." She bit her lip until the need to cry once again passed. "So the company I'm joining is not yours but Grandfather's?"

Papa rose, walked around the table, and pulled her into an embrace. "No, Buttercup. The company you're going to join is your own."

22

A man's wife is his treasure and a more than suitable
substitute for the treasure he must spend to keep
her happy.

—MISS PENCE

August 11, 1891
The Royal Greenwich Observatory near London

The calendar mocked Alex every time he looked at it, so he'd banished
the thing from his office and from the flat near Blackheath that he called
home. Still, each time the sun set on another day, he was acutely aware
of how quickly each hour passed.

What had seemed like an eternity in the future four years ago was
now exactly one day away. With the dreaded sands of time pouring
through the hourglass, tomorrow would be upon him far too soon. And
the grand irony of it all was that the Prime Meridian, the line where all
new days began, ran almost directly beneath his feet.

He slammed his fist on his desk and the inkwell rattled. The deal
he'd made four years ago stood despite all his efforts and prayers to the
contrary. Without the funds Daniel Beck provided, the Hambly family
debt might have crushed them all. And though the observatory on Summit Hill never materialized, the purchase of Beck Mining's Leadville
operations had brought profits beyond Alex's wildest dreams.

If only Daniel Beck had been reasonable and taken one of the many offers Alex had made over the years to settle the debt now coming due. What rational man of commerce refused double the amount owed to him?

Apparently one intent on marrying his menace of a daughter to the Viscount Hambly.

Alex pushed away from his desk and tossed his pen on top of his notes. The report, a treatise on cometary orbits and the probability that Comet Coggia-Winnecke 1873 VII and Comet Pons 1818 II were one and the same, would go unread until the next meeting of the British Astronomical Association anyway.

Alex leaned back in his chair. From this vantage point he could see the bright red Time Ball atop the Astronomer Royal's Flamsteed House and, in the distance, vessels plying the Thames.

While temptation prodded him to flee—to find some outbound ship and jump aboard, never to return—logic, or perhaps family honor, caused him to pick up his pen and go back to his work. Contemplating observations with the transit circle and the Sheepshanks Equatorial was a much safer way to spend the last afternoon of his freedom.

A movement out the window caught his attention, and Alex saw the red Time Ball jolt into motion. With a slow and even pace, the ball rose halfway up its mast, where it paused, indicating the time was now 12:55. In three minutes, at precisely 12:58, the ball would rise to the top. Two minutes later, it would begin its quick descent, indicating 13:00 hours.

The daily event, dating back more than sixty years, went unnoticed by most who toiled under the Observatory's roof, but some came just to see the sight. The onlookers were there now, a loose knot of people, their faces obscured by distance. Only when the winds were too high did the Time Ball fail to rise and fall.

Alex's stomach growled, reminding him that it was time for lunch. The upcoming move to the ancestral home at Hampstead Heath had resulted in bare cupboards and only the most basic of amenities in his Blackheath flat. Breakfast had been a meager affair.

He set his pen aside to consider his options. After one last look out the window to see the Time Ball declare the hour, Alex rose. A simple lunch from Greenwich Market would have to suffice.

He reached for his hat and headed for the door only to have it open beneath his hand, revealing a very grown-up Charlotte Beck.

Four years had been more than kind to her. And while she once wore her beauty with an unassuming air, it was quite obvious from her expression that the older Miss Beck knew exactly what effect she had on the male gender and reveled in it.

From the top of her carefully coiffed head—complete with feathered cap—to the tip of her well-shod feet, she looked as if she'd stepped out of a fashion magazine. And judging from the tiny waist of her dress, a fashionable frock of sky blue festooned with ribbons and adorned with ruffles at the neck and sleeves, her days of burning corsets were behind her.

And tomorrow morning, unless she'd found a way out that he hadn't, the American beauty would be his wife.

Then she smiled, and for the life of him, Alex could not think of a single reason why marrying her would be unpleasant. Ill-advised, yes, but judging from appearances alone, not altogether unpleasant.

The realization stunned him.

"What are you doing here?" he managed when speech finally ceased to elude him.

"We've business to discuss," Charlotte Beck said, "and I've been quite unsuccessful at securing an appointment with you since my arrival in London."

"Yes, well, I've been busy," Alex offered in explanation, though the truth was he'd found much to be busy with so as to avoid anything related to tomorrow's grand event. And, more importantly, to avoid Charlotte Beck.

Charlotte pressed past him, the blue feather on her cap tickling his nose in her wake. He recalled another hat and another blue feather, both of which were doused in a Leadville rainstorm. Ironically, that time he'd ended up shackled as well. She sidestepped a pile of books and moved toward his desk, then set a hamper on top of his papers.

"Considering the gravity of the situation, I hope you'll forgive the intrusion," she said.

Forgive the intrusion? Since when did Charlotte Beck apologize for thrusting herself into any situation, welcome or not?

An image rose of the ruined notes on his Jacob's Comet research four years ago, and Alex hurried to lift the hamper and gather up his pages. He tucked his notes into the topmost desk drawer, turned the key and put it in his pocket, then returned the hamper to the now-clear desk.

Charlotte laughed, and the sapphires at her throat caught the light. Alex dared to look into the green eyes of his future bride.

"I fail to see what you find so funny," he said as he began to recall why the two of them should never be considered a match. "You were once quite the menace where important research was concerned." He paused. "And telescopes."

"I have no idea what you're talking about," she said, though the humor in her voice belied her words. She opened the hamper. "You must be famished. Here. Chew on this while I set the table. Or what will have to pass for one."

Charlotte tossed him an apple, and he caught it. Before he took a bite, Alex lifted a brow.

"What?" she asked, pausing to regard him.

"I was just wondering if you might be ridding yourself of a groom with a poisoned apple."

Again she laughed. "Believe me, Alex, I've considered it. Ridding myself of a groom, that is." She gave the still-uneaten fruit a swift glance, then returned her attention to his face. "But not by poison. Too obvious."

"Well, that is comforting." He leaned against the desk and took a bite.

The apple was good, tart and tasty and just what he needed to hold his hunger at bay a few minutes longer, but watching Charlotte was even better. She moved with polished grace, a woman where once had been a girl playing at the endeavor. His eyes longed to slide down the length of her trim figure, but Alex didn't allow himself the pleasure. Instead, he watched her thoughtful expression, caught the afternoon sun as it spun gold into the curls that adorned her forehead, studied every nuance of her lips as they pursed in thought, of her gloved fingers as they worked to set plates and food for their makeshift feast. Then, slowly, his gaze traveled to her eyes.

"Do find your manners, Alex," she said evenly, "and stop looking at me as if I were the prize Christmas goose." She thrust a plate in his direction then gestured to the desk before taking a seat in *his* chair. "Enjoy your lunch while I offer a proposition that will benefit us both."

His chuckle of derision did not go unnoticed.

"You doubt me?" she asked.

"I doubt there is a solution I would agree to, and I assure you I've considered and discarded many options. As has my solicitor." Alex set the apple aside. "I refuse to break my promise, and your father refuses to accept anything other than a marriage in payment for what I owe him. Thus, tomorrow morning you and I will be wed."

"Of course we will," Charlotte said with far too much enthusiasm.

He gave her a perplexed look. "I'm sorry. I thought the point was to avoid marriage."

"The point," she said, toying with a sapphire earring, "is to keep our promise to my father, is it not?"

Alex considered his response carefully. "Yes, but—"

"But the mutton is wonderful." Charlotte smiled. "At least that's what I was told. So please, have your lunch while I explain." She paused. "I truly do believe I've found a way."

He complied, as much from hunger as curiosity.

She inclined her head in his direction. "Do you recall what we discussed in relation to marriage some years ago in my grandfather's parlor?"

Alex met her stare and one brow slowly lifted as a pleasant memory rose. "No, but I do recall a burning bustle and several memorable kisses. Were there two or three?"

The man was truly incorrigible. While she'd come here to solve their shared problem, her groom apparently preferred to bring up the embarrassments of the past. The temptation to remember those kisses tugged at her, but Charlotte held onto her dignity as well as her focus.

As she studied his features, every bit as handsome as she recalled, she forced herself to recall her purpose in making this visit.

"I'm going to ignore that." She smoothed her skirt. "Now, about my plan. Just as you suggested some years ago, I propose we go through with the marriage and then, after sufficient time has passed, have it annulled. Isn't that clever?"

"Clever." He repeated the word as if he were hearing it for the first time. "Are you serious? How could this possibly be a solution? We can't just go through all the fuss of a wedding and then announce we've changed our minds."

"Of course we can, though it's not as simple as all that," she said. "I did some checking, and you were correct. A marriage can be annulled if the couple does not..." She shrugged. "Well, you know."

"Yes, all right," he said slowly, "but how does this solve our problem?"

Charlotte warmed to the topic. "I promised Papa I would marry you if he allowed me to attend Wellesley and earn my degree. Unless I'm wrong, you're marrying me because Papa loaned you money to save your family."

"It's a bit more complicated than that," he snapped.

She'd hit a sensitive subject. Charlotte waved away his statement with a flutter of her hand. "With men it always is."

"I had a prior arrangement, and he made it possible to..." The viscount worried with his watch chain. Though her hand in marriage had been mortgaged to save the Hambly family from ruin, there were obviously limits on the details Alex intended to reveal.

Slowly, his gaze swung up to collide with hers. At that moment, Charlotte knew she had two choices. She could play the simpering female and hope to manipulate Alex Hambly back into good humor and into agreeing to go along with her plan. Or she could get right to the heart of the matter.

"Why so shy about this, Alex?" She toyed with the sapphire necklace Grandfather gave her for her last birthday. "I've sold myself too, and for a much less noble cause."

Charlotte sat very still and watched her future husband closely. Though he appeared to have dismissed her in favor of enjoying his lunch, Charlotte suspected the astronomer was preparing what he planned to say in response.

After a moment, Alex dipped his head. "Thanks to your father, I was able to settle some accounts without resorting to..." He paused as if deciding whether to continue. "Well, I was able to settle the accounts."

"And I was able to pursue a degree in mathematics." She watched his interest pique. "Which I plan to use in running my grandfather's company. And, eventually, my father's as well."

If Alex was surprised at the news, he did not show it. Rather, he seemed to be waiting for her to continue.

"So as you can imagine, a marriage and all that goes with it..."

"Such as a husband and children?" Alex offered.

"Yes. All good things, of course," she continued, "but I had hoped to put the things I've learned to use before considering them." She dared a peek in Alex's direction. "I'm sure you cannot understand."

Alex ran his hand through his dark hair, then shrugged. "It isn't mine to understand, is it?"

Charlotte thought only a moment. "No, I suppose not. So have we a deal? Will you help me? Help both of us," she amended.

Silence fell between them, punctuated by the occasional cry of seabirds outside the window. Unable to sit still any longer, Charlotte rose and went to the window. The view was lovely, just as she remembered. She spied a lone red ball atop one of the two cupolas on the building just beyond the lawn.

"Alex, what's that?" When he joined her at the window, she gestured toward the oddity. "There. The red ball on the roof."

He moved in close—exquisitely close—to follow the direction she pointed. Despite her best intentions to keep her distance, Charlotte leaned into him. The viscount smelled of soap and some sort of woodsy spice. Sandalwood, perhaps.

"That is the Time Ball," Alex said.

While he told her the tale of the timekeeping device, Charlotte closed her eyes and memorized his scent. Were she given to awakening each morning beside a husband—and she absolutely was not—she'd want him to smell as heavenly as this man.

"Do you wish to marry someone else?"

Charlotte's eyes flew open to the sight of Alex watching her. Though she hoped he'd asked in jest, she could find no trace of humor on his face.

"Someone else? No." She took a step back from the window. "I told you, Alex. I just don't think I'm ready to be some poor man's wife, and I know I'm not ready to be a mother. Not when I have so many ideas. For example, did you realize Beck Enterprises does not sell stock in the company?"

He shrugged in response.

"All right, well, my point is there are many things I wish to do, and marrying for love, then bearing my husband's children is high on that list. But honestly, that cannot be arranged, can it?"

He leaned against the windowsill and crossed his arms over his chest. "What do you mean?"

"I mean that love doesn't just happen because someone says it must. I know it isn't popular to ascribe that sort of requirement to a marriage, especially when so many of my friends gladly find a husband they barely know so as to call themselves Lady This or Duchess That. But I believe love evolves over time between two people who…" Charlotte allowed the remainder of the statement to remain unspoken. She'd already said too much.

Alex touched her sleeve. "There's nothing wrong with believing in love," he said gently. "I do."

Silence fell as Charlotte looked up at the man who had been nothing but a vexation when last they met. But now, standing so close to the only lips that had ever kissed her....

Charlotte took a deep breath and slipped from his grasp. Without comment, she turned her back on the Englishman and went to the desk to load the uneaten food into the hamper. Out of the corner of her eye, she spied Alex moving toward her, and her knees went strangely weak.

"Wait."

He placed his hand on hers, and she allowed it. Had she moved away, Alex might have seen her hands shaking.

"I still fail to see why you think this will work," he said.

"Papa wishes us to wed, and we shall. But my father, for all his money and power, cannot force us to live happily ever after, now can he?"

"No," Alex said thoughtfully, "I suppose not."

"Thus, if you were to sue me for lack of affection, or whatever it's called, then I could offer up proof to Papa that I am far too busy running the company to be married." She smiled and hoped Alex would as well.

He did not.

He removed his hand from hers. "So I am the one who will end what we shall begin tomorrow."

"Yes," Charlotte said. "I'll leave the details to you and your solicitor, but I hope this marriage of inconvenience will not last any longer than absolutely necessary. So," she said with what she hoped was her most congenial expression, "will you do it?"

The viscount paused only a moment. "Yes, Charlotte, I'll do it."

"Wonderful!"

Charlotte beamed at him, and then, before she realized what she was doing, she'd launched herself into his arms.

Inches away from the lips she'd kissed four years ago.

Twice.

He held her close, and once again she reveled in his scent. In the feel of his arms around her. In the way he dipped his head as if to kiss her.

Charlotte lifted up onto her toes to meet him halfway in a kiss that was every bit as memorable as the ones they'd shared in Grandfather's library.

Her mind finally caught up with her actions, and Charlotte slid from Alex's grasp. They stared at each other.

"Oh my," Charlotte whispered. "We will have to work on this arrangement, won't we?"

"Actually, Charlotte," he said slowly, "what we have to work at is not allowing that to happen ever again."

23

The bride should be the center of attention on her
wedding day and, as far as her groom is concerned,
on every day thereafter.

—*Miss Pence*

August 12, 1891
London

In light of the unfortunate kisses of the day before, when Charlotte met
Alex at the altar, which had been covered with fragrant orange blossoms,
pale pink roses, and lilies, she kept her gaze firmly on the clergyman and
not on her groom. And when the time came to present the bride and
groom as newly married, Charlotte presented her cheek for Alex to kiss.

Even though everything in her wished for just one more taste of
Alex Hambly's kisses.

Instead, she settled for taking his name, though upon its pronouncement by the dour white-robed clergyman, some of the bluster of
her grand plan evaporated.

Or perhaps the cause was the weight of the Hambly diamond, an
egg-sized stone set in a tiara of lesser diamonds and plunked on her head
in the early morning hours by Alex's enthusiastic mother. "All the Hambly brides have worn it," she had gushed.

And they all surely went to bed with headaches on their wedding nights.
Charlotte resisted the urge to pull the thing off her head and toss it
away.

To distract herself from the temptation, Charlotte looked up at the
canopy of roses and orange blossoms that covered the cathedral aisle,
then out at the sea of faces, most of whom were completely unfamiliar.
Her attention fell on Gennie, resplendent in embroidered violet satin
and matching feathered hat, beaming with joy while Papa tugged at his
cravat. Charlotte grinned as she spied her little brother, seated between
Gennie and Papa, mimicking the elder Beck. Grandfather and Uncle
Edwin completed the front pew, though neither seemed particularly
happy to be there.

Directly behind her family sat Colonel Cody, who winked when he
caught her looking. Charlotte returned the wink and added a sly grin.

According to Papa, the colonel had slipped away from his show, currently playing in Manchester, to attend. With him were several of his
performers, all former visitors to Papa's Colorado ranch. The sight of
these cowboys and Indian braves dressed in their Sunday best had surely
lifted a few brows of the stodgy Londoners in attendance.

On the other side of the aisle, Alex's mother, a vision of elegance in
gray silk, sat alone with no sign of the twin brother Charlotte had thus
far only heard about. Apparently the earl was not well. At least that was
what Alex's mother had offered in explanation.

Charlotte felt someone tug at her elbow and found Alex watching
her. "We've done it," he said.

"Yes," she managed to whisper as the last of the six bridesmaids filed
past, "we have."

She smiled at each of the Wellesley girls, all dressed in matching
pink chiffon Marie Antoinette-style gowns with frills of lace and bows.

If only Gussie could have been there, but she was far too busy with her own wedding. To George Arthur, of all people. Proof that there was a man for every woman who sought one. *And sometimes for the woman who did not.*

The viscount linked arms with her, and they followed the wedding party down the aisle and out into the gloomy British morning. Umbrellas were quickly raised above her, obliterating all but a tiny glimpse at the gray skies, while some poor soul kept the heavy duchesse satin train at the back of her dress off the soon-to-be-drenched ground.

As Charlotte allowed herself to be led to the carriage that would take her to Grosvenor Square for the wedding breakfast, she could only pray that the tiara balanced precariously atop her elaborate coiffure would not give her a splitting headache before the day was done. The tiny teeth of the tiara's combs were already jabbing her. But then, so was her conscience as she smiled and carried on the charade of being the adoring bride to Viscount Hambly.

Safely inside the carriage waiting to take them to breakfast, Charlotte watched Alex climb inside to take the seat across from her.

Just as the carriage door was about to close, Uncle Edwin reached inside to thrust a small package toward her. Along with the gift came the distinct odor of alcohol. Uncle Edwin's unsteady posture confirmed the source.

"For the bride on her wedding day," he said before peering up at Alex. "Care for her as if her uncle might find you and cause you great pain should you not."

"I shall, sir," Alex said with more deference than Uncle Edwin's behavior deserved. He passed the package to Charlotte without comment.

"Thank you," she told her uncle. "It was very kind of you to bring a gift."

His laughter once again sent the stench of alcohol wafting through the carriage. "I warrant you won't thank me once you've opened it."

And then he was gone. Charlotte looked down at the gift. A small book, it appeared, or something of similar size and shape.

She found Alex staring at her. "Are you going to open it?" he asked.

"Perhaps later." Setting the gift aside, Charlotte resisted the urge to tug at the tiara. "For now, I'll just sit very still and try not to ruin the Hambly diamond by tossing it out the window before the end of the day."

A short while later, the tiara still intact, Charlotte stepped out of the carriage and into the wedding breakfast, where she navigated the crowd of well-wishers, swelled to at least triple the number who attended the church service, to find her place at the bride's table.

By the time the second course was served, Charlotte could barely hold up her head, such was the pain from the diamond-studded instrument of torture. Somewhere, she thought, the dreaded Miss Pence was smiling.

The sun, what there was of it, indicated the lateness of the afternoon. Alex slid a sideways glance at his bride as they walked toward the waiting carriage. Gone was the defiant, green-eyed charmer whose talent to spark his temper was unmatched. In her place was a woman of docile temperament who neither spoke nor smiled.

The change in Charlotte Beck, now Lady Charlotte Hambly, was profound.

And slightly unwelcome.

Perhaps the Hambly tiara had done her in. Or maybe the hours of making polite conversation and greeting hundreds of guests was the reason. Whatever the cause, a meek and compliant Charlotte unnerved him. It was as if the earth had suddenly decided to turn on its axis and revolve the opposite direction. There simply was no precedent for it.

Daniel Beck followed them out into the London afternoon, clasping Alex's shoulder. "Congratulations, son."

Alex responded appropriately, but his attention—and his thoughts—centered on Charlotte.

"Buttercup," Mr. Beck called, but Charlotte continued walking. Her father stopped her, then enveloped her in an embrace that lasted only a moment before he handed her into the carriage.

When Charlotte was settled, Mr. Beck thrust his hand toward Alex. "I trust you understand you're to take only the best care of my daughter or you'll have me to answer to."

"I do, sir, and I shall. You have my word on it." For the brief time that Charlotte was his wife, he intended to do just that.

"I've arranged for a suite for you tonight." Mr. Beck met Alex's gaze. "My driver will see that you reach the ship tomorrow afternoon in time to sail to Venice. I trust you'll have Charlotte in Denver in time for Christmas."

"Yes, of course." Alex knew all too well their travel plans for the remainder of the year. How he would manage to pass the time in such close contact with his bride without kissing her again, he had yet to figure out.

Alex shook his father-in-law's hand, then climbed into the carriage, where he found Charlotte leaning against the cushions, eyes closed and the tiara in her lap. He left her alone until the carriage halted in front of the hotel.

When he touched Charlotte's knee, she swatted his hand. Startled awake, she gathered up the tiara and gift from her uncle and slid out of the carriage, leaving Alex to follow. Too soon he had retrieved the key from the front desk and arrived at the door to the suite, his silent spouse a step behind him.

"Shall I carry you over the threshold, Lady Hambly?" he asked to lighten the mood.

Charlotte ignored him, opened the door herself, then promptly attempted to shut it in his face.

Alex stuck his boot out to prevent it from closing. "Now that's the Charlotte I know," he said.

She moved away, the combined challenge of balancing the gift and the tiara apparently causing her to give up on both. Depositing the tiara on the nearest table, she tucked the gift—a book, Alex thought—under her arm and gave Alex a look that told him exactly how welcome he was in what she apparently felt was her own private domain.

In typical Beck style, their rooms were well appointed and lavish, as were the beautifully wrapped gifts languishing in piles in one corner of the sitting room. Alex watched Charlotte cross the expansive room, back straight and steps brisk despite the many yards of fabric in her wedding gown.

Their trunks had been delivered, as had an abundant feast. Charlotte reached for a grape with her free hand and popped it into her mouth, then moved toward the bank of western-facing windows without sparing Alex a backward glance. The orange glow of the setting sun cast his bride in shadows, preventing Alex from seeing her face.

The sound of voices in the hall behind him alerted Alex that he had not yet closed the door. When he did, Charlotte whirled and stepped into the circle of lamplight.

"Come no closer."

He ignored her. Instead, Alex shrugged out of his jacket and tossed it on the nearest chair. Next came his shirt collar, which he gladly deposited atop his coat.

"As per our agreement, I'll not share this suite or anything else with you, Alex Hambly," Charlotte said, eyes wide. "So you can forget any ideas you have. Do you understand?"

Alex held up his hands. "Trust me, Lady Hambly, I've entertained no such ideas."

Not exactly true, though he'd never considered his musings might actually turn into reality.

She seemed to relax as she threaded her fingers together. "Well, good. As long as we understand one another."

"Oh, I think we understand each other just fine."

He moved toward her deliberately and without removing his attention from her eyes, which widened with each step he made. Just before he reached her, Alex settled onto the settee by the window and affected a casual pose, though tension had him stretched taut inside.

If only he hadn't kissed her yesterday. Hadn't allowed himself a taste of the lips he'd been unable to forget.

On the table before him lay yet another platter of fruit, meats, cheeses, and several choices of breads, no doubt also courtesy of his bride's father. Had there been champagne or a bottle of wine, he might have poured a glass to bolster his courage. Or, perhaps, to dull the humiliation of marrying for money even though the marriage would soon be declared over.

When watching Charlotte ignore him became too much to bear, Alex turned his attention out the window, where the people of London went about their business, filling sidewalks and spilling onto streets clogged with all sorts of conveyances. Down there the noise was deafening, the stench ever present. But here in the honeymoon suite, the silence was deafening, and the room reeked of orange blossoms and lilies.

"Alex?" Charlotte's voice wrapped around his name and pronounced it with the slightest waver of uncertainty. When he met her stare, she continued. "It will benefit both of us to remember that ours is a marriage of mutual agreement."

Mutual agreement. Alex tried not to wince. Instead, he gestured for her to join him on the settee.

"I prefer to stand, thank you."

He shrugged. "Suit yourself."

"We really must stick to the terms as agreed upon yesterday."

"Immediately after which, you kissed me," Alex countered. Charlotte tried to protest, but he didn't let her. "And given your penchant for ignoring your end of our bargains, what assurances are you offering that this will not happen again?"

Charlotte shook her head. "Truly, Alex, you are insufferable." She moved toward the settee but made no effort to sit. "I'm serious."

"Then join me and let's have a serious conversation."

Alex watched her. After much deliberation, Charlotte perched on the edge of the settee, her back finishing-school straight and her entire demeanor stiff.

And yet her hair massed in wild curls at the nape of her neck, and a lovely flush of pink danced across her cheeks. From where he sat, Alex could see impossibly long lashes sweep closed, then open again.

Her fingers, still wearing the gloves she'd worn to marry him, worried with the trim on her dress. When he said her name, they stilled.

He itched to cover her hand with his. Instead, Alex rested his palms on his knees. "So, tell me how you plan to keep this proposition of yours."

There is an appropriate ensemble for each occasion.
A lady should always have several choices at the ready
should the occasion change.

—*Miss Pence*

Though her head ached, her feet hurt, and she could have fallen asleep standing up, Charlotte heard the humor in Alex's voice and almost smiled. Were she able, she might have made a joke worthy of sparring with him.

Instead, she settled for a simple answer. "I am no longer subject to my father's restrictions, I can come and go as I wish and be in complete control of my own life and my own funds. And I can now take my rightful position in Grandfather's company. These are ample reasons to keep my end of the bargain. However, this bargain has two participants, so you will have to carry your share of the burden as well."

Massaging her temples, Charlotte waited for the viscount's response.

One dark brow rose. "Might I remind you that as your husband, I have control now? Of your funds, of your social calendar. Even as to whether my wife will accept employment."

She met his even stare and laughed. "Oh, that's funny."

Alex remained oddly stoic. "Is it?"

"Yes, of course it is." And yet, even as she made the pronouncement, Charlotte felt the panic begin to rise. Surely the viscount meant to tease her. Though, as she considered his statement, technically he was correct.

Still, the thought that Alex Hambly might use something as ridiculous as the law to go beyond their agreement infuriated her. She let out a long breath and offered what she hoped was a calm expression. There was no sense baiting him when she only wanted to rid herself of his presence and take a very long nap.

"Honestly, Alex, did you not hear what Grandfather said at breakfast? Now that I'm wed, he's creating a new position on the board for me. It's all but done."

"How could I not have heard, Charlotte? He repeated it several times over." He paused to trace a line down the front of his gray striped trousers. "Your uncle, on the other hand, did not seem so pleased, though I did not engage him in conversation on the matter."

He looked up as if to judge her reaction. She offered none beyond a casual, "My uncle will get used to the idea."

Alex shifted positions. "Perhaps," he said, "though I wager the odds quite low. Edwin's not a happy man, is he?"

"Truly, I have no idea." Charlotte smoothed her hair with a trembling hand. "If only we could dispense with the trip to Denver," she said, "but I suppose there's no way around it. Gennie's determined to have her way in the matter, and if I know her, the parties are already being planned."

He shrugged. "And I promised your father I would see you safely to Denver so our marriage could be properly celebrated."

"And we do keep our promises," Charlotte snapped. A moment later, she shook her head. "I'm sorry. I'm just tired." She paused to see if Alex would do the gentlemanly thing and offer to leave. When he did not, she continued. "Regarding the grounds for annulment—would those same rules apply in Denver?"

"Perhaps." The viscount considered the question a moment. "I could have my solicitor research the issue."

"Yes, would you?" She leaned against her palm and closed her eyes. How easy it would be to fall asleep, but she couldn't do that with Alex still there. Then he'd never leave. "I would like to have this handled as soon as possible. As for your exit, I suggest now would be the proper time for it."

"My exit? From the marriage or the hotel suite?"

She removed Great-Grandmother Beck's pearls from her neck and placed them on the table beside her. "First the suite and then the marriage. Both with as much haste as possible."

Alex consulted his pocket watch. "Charlotte, we've been married less than half a day. Are you saying our love has run its course? Oh, wait…" He stuffed the watch back into his pocket, then made a face. "Forget you saw that watch. I had a terrible time with a pickpocket some years ago and I now take greater pains to keep my valuables safe."

His expression made her laugh in spite of herself, as did the recollection of how easily it had been to relieve the viscount of his prize possession. Likely she still could, though Charlotte had not used her talents in that area since that night in London four years ago.

"You have a nice smile. When you choose to show it," Alex said. "A pity our marriage didn't last."

"I shall always remember you fondly," she said with more than a little sarcasm. She pulled off the matching earrings and set them beside her pearls. Next came the bracelets, three in all, from the same set. Now the only jewel she wore was the wedding ring Alex had placed on her finger. She quickly rid herself of that as well.

If Alex noticed, he made no comment.

Charlotte suppressed a yawn. "I'm exhausted, Alex, and all I can think about is sleep. So, please, would you just go? We've said all we need to say."

"Go?" He shook his head. "Where would you have me go?"

"I don't know. Anywhere." She rubbed the bridge of her nose. "Home."

"Impossible," he said without inflection. "Surely the duchess told you about the extensive renovations she's undertaken so that our new home at the Heath will be comfortable for you." His chuckle held no humor this time. "As we're to be away for several months, the place has been stripped down practically to the rafters, and I've given up my flat."

She hadn't considered this. "Oh dear." An idea occurred to her, and she rose and forced her feet back into her shoes. "I'll have another room prepared for you. That should be simple enough."

"This suite has two bedrooms, Charlotte," he said wearily. "Is that not sufficient for you?"

She let out a long breath. "Just please find another room. How difficult can that be?"

Unfortunately, it was difficult, as every room in the hotel was booked. She returned to the suite to find Alex napping on the sofa nearest the window. Closing the door softly, she slid out of the hateful shoes and tiptoed toward her groom.

He lay sprawled across the settee, one foot on the floor and the other hanging over the end of the Louis XIV antique. The chime of the mantel clock caught Charlotte's attention. When she looked back at Alex, she found him studying her intently.

"Well?" He shifted to a sitting position and rubbed his face.

She shook her head. "There were no other rooms available."

"All right." Alex rose and walked toward her, and Charlotte steeled herself for what he might do. When he pressed past without comment, she was almost disappointed.

"Wait. Where are you going?" she asked.

He kept walking. "Good night, wife."

Charlotte watched Alex choose his room for the night, and the door shut behind him.

"Good night..." She couldn't bring herself to call him *husband.* Not when someday she hoped to have a real husband and a real marriage.

Someday. But not today.

She made her way into the empty bedroom, closing the door behind her. Before she fell asleep, Charlotte asked the Lord to forgive her for claiming a husband she did not want. She also asked Him to send another when the time—and the husband—was right.

25

Taking fresh air is a lady's best beauty secret, and the
air is always fresher when sailing first class.
—MISS PENCE

August 13, 1891

A knock at the door jolted Charlotte from her dreams, and she sat up
into a blinding ray of sunlight. Falling back onto her pillows, she mumbled a weak, "Go away, Alex."

"I'm sorry," a woman called. "Mrs. Beck sent me to help. 'Tis time
to prepare for your voyage."

"I'm not going," Charlotte muttered as she covered her head with
the pillows. "So please thank Gennie for sending you. I promise to call
when I've had my rest."

Despite her instructions, the door opened anyway, and heavy footsteps crossed the room toward her. Charlotte lifted the edge of the pillow to see Alex standing at her bedside, the maid cowering behind him.

"Do go away," she said, once again covering her head with the pillow. "I've told you I don't—"

"And I've told you I have control in the marriage until I relinquish
it." At her shocked look, Alex's expression softened. "Relax, Charlotte.
It's far too early in the day to begin running the Beck empire for you.

I'm more concerned with getting you and all your trunks aboard ship before it sails."

"I'm not going to Venice." She looked past Alex to the maid, who had inched her way back out into the hall. "Might I trouble you to return in a few hours after I've had more sleep?"

With a nod, the timid woman was gone, skittering out the door and leaving a loud slam and then silence in her wake.

"Well, she was something, wasn't she?" Charlotte grumbled.

"As are you," Alex said. "Now get out of bed and put on your traveling clothes before I'm forced to assist you."

When she rolled over and attempted to return to sleep, Alex yanked the blankets off the bed.

"Have you lost your mind?" she demanded.

"Just my patience." He tossed the blankets in a heap at his feet then crossed his arms. "Look, I don't want to see Venice any more than you do, Charlotte. At least not with you in this sort of ill humor."

Charlotte hauled the mess that was her hair out of her eyes and regarded Alex with irritation. "My ill humor comes from being awakened at the crack of dawn by a man I did not want in my hotel room. What's the cause of yours?"

"Mine comes from dealing with a woman who, even when she gets what she wants, still manages to complain about it." He held up his hand to prevent her response. "It also comes from the fact that you seem to think you're in charge around here. As I recall, this annulment is to be had by me, not you. Am I correct?" When she nodded, he continued. "Then I suggest you be a bit nicer, Charlotte. And while you're at it, stop trying to order me around."

"You *are* cranky this morning." Charlotte tugged at her nightgown and then yawned.

"It isn't morning," Alex said. "It's half past two."

Charlotte sat up. "What? But then we've missed our boat! Why didn't you wake me sooner?"

"I thought you didn't want to go to Venice."

"I don't," Charlotte said stiffly, "but if we're not going to Venice, what's the hurry?"

"Well," Alex said slowly, "I spoke with your father at length this morning over breakfast. He understands how homesick you are for Denver, and he's completely amenable to our postponing our Italian honeymoon in order to return with your family to Denver."

"Really?"

"Really," Alex said, "but only if you don't make us late. The *Teutonic* will sail with or without us, I'm afraid."

She bounded from the bed, then gave Alex a look. "Out," she demanded. "Lest *you* make us late. And call back that maid, would you? I'll never get my hair to look decent if left to my own devices."

Dressing in record time, Charlotte stepped out of her bedchamber just as the last of their trunks disappeared with the porters. She slid the cords of her reticule over her wrist, reached for a handful of grapes, and followed Alex into the hallway.

"Wait," she said. "I've forgotten Uncle Edwin's gift."

Alex continued walking, his broad back disappearing around the corner. "It's packed in one of the trunks," he called. "And so your concern doesn't keep you awake tonight, the Hambly tiara is on its way back to the bank vault in the capable hands of my solicitor."

"That thing I hadn't worried about," she said as she caught up to her husband.

The viscount spared her a swift glance. "That *thing* is a valuable heirloom, Charlotte. Handed down and prized by the Hamblys."

"Prized by the Hambly men, perhaps." She rubbed her still-sore temple. "Likely the Hambly women who've worn it would have a different opinion."

Alex sighed. "Apparently it is the curse of Hambly men to marry women who have no trouble voicing their 'different opinions.' Wives in this generation and the previous one certainly bear out the theory."

"Yes, well, I won't be your wife long enough to remember," Charlotte snapped. "So rest assured whatever opinions I hold, I shall keep them to myself in the future."

"Oh, that's rich," he said, his tone sarcastic and his expression dour. "I doubt you've ever held an opinion that you haven't shared."

Charlotte adjusted the strings on her reticule, as much to loosen the tight knot as to have something to do other than look at the man beside her.

Thankfully, Alex did not comment further. He seemed to have lost interest in any conversation at all, leaving Charlotte to her own thoughts. As much as she'd almost enjoyed sparring with the viscount in the past, being wed to him was another thing altogether. Hopefully the situation would be remedied soon. A man like Alex Hambly should be married to a woman who wanted to be his wife.

As their carriage rumbled toward the docks, Charlotte slid her groom a covert glance and found him studying her. "What?" she asked.

"I believe your father is on to us."

She shook her head. "What do you mean?"

Alex toyed with his cuff. "I think he suspects our plan to have the marriage annulled."

"Because we're not going to Italy as planned?" Charlotte shrugged. "I can remedy that. I'll just tell Papa I wanted to get whatever Gennie's planning over with before I considered any further travel. That's certainly the truth."

The last thing Charlotte wished was to stand among her Denver friends as the fraud she knew herself to be. Better to get it behind her rather than languish away on an Italian honeymoon, dreading it.

"We should have anticipated that my father would be suspicious. We did agree to this ridiculous plan of his far too easily."

"Perhaps," Alex said. Silence once again fell between them.

"So, Alex," Charlotte finally said, "how did you come to have breakfast with my father this morning? Wouldn't he expect you and I to be…"

An image of the two of them entwined beneath the silken bed linens she'd recently vacated rose unbidden. She pushed it away but not before heat flushed her cheeks. Alex's grin did nothing to help her embarrassment.

"Actually," he said, "he sent a note."

"My father invited you and I to breakfast the morning after our wedding?" She leaned back against the cushions to absorb the news. "You're right. He's on to us." Charlotte let out a long breath. "Did he say anything that hinted at what he's planning?"

Alex grinned. "I didn't give him time. I arrived at the appointed time looking, shall we say, a bit worse for wear and excused myself after a few minutes, pleading extreme angst at being separated from you."

"You did not," she said with a chuckle.

"I did." When she glanced his way, Alex lifted one dark brow. "Whether he's on to us or not, I did at least throw him off track."

"And you got us passage home on the *Teutonic*. As I recall, it's a lovely ship."

"Charlotte, he already had passage booked for us when I arrived at the breakfast table."

"My father bought our tickets home?" She shook her head. "Why?"

Alex's look was answer enough.

"All right, then," she said. "I shall thank him when I next see him."

"That won't be long," Alex responded. "Remember that he and the rest of your family are on the same ship."

Charlotte thought a minute. She touched Alex's sleeve. "Don't you see what an excellent opportunity this is?"

Her groom looked down at Charlotte's hand until she pulled away. "No, I don't," he said.

"Papa will expect us to behave as two strangers forced to wed."

"Which we basically are," Alex interjected.

"We are not. I do not kiss strangers, Alex." Again the heat rose in her cheeks. She hid it by looking away until the feeling passed. "So," she continued when she could manage it, "if Papa hopes to catch us trying to escape the marriage, then we shall do the opposite and behave as if we wish to be married."

Alex shook his head. "That doesn't make a bit of sense. How can we then claim grounds for annulment?"

"This way Papa won't expect it, and thus he will have no plan against it." She grinned. "Isn't that brilliant?"

"Brilliant," he echoed, though Charlotte couldn't tell whether she heard sarcasm or enthusiasm in his tone.

"First lesson in business, Alex," she said as she spied the entrance to the docks and the twin smokestacks of the *Teutonic* ahead. "I learned at Wellesley that a good plan takes the competition by surprise."

"But this is your father," Alex said. "And we're not planning some business transaction."

"Actually," she said sweetly, "we are." Charlotte paused. "It's a contract between companies. Just signatures on paper."

But as she said the words, Charlotte felt the slightest twinge of conscience. It was true, wasn't it? Paperwork didn't make a marriage. Only the Lord could make a marriage. And surely a sovereign God would never join her in marriage to Alex Hambly.

Surely.

26

A lady never carries her own money. Unless she has
no one else to carry it for her.

—*Miss Pence*

Diamonds were everywhere: circling his wife's throat and wrist, dangling
from her ears, and even woven into her hair in the form of a crescent-
shaped comb. More stones of a lesser quality decorated the front of her
gown and, to Alex's amusement, dangled from her sleeves like the
adornments on his mother's favorite lampshade.

Charlotte reached for her perfume bottle, and the resulting collision
of sun with jewels sparked a galaxy of lights that danced around her. The
scent of Violette de Parme filled the air, and Alex's heart seized. Were she
not his unwanted wife, his forced companion, Alex might have allowed
himself to lose his heart to her.

Instead, he held his heart in close check, just as he held his feelings
in these close quarters. Though Charlotte pretended not to notice upon
their arrival, Alex was keenly aware that this suite contained only one
bed.

No place to seek solace from the woman who dogged his musings
even as he slept. There was no claim of love in his addled thoughts, and
no wish to find any such emotion. Rather, his American bride rose
unbidden in Alex's musings to taunt him not only with what he had, but
also with what he would never possess.

And he wanted neither. At least that was what he told himself.

A life spent with Charlotte Beck would be a life spent in perpetual turmoil. It would most certainly be the exact opposite of the sedate life of research he desired, with only the occasional trip to present his findings at conferences before others who valued the study of the stars to interrupt his solitude.

Yet when he saw her profile—the upturned nose, the lashes that dusted high cheekbones, the lips he'd kissed—he was powerless to forget how very much she both irritated and interested him.

In her presence, at least when he could forget the ire she drew when she spoke, Alex felt like a bee drawn to honey, stars to constellations, galaxies to—

"You're staring again."

Alex snapped to attention and realized Charlotte was looking at him. "What? Oh, sorry," he muttered. "I wasn't staring. I was...I was contemplating galaxies and constellations."

"I see."

She swept into a standing position and smoothed the front of her dress, leaving the bow decorating the back askance. He didn't dare adjust it. While his eye preferred symmetry and balance, his hands knew to keep their distance from Charlotte, especially given the burning bustle debacle.

Charlotte slid the jeweled ties of her reticule over her gloves and into the crook of her arm. "Show time," she said with an impertinent grin.

"Show time?" Alex echoed.

"Yes, of course." Charlotte leaned down to look once more into the mirror, and her bow tilted even further. Ignoring it was impossible.

"You're crooked." Alex gestured to the general vicinity of the bow. "Though thankfully not on fire."

"Funny." She righted the bow. "Show time," she explained, "is what Colonel Cody says when presented with a room of people he doesn't know." She tossed her head. "Or even when he does, actually."

"I see." Alex had almost forgotten his bride's connection to the Wild West star, at least until the fellow showed up at their wedding. It appeared the man was practically family, which impressed Alex's mother immensely.

Charlotte walked toward the door then turned to face him. Alex barely managed to halt his steps in time.

"Remember, we need to make Papa and Gennie believe we're in love. It's the only way." Impossibly green eyes peered up at him and, for a second, Alex thought he saw a tiny spark of fear. "If Papa thinks we're acting, he will know something's up. And if he knows something's up, he will move to stop us."

"I still fail to see—"

She silenced him by pressing her finger to his lips. He looked down at the ruby he'd placed on her left hand just yesterday, which now glittered atop her gloves.

"Show time," she said again. "Say it with me."

"Show time," he echoed just a beat behind her.

"That's better." Charlotte studied him for a moment as her golden brows wrinkled. She reached up on tiptoe to straighten his collar, bringing her far too close for comfort. "There, now you're ready."

Though he was far from ready, Alex followed two steps behind his wife as she led the way.

"Have you sailed the *Teutonic* before?" she asked over her shoulder. "It's positively lovely, isn't it?"

"No." He watched the bow bob its way back into crookedness. "And yes, lovely."

The trip to the dining room proved thankfully brief, and Alex was able to keep his mind occupied with things other than his wife. Ahead, he heard the low hum of voices and the scrape of a bow against violin strings as the orchestra struck up the first notes of a Vivaldi concerto.

Charlotte slowed her brisk pace to primp in front of an oversized mirror framed with ebony likenesses of Zeus and Apollo. Alex stood back, not to watch, but to pray for the strength to get through the evening. Daniel Beck would be a hard man to fool.

Alex patted his pocket. The wedding gift he'd brought was a joke meant to make a point. A bauble plucked from the treasure trove of his mother's jewels, which Alex had bought back piece-by-piece over the past four years. When the duchess offered up anything in her vault as a gift for his bride, Alex easily settled on the pearl and diamond piece. Under the circumstances, however, he'd have to be much more clever—and more public—in its presentation.

Charlotte motioned for him to join her, and Alex complied. Ahead, the double staircase leading to the dining room beckoned.

"Just as a reminder," she said, toying with the walnut-sized diamond at the center of her necklace, "anything said or done aboard ship is completely in the interest of—"

A well-dressed couple approached. Charlotte turned a radiant smile toward them.

"Good evening, darling," the fur-bedecked matron said, enveloping Charlotte in a polite embrace. "I heard all about your wedding. What a wonderful event it must have been. Are your parents here?" Her portly companion stood a few feet away and seemed to be studying Charlotte's bow, though from his expression he found no flaw in its lack of symmetry or poor position.

"Darling," Charlotte called, "come and meet the Cadwalladers."

Once introductions were dispensed with, Charlotte made their excuses, and they moved toward the dining room. "A business associate of Papa's," Charlotte explained. "Now, shall we?"

Alex offered his arm, and together they turned the corner and paused at the top of the wide, double staircase. Two full floors below lay the dining room, glittering beneath a multitude of chandeliers. Waiters milled about, seeing to those passengers who were seated and urging others tarrying in conversation to take their places.

A light flashed, and Alex nearly tripped. "What the—"

"Miss Beck! Miss Beck! Here!" a fellow in a dark, working-man's suit called. "A few words to go with the photograph, please? And if you would, maybe pose with your new husband?" Charlotte turned toward the gentleman, who identified himself as a journalist for the *New York Times*. "Nate and I covered your wedding," he said.

Apparently Nate was the photographer, for the man with the camera lifted his hat in greeting. Alex gave him a curt nod.

"Your father was kind enough to allow me to slip in as his guest for the evening. I hope you don't mind. I'd love to ask a few questions about how you and Mr. Hambly met."

"That's *Viscount* Hambly," Charlotte corrected with a smile, "and of course, we wouldn't mind." She turned to Alex. "Would we, dear?"

"No, of course not, dear." His smile beat hers. "Though I'd prefer if you told the story. You know how prone to misspeaking I am."

Charlotte tilted her head and waved at someone in the crowd below. He followed her gaze and spied Eugenia Cooper Beck watching them. So was Daniel.

"After you, sir," Charlotte said to the reporter and his photographer companion.

"Yes, of course. The better to capture you coming down the steps, perhaps?"

After two stops for photographs, the trek down the stairs and across the dining room was accomplished. Greetings were exchanged all around, and Daniel motioned for Alex and Charlotte to find their seats. Thankfully, Charlotte sat beside her father, sparing Alex any sort of private conversation with the man.

As course after course arrived and disappeared, Alex tiptoed through the delicate minefield of conversation, knowing that Daniel Beck and a reporter from the *Times* documented his every word. It was a miserable meal, and one he vowed not to repeat.

As the second round of dessert dishes was cleared, Alex reached for the box in his pocket and cleared his throat, preparing to speak his first words in nearly half an hour.

"Your attention, please."

Charlotte and her father continued their discussion with the reporter while Mrs. Beck held a lively dialogue with the photographer. Alex waited a moment then made another attempt to gain their attention with the same result. Finally, he rose.

"Your attention, please."

All eyes turned his direction.

"Thank you." He looked down at Charlotte, whose wide-eyed expression revealed unmistakable terror. "Darling, do you mind?" He helped his wife to her feet.

The American beauty leaned up as if to kiss his cheek. "What are you doing?" she whispered into his ear.

"Relax," he said only loud enough for her alone to hear. "I'm merely giving my wife a wedding gift." He turned to the diners still seated. "It would be redundant to remind you that my bride and I exchanged vows only yesterday."

Mrs. Beck giggled and touched her husband's shoulder. Daniel Beck, however, affected a stern look, his arms crossed over his chest. The reporter made a grab for his notebook, which he'd hidden beneath a damask napkin, while the photographer merely looked bored.

"And as such," Alex continued, "I felt compelled to mark the occasion of our first day as husband and wife with a small token of my affection." He worked up his most romantic expression and hoped the others at the table believed it. "Darling, reach into my jacket pocket, would you?"

"Wait. Get the camera, Nate," the reporter demanded.

Charlotte gave Alex an ambivalent look.

"Go on," he said, affectionately patting her head. "It won't bite." Alex paused as Charlotte slipped her hand into his pocket. "Or maybe it will," he said quickly, causing her to squeal.

His bride quickly withdrew her hand then gave Alex's arm a swat. "That wasn't funny."

"Perhaps you will give me the opportunity to make amends later," he said. "But for now, darling, retrieve your gift."

Charlotte reached more slowly this time, but when her fingers found the pearls, her eyes widened. "Alex?" she said with what sounded like the last of her breath.

"Go on," he urged.

She lifted the strand slowly, each perfectly matched pearl on the rope revealing the next until she could reach no higher. And still there were more pearls—and another surprise—in his pocket.

"Look this way, please, and don't move until I give the signal." Nate aimed the camera at them. After what seemed like an eternity, he nodded, and Alex could move again.

Charlotte cradled the pearls in her palm. "They're lovely," said softly, "but you shouldn't have been so extravagant."

The statement was meant as a reminder of which family held the bigger bank account, no doubt. He'd not disabuse her of her erroneous belief. At least, not in front of her father.

Alex reached into his pocket and pulled out the remainder of the pearl rope, a full five feet in length. The same as her height. He tripled the rope then placed it around her neck. "Beautiful," he said before realizing he'd spoken aloud.

When the diamond and emerald egg that hung at the end of the pearls caught her attention, Charlotte gasped. "What's this?"

Alex captured the jewel and placed it in her hand. Ten carats of diamonds, three carats of emeralds, and one very special surprise made up the adornment. "Open it."

She shook her head. "How?"

"Like this." Alex showed her then waited for her reaction.

"It's…" She giggled then held it up for the other diners to see. "There's a watch inside."

Alex slid Charlotte's father a look before returning his attention to Charlotte. "Yes, darling. Can you guess why I've gifted you with a watch?"

Daniel Beck started to laugh. Mrs. Beck soon joined him.

"I fail to see what's so funny," Charlotte said. "This necklace is absolutely lovely."

Alex wrapped his arms around his wife's waist and hauled her closer. "Darling, I present this watch to you not only as a token of my love and undying affection and as a commemoration of our first full day as husband and wife, but also so that you shall never feel the need to appropriate mine."

"You're not the least bit humorous." Charlotte clutched the watch in her hand. "However, in the spirit of keeping harmony in our home, I accept your humble gift."

"Isn't that wonderful of her?" Alex asked Mrs. Beck.

"Truly wonderful," she responded with a laugh. "But that's our Charlotte."

"Actually, she's my Charlotte now." When Daniel's smile disappeared, Alex continued. "And as such, I'm sure you will understand I mean no disrespect when I inform the both of you that for the remainder of the voyage, my wife and I will be taking our meals in our stateroom."

"But darling, I—"

"I'll have no argument, Charlotte."

Alex looked down at his temporary wife with what he hoped would appear to be deep affection. Charlotte, however, saw nothing of the sort, for as their gazes met, her eyes narrowed. There would be some discussion about his behavior once they returned to the privacy of their stateroom, of this Alex was certain.

She stood on tiptoe and leaned in to kiss his cheek. "You won't get away with this," she whispered against his skin.

"I already have." He captured her chin in his hands. "Watch this."

He kissed her. Soundly.

At some point, either Nate the photographer captured the moment for the *Times* readers or the mingling of their lips set off fireworks in the dining room. With Charlotte leaning breathless against him, Alex would have believed either possible.

"Now," he managed as he steadied his bride, "say your good nights to our family and friends."

When she did not, he said them for her, then took her elbow and guided her from the table.

"Hambly." Daniel Beck caught up to them and clasped Alex's shoulder.

Alex went eye to eye with his temporary father-in-law. "Yes?"

A moment passed as Beck stared him down. Alex returned the look, his shoulders squared. The orchestra struck up a Tchiakovsky overture. Thankfully, Charlotte kept her mouth shut.

Slowly, Daniel Beck nodded. "Congratulations, son." He shook Alex's hand. "I'm glad I wasn't wrong about you."

"Thank you, sir," Alex mumbled. He guided Charlotte away, his bruised conscience trailing behind him.

27

A lady's best beauty secret is a good night's sleep.
——*Miss Pence*

Long after Charlotte's head landed on the pillow, her eyes refused to shut. Whether it was anger or just plain annoyance at being treated like property, she found a dozen smart responses to Alex's behavior that demanded to be said. But Alex had taken his blanket and pillow to the sitting room and was now happily snoring away, oblivious that she'd finally found her voice and wanted to state her opinion.

How dare he kiss her in front of a reporter, then tell her parents she would not be seeing them the remainder of the voyage?

Then again, other than the fact that he hadn't consulted her on the matter, Alex's choice of isolation over continued contact with Papa and Gennie was brilliant, which just made her angrier.

She balled her fists and counted to ten. Why did it bother her so much that she'd be stuck in close quarters with the infuriating man for the next week?

"Because he snores," she muttered. Not in that awful rumbling-the-roof way, perhaps, but softly, making just enough sound to remind Charlotte that a man slept in the next room.

Throwing on her wrapper, Charlotte slipped out of bed and navigated the treacherous distance across carpet and around tables to the sitting room. The viscount lay curled up on a sofa half his length, his face bathed in silver moonlight and partially obscured by a lock of dark hair that had fallen across one eye. The blanket had fallen to the floor in a puddle, and both his arms were curled around his pillow.

Something about the innocence on his face stopped Charlotte cold. For four years she'd thought of Alexander Hambly as that awful fellow Papa was so fond of, the man she was doomed to wed.

But now, as his even breathing continued, Charlotte felt compelled to reconsider these judgments.

She moved closer, picked up the blanket, and covered him with it. The snoring stopped. Charlotte froze, her arms wrapped around her waist, as she prepared an excuse for her intrusion on what was now Alex's bedchamber.

He did not move, nor did his eyes open. Charlotte whispered a sigh of relief and turned to retrace her steps.

"Wife," Alex called, stopping her in her tracks.

"Stop calling me that," she shot over her shoulder as she picked her way through the darkened cabin.

The sofa creaked, and she heard his feet hit the floor. "And yet you are," he responded, "whether either of us likes it or not. So what are you doing out of bed at such an hour? Were you spying on me?"

She was, of course, but she'd never admit to it.

"Charlotte?"

"Oh, don't be ridiculous." Charlotte hurried toward her bed. The floor beneath her shuddered as the ship gently listed to port. When it righted a moment later, Charlotte slammed her bare foot against something hard. She cried out, then covered her mouth with her hand and dove under the blankets without bothering to discard her dressing gown.

"Charlotte? What happened?"

She ignored him though her toe throbbed and she longed to complain. Again Alex called her name. She looked out from behind her bed's velvet curtains and bit her lip as a lone tear traced down her cheek.

The shadow of her husband appeared at the door. He leaned against the frame, hands in the pockets of his robe. "You've hurt yourself. Can I help?"

"No," she managed. "I'm fine." Then she gave herself away by sniffling.

"You're not."

Something in his voice, softened with sleep and warm with concern, caused more tears to fall. She'd never been good at suffering in silence, though admitting that or any other weakness to the Englishman was unthinkable.

"I will be fine if you'll just go away," she said gently. "Please."

But as Alex Hambly generally did, he ignored her. A moment later, he'd arrived at her bedside and found the lamp. The blaze of light blinded Charlotte, and she struggled to find her focus. When she did, Alex was staring at her with concern.

"You're bleeding," he said, gesturing to the floor next to the night-stand where a few drops of blood marred the rug. Nothing to fuss over.

"My toe," she said. "But it's just a scratch."

"I'll be the judge of that. I've had a bit of medical training. I think I can manage it."

Charlotte shrank back from him. "You're an astronomer. What possible training could you have that would help?"

"My brother is not the only one who went to war, Charlotte. I've seen my share of field repairs, as it were."

"Field repairs?"

Alex's lips turned up in the beginnings of a smile, and she knew he was teasing.

"How lucky I am to be in the presence of a professional," she said, though without as much sarcasm as she intended.

"Indeed you are. Now stop being uncooperative and leave this to me." He studied the curtained bed then allowed his attention to drift up to Charlotte's stare. "Are you decent?"

She tugged her wrapper down over her ankles then nodded. "I am."

"All right. Let's see what we've got here."

Alex threw back the blankets and reached for her foot. With the gentlest of touches, he turned it first to the right and then to the left. "Nothing's broken," he said, "but you've made a mess of your bedding, and you're still bleeding a bit." He went to find cloth and a basin, and returned a moment later.

At the touch of the cloth on her cut, Charlotte flinched. Then, by degrees she became aware of Alex's close proximity, of the feel of his fingers as they slid down the back of her ankle, the set of his mouth as he remedied the damage she'd caused by stumbling about in the dark.

With Alex's attention elsewhere, Charlotte could study him. Little had changed about the viscount in the four years since they'd last met except, she noted, the tiny crescent-shaped scar on the left side of his chin.

His hands stilled. He'd caught her staring.

"Something wrong, Charlotte?"

She tucked her dressing gown back around her ankle then leaned toward Alex. "Actually, I was wondering…," she touched the scar, "what happened here?"

The ship rumbled beneath them while the sound of the night bells drifted toward them. Charlotte's hand fell to her lap as she waited, watching Alex's face.

"I'm sure you already know." Alex gave her a look that told her he'd take no foolishness. "Now allow me to complete my doctoring, please."

While he worked, Charlotte watched her temporary husband. His care of her injury was gentle and efficient, his touch firm but quick. Once he'd stopped the bleeding and applied a small bandage, he disposed of the cloths and then returned to her bedside to tuck the blankets around her.

"Stay in bed, Charlotte," he said. "I will be fine without your supervision."

"Supervision? I assure you I intended no such thing."

Their gazes met. "What did you intend, wife?"

She tucked a strand of hair behind her ear and looked away. "Stop calling me that."

"Fine, but mind my words please, and stay put." He extinguished the lamp. "Good night."

Alex had padded all the way back into the other room before Charlotte recalled the question he had not yet answered.

"You're not done here," she called. "About that scar. You never told me how you got it."

"Sleep, Charlotte," he said, his voice tired.

"As soon as you answer me," she replied.

His shadow once again filled the doorway. "Didn't your father tell you about the meeting we had after you left for Wellesley?"

Curiosity chased surprise up her spine. "Did my father do that?"

"No, of course not." In the dim light she spied Alex's hand touching his chin. "I just assumed he'd spoken to you."

"Oh, no. Papa didn't dare mention you in my presence." Charlotte ducked her head then peered up at him. "Nothing personal. It was the *idea* of what you represented."

"What I still represent."

"Yes." She snuggled down into the pillows, feeling a sudden, strange desire to hide.

"You probably do not recall that when your father first offered your hand in marriage, I declined because I had another offer."

She did, but Charlotte wasn't about to admit it.

"Before I could accept the offer the second time it was made," Alex continued, "I had to decide whether to end my association with the other young lady."

Charlotte's heart jolted, an odd feeling for one so intent on ridding herself of the man.

"The young lady and I had not met, but her father had been in discussions with my solicitor. Thus, when the time came to withdraw from our tentative agreement, the news was not well received by the young lady's father." Alex paused. "Mind you, the man had proven quite difficult to pin down when it came to negotiations, so I was well within my rights to step away from the table and end the discussions."

The moon went behind a cloud, plunging the bedchamber into darkness. Charlotte heard rather than saw her companion shift positions. Her gaze went to the window where the sprinkling of stars beckoned. Had she not allowed her paints and canvases to be packed away...

Charlotte shook away the thought. Painting was something she hadn't attempted in years. Four years, to be exact. Not since she left the ranch for Wellesley. And while Colonel Cody had understood that her studies came first, Grandfather still asked on occasion if she'd taken up the hobby again.

"So the girl's father did that?" she asked Alex when the silvery moon returned.

"He did," Alex replied. "Now, if you're done with the questions, I suggest you allow me my rest."

Without waiting for a response, Alex turned and disappeared into the sitting room. As she heard the creak of the sofa that indicated the Englishman had returned to his makeshift bed, it was all Charlotte could do not to ask who the other girl was.

"Better I don't know," she said as she closed her eyes. "Not that it matters. He'll be free to marry her soon, should he wish."

But even as the whispered words escaped her lips, Charlotte knew she didn't want her husband to run to the welcoming arms of another woman. Even if he wasn't her husband anymore.

Not that she would ever admit this to Alex.

Or anyone else, for that matter.

28

A slow and measured pace indicates a well-bred lady.

—MISS PENCE

August 21, 1891
Denver, Colorado

The *Teutonic* sailed so fast across the Atlantic that a new speed record was set, and yet the voyage had seemed interminable. After five days of sea air and close quarters with her polite but distant traveling companion, Charlotte was more than ready to board the train for home.

The size of the Beck rail car allowed for little privacy, a welcome change from the first class ship cabin that had become her prison. With Alex spending much of his time reading his charts and books and making notes in the mountain of journals he'd brought along, Charlotte had been left to fill her days reading or staring out at the ocean.

At least she managed to give Alex the impression she'd done these things. Each time she turned a page, Charlotte would have been hard pressed to tell anyone what she'd read. And while the ocean unfolded in a shifting hue from green to gray to blackest ink, her thoughts wandered as she watched the waves drift past.

Now she could talk with Gennie and Papa and play games with little Danny. Always, however, her husband was present, and with Alex so near, her focus fractured.

The only time Charlotte could truly take her mind off her temporary marriage was when she and Papa talked business in the private study in the farthest section of the rail car. On those rare occasions when her father was amenable to answering her questions or debating the benefits of public offerings over private ownerships, all other worries vanished. With the door closed to interruptions and the scarlet curtains swaying with the rhythm of the rails beneath them, Charlotte finally felt worthy of the Wellesley education Papa had allowed her.

Today, however, with Denver practically in sight, Papa had banished Gennie and Danny to the sleeping chambers so that he might meet with Charlotte and Alex on some matter. But first, he'd asked that Charlotte come into the study alone.

She sat across the desk from Papa, the vast golden plains of Colorado sliding past outside and a poster from a show Colonel Cody had done back in 1887 staring at her from a frame on the wall behind her father's head. She shifted her focus to her father.

Papa wore a troubled look, putting Charlotte on her guard. Apparently today's discussion would not be about business. Or, worse, it would be about some mistake she'd made in the affairs she already handled for Grandfather. Only the request that Alex join them as soon as he could manage it kept Charlotte from believing she'd been unseated from the Beck Enterprises board before she could make any sort of go at the position.

Speaking first would betray her nervousness, so Charlotte settled into a more comfortable position to wait her father out. She allowed her gaze to slide past the poster to a collection of books, safe behind glass and shelved floor to ceiling on either side of the window. When Papa first purchased the rail car, long before Gennie came into their lives, the lower two shelves had been filled with books just for her. A smile rose at the memory of the many times she'd curled in the corner, a book in her hand, while meetings or visits of some importance took place around her.

Her father sat back and studied the ceiling, one hand on his chin. After a moment, he swung his gaze to meet Charlotte's nervous stare. This time she could no longer keep quiet.

"Something wrong, Papa?" she asked, working hard to keep her posture straight and her expression calm.

"I'm wondering something this morning, Buttercup." He paused. "Hambly—does he treat you well?"

Not what she expected. "Yes, I suppose he does."

"You suppose?"

She shifted positions. "He does," she said with what she hoped was the proper amount of enthusiasm. "Very well." She recalled his tender touch while seeing to her injury aboard ship.

"But you do not yet love him." Papa waved away any response she might offer. "No, of course, you don't. It's too soon."

Her father's admission of that fact surprised Charlotte. Rather than continue the charade, she decided to attempt the truth.

"No, Papa. You're right, I do not love him. Nor, truthfully, do I see that love is something Alex and I could achieve over time. We are simply far too different, and we want things that have nothing to do with marriage and children." Having said more than she intended, Charlotte clamped her mouth shut, and her fingers worried with the trim on her sleeve. When Papa didn't respond, she added, "But love wasn't a consideration when you insisted on this transaction, was it?"

"Not the sort of love you're thinking of." He turned toward the window. "But understand that anything I have ever done with regard to you has been out of love."

Again not what she expected.

An inexplicable spark of anger rose inside her. "So you insisted I marry Alex Hambly because you love me? You used my desire to attend Wellesley to force a marriage upon me because you love me? Well, that's just wonderful."

If Papa was upset by her outburst, he did not show it. He simply waited in silence until she shook her head.

"If you're looking for an apology for my feelings," she said, "I refuse. I will, however, apologize for the disrespectful tone."

"Apology accepted." He paused. "And for the record, you had a choice, as did Hambly. Nothing was forced on either of you."

She opened her mouth to offer a rebuttal but found no argument against what he'd said. An uncomfortable silence fell between them.

"So," Papa finally said, "is there anything you wish to tell me?"

"About what?" Guilt made her heart jolt, but she covered by offering a smile. "I don't know what you think I might have to say."

He shrugged, then removed his spectacles and set them aside, rubbing the bridge of his nose. Outside, the train's whistle sounded, filling the room with the reminder that with every crossing, with every mile of track, they were closer to home.

Closer to freedom.

"I'm concerned," Papa said.

Charlotte shifted positions and focused on the swaying, scarlet curtains to her right. "I can't imagine about what." She remembered her earlier worry. "Is it Grandfather's company? Have I done something wrong? I assure you we aren't going to compete with anything Beck Enterprises is doing here in the States. And I've already spoken to Grandfather about going public with a stock offering, which would not only bring in some cash but would also—"

"Charlotte."

She leaned back and folded her hands in her lap. "What?"

"My concern does not extend to any business arrangements you've made with your grandfather. In fact, I'm quite pleased that you've taken hold of your position with such enthusiasm, and I'm certain you will do whatever you set your mind to with great success. You always do." He put his spectacles back in place, then rested his elbows on the desk. "As your father, my greater worry is for the condition of your faith."

Wonderful. This discussion again.

Charlotte exhaled a long breath. She and Papa hadn't broached this topic in quite some time. Not since the summer of her third year at Wellesley, when they'd had a terrible row over her reluctance to believe that she did not chart her own course in life without a heavy measure of divine assistance.

Why couldn't Papa accept that, while she loved the Lord as much as the next person, Charlotte had found little in the way of proof that hard work and determination was not what caused a person to succeed. Indeed, she found her father's unwavering belief comforting, even if her years at university had offered up too much proof that his faith was a bit antiquated for the modern world. After all, in a few years there would be a whole new millennium upon them. And didn't Papa always teach her to think for herself?

All of this she might have said had she the means to form the words. Though she held her beliefs, Charlotte had not yet found a way to express them to her father.

"My faith is fine," she quipped. "Though I'm sure you've an opinion as to—"

A knock interrupted what would have been a brilliant statement. When Alex opened the door, she gave him a look that told him exactly how welcome his entrance was. Papa, on the other hand, rose to welcome the Englishman as if the prodigal had returned.

"Do sit down." Papa indicated the chair nearest Charlotte.

She slid her husband a sideways glance. He'd obviously come from working on his charts again, for he had ink smudged on his sleeve. When he swiped at his forehead, a smear of it landed just above his left eyebrow.

She reached into her pocket for her handkerchief and handed it to him. When he appeared reluctant, she gestured to the ink stain. "Go ahead. Take it." She lifted a brow and almost smiled. "It's clean."

Their gazes locked. Slowly his hand covered hers, and Charlotte could feel the warmth of his touch down to her bones. And then, slower still, he slid the handkerchief from her palm. Finally, he lifted one side of his mouth in a crooked smile.

"Thank you, wife."

And with three words, the sweet mood was ruined. She opened her mouth to snap at him, then thought better of it. Instead, she continued to stare at him, making the best of their childish refusal to look away.

"If you don't mind," Papa said, "I'll go on with what I'd like to say while you're attending to yourself, Hambly."

Alex broke the stare first, turning to face Papa as he dabbed at the spot on his sleeve. "Yes, please do."

"Charlotte, your attention please."

Rolling her eyes, Charlotte settled back in her chair and offered Papa her best version of an attentive look. When he seemed satisfied with her performance, he nodded.

"I've spent four years planning, not for the wedding—that was Gennie's job—but for the day I would speak to the two of you as husband and wife." He shook his head. "I'm sure you both thought I was mad for considering this arrangement at all, much less for insisting that the two of you agree to a wedding in order to achieve the goals you'd set for yourself."

"Papa," Charlotte said gently, "you don't have to say anything. We know—"

"You're wrong," he snapped. Then, ducking his head, her father seemed to collect his thoughts. When he looked at her again, his vision seemed clouded by tears. But surely not.

When Papa shifted his attention to Alex, Charlotte let out a breath she didn't realize she'd been holding. What was it about her papa that reduced her age by half every time she felt his disapproval?

"Hambly, you took on the responsibility that belonged to your brother. I applauded that then, and I still do. Rather than wait for Summit Hill to be chosen as the site for the observatory as I would have done, you were clever enough to sell high and reap the profits. The truth, though—did you have inside information that the observatory would be built elsewhere?"

Alex shrugged, her ruined handkerchief wadded in his fist. "No, sir, but I had a gut feeling when the investors continued to stall after you and I made our deal that something was going on. Maybe another deal in the works."

"Or perhaps just stalling to drive down the price?"

"I considered that, but I couldn't convince myself of it." Alex opened the handkerchief and then folded it in half, then in half again.

"Why not?" Papa shrugged. "It's a logical conclusion."

Alex hesitated. "I don't know if you've ever been to war, sir."

"I have," Papa said softly.

Charlotte blinked hard to hide her surprise. Papa had never mentioned military service.

"Then you know, Mr. Beck, that when a man's responsible not only for his life but the lives of those around him, he learns to listen to his gut." Her temporary husband paused. "And to pray, of course."

Her father swung a triumphant look in Charlotte's direction. "Of course," he said to Alex. "But it still took no small measure of skill to make that decision, considering what you had to lose. And now you've parlayed the small amount you received from me into something quite impressive."

"Sir, your contribution was no small amount," Alex corrected, "and I hope you understand I'm grateful."

Charlotte felt her brow wrinkle as she listened to Papa laud her husband's business acumen and his loyalty to home and family. In all those times she'd attempted to speak to Alex about her passion for the corporate world, he'd never once mentioned his skill at negotiating this deal. A deal that, by Papa's admission, would have gone sour had he been the one handling it.

And apparently, the man to whom she was currently wed had become quite well off in the four years since they'd last met. Why hadn't he told her as much?

"But above all that," her father said, "I'm struck by the fact that you're a praying man."

"I am, sir."

A praying man? Interesting. What else hadn't Alex Hambly mentioned?

29

A lady's smile is her calling card, her calling card her smile. Never waste either.

—Miss Pence

Alex felt the weight of Daniel Beck's praise settle heavily on his shoulders. Worse, however, was the jab of his conscience when he admitted to being a "praying man." Especially since he had done precious little praying lately.

"So," Mr. Beck continued, "before I leave my daughter in your hands, might I pray a blessing over the two of you?"

While Daniel waited for a response, Alex looked at Charlotte. Her wide-eyed expression told him the question had hit a nerve with her as well.

"Very well then," Mr. Beck said, and then he began to pray. He spoke about a husband's leadership in the household and petitioned the Father to assist Alex in carrying out the promise he had made before Him in the church in London. He ended the prayer by thanking God for bringing Alex into the family.

Alex tilted his head slightly and opened one eye to spy on his wife. Charlotte sat very still, her hands folded in her lap and her head bowed. Despite her beauty and the air of innocence she portrayed, the woman was irritation personified. No other female, including his mother, could cause him to lose his patience faster, and certainly none had wreaked as much havoc in his life in so short a time. And yet, she had somehow managed to work her way into his mind and his heart. Her kisses, her smile, and those beautiful green eyes chased him wherever he went.

How the Lord could have intended this match was beyond him. And yet, as Daniel Beck continued to pray, Alex knew he had little left in the way of an excuse for leaving this sham of a marriage. His conscience wouldn't allow it. And neither, perhaps, would his heart.

By the time the amens were said, Alex had made peace with the fact that he was a married man. It felt good telling the Lord that the promise he'd made would be one he kept.

Telling Charlotte would be another thing entirely.

Beneath his feet, he felt the train begin to slow. Alex looked out the window and saw the landscape of Denver.

Mr. Beck gave a passing nod to the scenery outside, then returned his attention to Charlotte. "And now for the final purpose for our little meeting. Buttercup, I know how you've always loved our home in Denver, but as a married woman, I think you've earned a place of your own." He paused. "A place where the two of you can raise your children when you're away from London."

The soft intake beside him told Alex his wife hadn't expected this. "Truly, Papa, that isn't necessary."

Mr. Beck regarded Alex with a grin. "It appears you've already had a positive effect on my daughter, Hambly. The old Charlotte would have been thrilled with a home of her own, given the lengths she went to in trying to escape the torture of living under our roof."

Charlotte chuckled nervously. Alex turned to face his wife and saw her perched on the edge of her seat. "It wasn't torture, Papa. Don't be silly."

As the train's whistle sounded and the brakes squealed, Mr. Beck studied Charlotte a moment before shaking his head. "In any case, I'm sure you'll want to do some decorating, Buttercup, but the home is quite serviceable as it stands." He opened his desk drawer and pulled out a file, then handed it to Alex. "You'll see from the address that it's near enough to our home without standing in its shadow. I believe a man has the right to start his marriage without his wife's parents watching his every move."

The train jolted to a stop, causing the ink bottles on the desk to rattle in their stand. Alex accepted the file, then placed his palms on top of it. After a petition to the Lord for the correct response, he rose and thrust his hand across the desk.

"Thank you, Mr. Beck, for the home and for trusting me with your daughter's hand in marriage." At the older man's nod, Alex continued. "I want to assure you I'm taking the promise I made before you and the Lord seriously. Charlotte will never want for anything."

Daniel Beck stood to offer a firm handshake. "I'll hold you to that, Hambly."

With a knock, Gennie opened the door. "I'm sorry for the interruption," she said, "but we've arrived. Shall I have the driver load up our things or will you need more time, dear?"

"No, that's fine," he said. "Your son-in-law was just thanking us for the wedding gift. Charlotte, however, is apparently speechless."

And pale, Alex noticed, though he was careful not to meet her gaze. If he did, he might say in front of her parents how very sorry he was not to be able to continue with their plan.

He watched as Mrs. Beck embraced Charlotte and began to chatter about the finer points of the home that would apparently be subjected to a complete redecoration. Mr. Beck moved around the desk to clasp Alex's shoulder.

"A moment alone, son." At Alex's nod, Mr. Beck added, "Walk with me."

They left the office together, crossing the length of the railcar to emerge onto the platform, where half of Denver appeared to be milling about. Mr. Beck gestured to one of two waiting Beck family carriages, and Alex joined him inside.

The elder Beck waited until the door closed behind them before leaning forward to give Alex a curious look. "So," he said slowly, "that was a nice performance. A pity my daughter was not as prepared as you."

"Prepared?" Alex's gut twisted. "What do you mean?"

"Do you think I am unaware of my daughter's desire to rid herself of this marriage?" When Alex did not respond, Mr. Beck clenched his fists. "Know this, Hambly. Nothing remains hidden forever. Whatever plan the two of you have hatched will be found out as fraud. I understand this, don't you?"

"Mr. Beck," he said slowly, "I admit there has been some discussion of how best to end this marriage."

"My guess is annulment," Beck interjected.

"True enough," Alex admitted.

Mr. Beck's eyes narrowed. "I won't allow it."

"With all due respect, sir," Alex said, "neither will I."

Obviously Mr. Beck had not expected that answer. "So I am to believe you've suddenly changed your mind about whatever deception you and my daughter have planned?"

"I have," Alex said.

Leaning back, Mr. Beck crossed his arms across his chest. "Just like that? Need I remind you once again that I am no one's fool?"

Alex offered a look of his own, one he hoped conveyed exactly how he felt about being questioned on the first real truth he'd told regarding his marriage. "Sir, need I remind *you* that I am a praying man? Since you reminded me of that fact not half an hour ago, I've had the distinct displeasure of being forced to change my plans."

"So you were not just discussing an annulment. You were planning one."

Alex spied Charlotte watching from the window of the railcar. "On grounds that I'd prefer not to discuss," he said as she disappeared behind the scarlet curtains.

"Grounds that I warrant still stand," Mr. Beck said.

After another long breath, Alex reached for the door handle. "If you'll forgive me, sir, I prefer not to discuss private matters. I am husband to your daughter, and as long as I draw a breath, I intend to remain as such. Now, if you've no further concerns on the topic, I'll claim my bride and take her to the home you've so generously given us."

"Very well, then." Mr. Beck opened the door and gestured to the driver. "I'll send your wife out. You see, this carriage comes with the home."

When Mr. Beck had climbed out, Alex followed. "No, thank you, sir. I'll get her myself."

Charlotte's father chuckled. "While I applaud your enthusiasm, might I do you one last favor and fetch her myself? I'm not sure my daughter's going to be as amenable to your new attitude toward the marriage as you would like."

Alex thought only a moment before returning to the carriage. He had little time to prepare before Charlotte threw open the carriage door.

"'I want to assure you I'm taking the promise I made before you and the Lord seriously'?" she said as she allowed the driver to help her inside. "'Charlotte will never want for anything'?" She settled across from Alex and tossed her reticule on the seat beside her with a flourish. "You're going a bit overboard on this, aren't you?"

"Actually, I'm telling the truth. I do not intend to go through with any of the plans we made." He paused, reaching across the gap between them and placing his hand on top of hers. "Beyond the one where we planned to marry, of course."

Charlotte yanked her hand away. "You and I had a deal, and now you're changing your mind?" She gave him a sideways look. "Wait," she said with the beginnings of a grin. "Oh, you're good, Alex. Really good. I almost believed you."

Alex opened his mouth to explain, then thought better of it. By the time the carriage turned onto Grant Street, he knew it'd be best not to explain his new position on their marriage until he absolutely had to.

Charlotte turned her attention to the parade of lavish homes rolling past. "I wonder which one is ours." She shook her head. "Mine, that is."

Alex chuckled as he patted the papers beside him. Wouldn't his bride be surprised to know that the Grant Street property was deeded to him? Another detail Alex would reveal when the time came and not before.

"Driver," Charlotte called, "can you tell me which one is ours?"

"Yes'm," he said. "It's the one up ahead on the left. With the iron fence and the crown atop the turret."

She craned her neck, and a smile slowly curved her lips. "Oh, there it is. Alex, look. It's lovely."

He followed her gaze to a rather interesting, three-story, limestone block home of larger than modest size. The ground floor entrance was covered by a portico that curved around the left side of the house, beneath an upstairs balcony finished in ornamental fashion. On the right, a turret rose two stories high and ended with a crown-like cap on the topmost floor. A fence of black iron situated atop limestone circled the entire structure. Were the grounds greener and the backdrop not the

Rocky Mountains, the home would have put Alex in mind of an Irish castle he'd visited in his childhood.

A uniformed servant met the carriage at the gate. "Welcome," he said as they rolled past. Before the carriage stopped, the gate had clanged shut. When the driver opened the door, Alex climbed out, then offered his hand to Charlotte.

"It's lovely," Charlotte repeated as she allowed Alex to help her down.

"Lovely, yes," Alex echoed, though his attention was not focused on the pile of limestone he'd inherited in this bargain. Rather, he fell head-first into the wide green eyes of the woman to whom he'd promised the Lord he'd play husband.

Though he did not intend to fall in love with her, he found her enthusiasm enchanting. Especially when she forgot her ladylike airs and hurried toward the grand front entrance like a little girl rushing to her first tea party. The last time he'd seen such childlike innocence in her was when she'd bested him to the door at his father's home in London. And even then the silliness was quickly replaced by the coy ingénue who'd tricked him into doing exactly what she wished.

"Alex, come see the gargoyles," she called.

"Gargoyles?" Alex shook his head. "Whatever are you talking about?"

She pointed to a spot on the roof. "See, right there next to…" She looked over her shoulder to smile at him. "Right next to the telescope."

He looked in the direction she pointed. Sure enough, situated mid-way between two carved creatures of medieval vintage was a telescope.

"Looks like we're even," she said as she climbed the steps leading to the double front doors.

Alex hurried after her. "Even?"

Charlotte stopped short and Alex almost ran over her. She smiled sweetly up at him. "Yes. You claim I ruined your favorite telescope." She shrugged. "Well, it appears you've gained another."

Before he could respond, he'd lost his wife to the open door. He heard a squeal of delight.

"Do come and see," she called. "The home is quite lovely."

"Lovely," he again echoed. "Indeed."

While Charlotte busied herself going from room to room to exclaim over the wonders of their new home or complain about its faults, Alex went straight toward the roof.

The third-floor landing opened directly onto a library. Shelves extended from floor to ceiling, already filled with leather-bound volumes that, upon closer inspection, revealed books on science and astronomy that he'd longed to purchase. A desk large enough for two anchored the center of the room with marble fireplaces on both the northern and southern ends of the oversized room. Chairs clad in hues of scarlet and gold flanked the fireplaces and provided seating at the desk, and a tableau of the constellations decorated the ceiling above the glittering chandelier.

Between the bookshelves on the eastern wall stood a set of double doors flanked by velvet curtains the color of the night sky. One of the doors had been thrown open, offering a view of the place he'd come to inspect: his rooftop laboratory.

He found a telescope with a four-inch refractor set securely into a base that offered a panoramic view of all Denver. Alex ran his hand down the metal exterior, then lowered the treasure to peer up at the snow-topped mountains on the horizon.

"Magnificent," he whispered. He swung the instrument around and spied the silver dome of the newly completed Chamberlin Observatory. "Absolutely magnificent."

"Alex," Charlotte called. "Where are you?"

"Out here," he responded as he saw his bride moving toward him.

"Oh my," she said. "Look at this." She found the ledge and leaned over it to peer down, causing Alex's gut to roll as he witnessed her daring. "What a view," she called.

"Come and see this." He swung the telescope around and waited for her to join him. "Don't touch it," he joked when her fingers found the edge of the eyepiece.

Charlotte jumped, then laughed. "Stop teasing me," she said as she bent to look through the telescope. "Oh, Alex, I can see all the way to Leadville."

"Almost," he said with a chuckle.

The wind teased her hair and lifted the lace on her collar as her long lashes dusted cheekbones of palest ivory. She pushed a golden curl from her eyes then took a step back and regarded him with that childlike expression. "Oh, won't it be lovely to look at the stars?"

"Yes," he said softly. "Lovely."

And she truly was.

"Perhaps I could paint them." Her laughter caught on the breeze and faded far too soon. "How funny. I wouldn't know where to find my paints if I tried." She shrugged. "Perhaps another time. Once the trunks have been unpacked."

As he watched her walk back inside, it was all Alex could do to keep from tearing through every one of the twenty-odd trunks now being delivered in order to find the paints his wife required.

"Yes," he said to her disappearing back, "perhaps another time."

30

If it be humble, it is no home for a lady.

—*Miss Pence*

September 1, 1891
Denver, Colorado

Alex looked up from his notes when Charlotte walked into his study. Today his bride wore a shade of pink that matched the color in her cheeks, and her hair was fashioned in a simple coil at the nape of her neck. Draped over her arm was a collection of lengths of cloth.

He noticed the letter he'd received yesterday lying within reach. And within sight of his wife. Alex snapped it up and tossed it in the top drawer of his desk. Until he decided what he thought of the University of Colorado's interesting but unsolicited offer to join their staff, Alex intended to keep the information to himself.

"And I thought I married a businesswoman bent on ruling the world one company at a time." He set aside his pen and journal to give her his full attention.

"You did, and perhaps I will, but first I've a few samples here I'd like to show you." She laid the fabric across the edge of his desk. "The colors in here are so dark and dated. What do you think of this one?"

Nothing about his third-floor space seemed displeasing, and there would be no painting over of the constellations above him. He did his best to study the woodsy green material with some measure of interest while he decided whether to assert his preferences now or later.

"Yes, it will do fine," Alex said when he figured he'd shown enough interest. "Now if you'll excuse me, I've some things to attend to."

"Truly, Alex, if you have no opinion, it's fine to say so."

"What?" He looked up as Charlotte wandered to the bookshelf and selected a volume by Voltaire. "No, really, I don't mind the green at all."

"You don't mind it?" She replaced the book on the shelf and turned to face him, one hand on her hip. "Why bother changing anything if there's nothing to be gained by it?"

"An excellent argument for more than just fabrics."

Charlotte huffed. "Why am I even asking you? We won't be married much longer." She moved toward him, sweeping past the trunks of still-unpacked journals and charts to settle easily in the chair across the desk. A knock sounded at the door, and one of the small army of household staff peered in.

"The mister's tailor is here for a fitting," the maid said.

"My tailor?" Alex shook his head. "I ordered no clothing."

Charlotte's gaze pointedly swept the length of him. When Alex's eyes met hers, she shrugged. "I took the liberty of choosing a few things that were a bit more appropriate."

"Appropriate for what?"

"The reception, of course." Charlotte looked past him to the maid. "Thank you, Mary. Please let the tailor know that Viscount Hambly will be down for his fitting in a few minutes."

"No, Mary," Alex said. "Tell the tailor to give me ten minutes with my wife, and then he can come up here for the fitting."

"But Alex, I…" Charlotte apparently thought better of her protest. "Never mind. Yes, Mary, please do as the viscount asks."

Alex returned his attention to Charlotte. "Have you found your paints?" he asked.

"Not yet." She smoothed her skirt, then rested her palms in her lap. "Alex, it is September today. Did you realize that?"

"I did, actually."

"Grandfather has asked when I'll be returning to work in London."

Alex felt an odd flash of temper. "Likely he asked when the two of us would be returning."

She met his stare. "In any case, I'm anxious to meet with his board again. Other than the day before the wedding, I've had little contact with anyone but Grandfather. Of course, under the circumstances I suppose he's really the only one I need to speak to."

Alex watched his wife as she absently turned the wedding ring that meant so little to her. Already she'd said more to him in this conversation than in all the past week put together.

"Perhaps I'll take a house in London after the first of the year," she said.

"Does your grandfather's home no longer meet your needs?"

She gave him a sideways look. "A place of my own."

Alex nodded. This uneasy truce of theirs would end as soon as she learned he would not seek an annulment. Knowing Charlotte had a place to live that did not involve sleeping under the same roof as him might be beneficial to both of them.

And yet, that was no marriage, was it?

"Have you had any further correspondence with Mr. Pembroke?" Charlotte asked.

The question hit a nerve, and Alex winced. "It has been some time since I've received a letter from him, actually."

"I see. Might a telegram be in order?"

Though he knew the answer all too well, Alex decided to broach the topic anyway. "Why the sudden interest in Will Pembroke, Charlotte?"

She shifted positions. "Only to see if perhaps anything important has gone missing between his office and yours."

"Charlotte," he said slowly, painfully aware of the trouble he was about to dive into, "what is it you'd like to know?"

Her fingers drummed a rhythm on her knees, and she lowered her gaze to study something in her lap. Then she abruptly returned her attention to Alex.

"I would like to know when I am free of this marriage."

"I see." He exhaled slowly. "Then I shall inform you of any further information I receive on that topic in as timely a manner as I can manage."

There. He'd answered her concern with a mostly truthful statement.

Alex sighed. Mostly was not good enough. A partial truth was still a lie.

"Look," he said. "I've not heard from Pembroke because I've informed him I no longer wish for him to look into an annulment through the London courts."

"What?" Her eyes widened. "Stop teasing me, Alex."

He waited a moment before speaking. "I'm quite serious."

"I see." Charlotte rose and gathered up her fabrics. "It appears you've forgotten that we had an arrangement. As part of that arrangement, I have pretended to be your wife. And because of that, you now have this lovely office and that telescope. You also have a standing in this town that only an association with the Becks could have achieved."

"A standing in this town?" Alex looked up at his wife. "I have no idea what you're talking about, Charlotte. You know I don't give one whit for social standing, but if I did, an Englishman and his titles are always welcome in the drawing rooms of Denver."

To her credit, Charlotte only let her haughty expression slip for a moment. "I've a mind to tell you exactly what I mean, but I fear I shall only cause more harm to what appears to be an endangered arrangement." She lifted her chin. "I shall forgive you for considering the breaking of your promise."

"You shall?" He stood and looked down on her from his superior height. "That's quite magnanimous of you, Charlotte."

"As is allowing you to live in *my* home when you have acted so dishonorably."

She took his laughter no better than the news of his lack of interest in the annulment. Dropping the fabrics at his feet, Charlotte stormed toward the door.

"Come sit down," he called.

"I won't."

"Fine," Alex said, "but you should know it is *I* who am allowing *you* to live in my home."

He waited for her footsteps to slow, and she returned to stand before him.

Alex shrugged. "I've the proof if you're interested." He retrieved the file Daniel Beck had given him upon their arrival in Denver. "I had hoped to spare you this."

Charlotte looked at the file with disdain and refused to take it. The expression she offered him was no better. "I wish no proof from you, Viscount Hambly. If you're not to be trusted with the annulment, then you're certainly not to be trusted with this."

She squared her shoulders, but something in her eyes held the slightest bit of fear.

"Then go and ask your father," he said. He'd already told her more than he'd intended. What was it about this woman that made him do things he wished he hadn't? "And send the tailor up. Being poked with pins sounds like a slice of heaven compared to continuing this conversation."

"All right," Charlotte said. "I shall."

Later, as the tailor took his measurements, Alex heard the carriage leave. Exactly one hour and ten minutes later, it returned. Alex moved to the window and watched as the driver handed Charlotte out of the carriage. While she made her way up the stone walk to the door, he slipped back so that Charlotte would not see him observing her.

When the front door slammed shut, he heard it. And when she stormed up the stairs to slam yet another door, likely the one to her bed-chamber, Alex heard that too.

He went back to his desk and retrieved the letter from the university. Request to teach. Offer to research. Plans to extend the current pro-gram. He read the letter from the dean in phrases, two or three words here and there, until he reached the end. "Must have your reply before 15 September."

Two weeks from now.

Another door slammed, and he heard footsteps on the floor below. Charlotte seemed to be pacing, as the steps continued but she did not seem to make any progress.

And then, suddenly, everything went quiet. He shifted to listen. Nothing split the silence except the tick of the clock behind him.

Alex rose to find the book he'd been reading, Mr. Langley's *The New Astronomy,* but he had no mind for concentrating. His addled brain kept wandering back to the floor below, where his wife likely plotted either his imminent demise or her imminent departure.

When the carriage once again pulled around to the front of the house, Alex did not need his telescope to see who climbed inside. He watched from the ledge between the two gargoyles as his wife and a half-dozen of her trunks disappeared down Grant Street.

He waited a full two hours before sending one of the staff down to the Beck home after Charlotte. When that failed, Alex debated whether to search for her at the Windsor Hotel. Surely she would not wish their marital troubles to become public knowledge.

But where else could she have gone?

31

A lady never forgets her manners or her mirror.
Both serve her well in all occasions.

—MISS PENCE

September 7
Beck Ranch outside Fort Collins, Colorado

Another letter from Gussie. The second one in the four days since Charlotte had arrived at the ranch after spending a few nights with her friend. She stared at it from across the room and willed it to disappear, wishing she hadn't asked for her old friend's help in escaping.

Though Charlotte held Augusta Miller in high esteem, reading in exquisite detail about her preparations for her wedding to George Arthur was the last thing she felt like doing this afternoon. For all Gussie's enthusiasm, she failed to grasp that now that Charlotte was a married woman, the New York social season would go on without her.

For that matter, *life* went on without Charlotte as she waited for Alex to respond to her demand for an annulment. In the meantime, everyone on the ranch believed she'd returned to help Gennie prepare for the ridiculous wedding reception.

The only person she hadn't offered an excuse or explanation to was Alex. She didn't care what he thought, and any questions regarding his absence went unasked by Papa and Gennie.

While enduring endless chatter from Gennie regarding every detail of the reception drove Charlotte mad, it was preferable to explaining why her husband was more than fifty miles away. The few times she'd been stupid enough to cry, Gennie had mistaken the tears for those of a bride longing for her groom rather than a woman wronged by a man bent on breaking the one promise that had gotten him married to her in the first place.

A knock sounded at the door, and Papa peered inside. "A moment of your time, Buttercup?"

"Of course." She watched while he settled onto the settee nearest her window. He studied her as she sat beside him, then gathered her into an embrace that nearly set off a fresh round of tears.

"A father wonders why his daughter's husband is nowhere to be found."

Charlotte put on a smile and faced her papa. "He's a busy man," she said. "And I'm a busy woman."

"Of course. Though I wonder if you've given too much thought to business and not enough to marriage."

When he said nothing further, Charlotte rested her head on her father's shoulder and sighed. How many times had she and Papa sat like this? Too many to count.

Finally she straightened and squared her shoulders. Best to say something before Papa did. "I know Alex," she said. "He wants me to be happy."

"A bride ought to find her happiness somewhere other than the boardroom," Papa said. "But I'm just your father, so what do I know?"

With a knock, Elias stepped inside. "Beg pardon, but Mr. Hiram's got a list of questions longer'n my arm. One of you ought to go down and answer 'em." He looked at Charlotte and winked. "The other might want to find something to do besides sit in her room and mope. Not that you're asking, and nor am I suggesting it."

Papa's laughter echoed in the hall as he pressed past Elias. Papa's old friend remained in the doorway. "Something bothering you that I can help with?" he finally asked.

Charlotte sighed. "No, but thank you for asking."

"Remember, even when I'm not asking, you can still tell me. Tova, too."

"Thank you," she managed.

Elias gave her another wink. "I've got to get downstairs and see if I can calm my wife down. Bill Cody's making his annual visit soon, and you know how she gets when that circus comes to town. She cleans every surface in the place and frets over what sort of mess they'll make. Seems a contradiction, but what do I know?"

"Can you blame her?"

"Not really." He lifted his cap and swiped his hand through iron gray curls. "But that don't make it any easier to listen to."

She smiled until Elias closed the door, and then tears threatened again. "Well, there's nothing for it." She stormed into her wardrobe and yanked off her afternoon frock.

The sun was out, and the sky was blue. With nothing else to occupy her time, Charlotte decided to take a ride and perhaps put the paints she'd finally found to use while the light was just right.

A change of clothes and a pair of boots later, she'd donned her favorite riding attire, tossed Gussie's letter into her bag, and found her way down to the barn, where she tucked her mother's paint box into her saddlebag.

The breeze bit as it slithered down her neck, so Charlotte shrugged closer into her buckskin jacket, glad she'd brought it, as they seemed to be in for one of the strange, unseasonable cold snaps that occasionally happened in Colorado. The heavy leather coat was a favorite, especially for rides across the plains in search of just the right scene to paint, and had always kept her warm when no other could. Though Gennie swore it was once hers, Papa refused to confirm or deny the allegation. Charlotte suspected it might have been a gift from Colonel and Mrs. Cody. She couldn't imagine her very proper stepmother ever willingly purchasing such a garment.

She rode through the paddock and out the gate, and then Charlotte spurred the mare into a gallop. The sorrel was a young horse but fast as the wind, and soon the ranch was merely a speck on the horizon behind them.

Charlotte dug her boots into the stirrups and headed for the stand of junipers at the edge of the canyon. There she would find the best view of the sunset as it stretched golden fingers across the canyon. Wood roses grew thick there, and though the ground would likely be covered in a light dusting of snow, she still wanted to capture it in the golden light. There was something about painting a fall afternoon in Colorado that almost made her forget about everything else.

If she didn't think she would freeze to death, Charlotte might have attempted to paint the night sky, with its pulsing planets and endless stars, from this vantage point as well. But the air temperature seemed to be dropping by the moment as the wind grew stronger. Perhaps she'd come back in late spring, when a blanket wrapped around multiple layers of clothing would not be required to keep warm.

As soon as the idea occurred to her, Charlotte shrugged it away. By then she would be in London, and though there were many things to recommend the English city, the night sky was not among them.

Ducking her head to keep the cold wind from stinging her eyes,

Charlotte held on tight until the mare slowed near a copse of silver birch. She reined in the sorrel and set about finding a spot in the snow for her easel and folding stool. As she ran her hand over the enameled paint box, she thought of her mother. Of how Mama's hands likely traced the same path across the wooden surface. This box was the only tangible connection Charlotte still had to her mother, her only inheritance.

Shaking away the memories, Charlotte lifted her head and lost herself in the beauty that was this part of Colorado. With long brush strokes, she painted a sky of the bluest blue, then dabbled on the myriad of colors that made up the canyon floor. Though the wind occasionally gusted past and the ground was so cold she had to stamp her feet to regain feeling in them, Charlotte continued to paint.

Finally she set her brushes aside and rose to take a step back. Something wasn't quite right. She looked past the oil on the easel to the canyon beyond. She'd captured all she saw.

Perhaps a few clouds to decorate the horizon would give the painting what it needed. Charlotte went back to work, painting in wisps of white that trailed across the horizon and evaporated into the endless sky. When those did not appeal, she turned the cirrus clouds to cumulus with great thundering tops in the darkest gray.

Charlotte once again stepped back to admire her handiwork. Still she hadn't managed to capture an image worth keeping.

An idea occurred to her, and she went to her paints to mix colors. Before the shadows of the junipers reached her feet, Charlotte had turned the painting of an autumn afternoon into a glorious nighttime scene with only a sliver of moon and a sky full of tiny stars.

Now to place the constellations. She closed her eyes and tried to remember where to put them. Perhaps tonight she would slip out after all and take a quick peek at the sky, just a fast visit to get the image

straight in her mind. Once the sun went down, the canyon would be
bitterly cold, but what was necessary must be endured.

The mare began to complain, and Charlotte opened her eyes, trying to see what caused the placid horse to stomp and snort. Snakes were
an ever-present threat, as were strangers, though she'd rarely been both-
ered by either.

Only a fool traveled alone and unarmed, so there was a pistol tucked
into her saddlebag. With care lest the intruder be a snake, Charlotte rose
and inched toward the still-complaining sorrel. Something rustled
beyond the thicket, so she reached inside the saddlebag and wrapped her
fingers around Papa's old Colt. With her free hand, she scratched the
mare behind the ear.

At Charlotte's touch, the horse quieted. "Good girl," she whispered.

She leaned against the animal's neck to hide as best she could, then
slid the revolver out and placed one boot in the stirrup. Now she could
either shoot from where she stood or, as Colonel Cody had taught her,
jump into the saddle and take aim on the fly.

Again something rustled.

"Shhh…" she whispered to the fretting horse.

For a moment, only the whispers of a September breeze and the call of
some faraway bird interrupted the silence. Even the mare stood stock-still.

Carefully, Charlotte cocked the revolver, and the click seemed mag-
nified a thousand fold.

Then, from behind her, she heard the same click.

And then footsteps crunching on the rocks.

Charlotte froze. Shooting meant turning around. Fleeing meant
making a move with someone behind her, likely aiming a weapon in her
direction.

In the silence, she heard the familiar rattle.

ॐ

Alex took aim at the snake, mindful of the fact that the creature was close enough to Charlotte and her horse to strike either should he miss. Then there was the problem of Charlotte shooting him whether he missed or not.

From the look on her face, she felt he deserved it.

Slowly he pointed to the ground then, even slower, put his finger to his lips. When Charlotte nodded, Alex steadied his aim.

The blast killed the rattler instantly. Unfortunately, it also sent Charlotte's mare skittering across the prairie and out of sight beyond the junipers. Thankfully she had the good sense to jump back. After one more shot to be certain the snake was dead, Alex grabbed a stick and shoved the carcass away from his wife.

"Shall I skin it or do I risk my own life by allowing a knife within your reach?" Alex turned to see that Charlotte still held her pistol, though she'd lowered her arm and no longer pointed it at him.

In the overall scheme of things, that was progress.

"Did you bring the annulment papers?" she asked.

He shook his head. "I've told you what I think on that, and it's not changing. But at least I brought my gun. You'd have been bitten had I not found you."

"Thank you," she said as she holstered the gun. "Though I'm now on foot."

"Will the mare come when you call?"

Charlotte gave him a look, then turned her back on him and walked toward her paints. "About as well as I do."

Alex followed and peered over her shoulder at the painting. "Very nice." He pointed out a few of the constellations, then paused. "I'm sorry. I tend to get carried away when it comes to the stars."

She shrugged. "I don't mind, actually."

He gave the canvas another look then turned his attention to Charlotte. "You did an excellent job of conveying the night sky. It's beautiful this time of year."

Charlotte banged the small folding stool shut, interrupting his conversation. When he attempted to repeat his statement, she banged it again. He took the hint and kept his mouth closed.

She set the chair aside, then went to gather up her paints. He tagged along behind her like a puppy until she turned abruptly and nearly swiped him with her brush. Charlotte gave him a hard look, then stamped her feet.

"Cold?" he asked, but she ignored him. She made short work of cleaning her brush and returning it to the case. "It will be dark soon," he added, having nothing else to say.

She put away her canvas and easel without sparing him so much as a glance. When she was done, she walked a few yards to the ridge and whistled.

A moment later, the errant horse returned.

"I thought you said she didn't come when you called," he said.

Charlotte gave him an even stare. "I said she responds about as well as I do." She paused. "At least to people she doesn't want to listen to." She stowed her painting supplies in her saddlebags, then fitted her stool into place. "And truly, Alex, I don't want to listen to you anymore. Just get the annulment."

"Wait," he said as he watched her climb into the saddle. "It's not that easy."

"Of course it is," she responded. "You and I just stay away from one another until the paperwork is done. Then we ask a judge to declare our marriage void." She grasped the reins tightly. "How difficult can that be, Alex?"

And off she went, riding like the wind over a prairie dulled by shadows, the first stars of the evening twinkling overhead. This time when Alex followed her, it was less like a pup and more like a man with a mission.

No matter what Charlotte Beck Hambly said, he had no plans to declare their marriage null and void, and Alex planned to shadow his wife until she gave up her desire to leave the marriage.

The only thing he hadn't figured out yet was how exactly to convince her to stay.

A lady should never leave home unprepared for
emergencies. Generally it is best to bring a comb,
a mirror, and at least one strong gentleman of good
character and pleasant appearance who can be relied
on to handle any other eventualities.

—*MISS PENCE*

Charlotte didn't look back to see if Alex followed her. The fact that he'd
come for her should have meant something, but all she could think of
was his refusal to keep his promise regarding the annulment.

Unlike her leisurely trip to the foothills, Charlotte urged her horse
to fly over the flat land. Soon, however, the rocky terrain near the river
caused the mare to slow. Charlotte was forced to allow it, for as much as
she wished to be rid of Alex Hambly, she did not wish to land in the icy
water in the process.

She kept a tight grip on the reins and focused on the trail as the rising moon traced a crooked silver path down the center of the river. The
mare's breath was visible in the chill air, as was Charlotte's own, but the
borrowed leather jacket kept her from the cold.

She shrugged down into the warmth and allowed the hope that Alex
had gone home by another way to take hold. Unfortunately, the sound
of a horse echoed behind her. Resisting the urge to turn and face him,
Charlotte kept her eyes on the trail ahead.

Until Alex rode up and blocked her path. Looking more like a member of Colonel Cody's Wild West show than the nobleman she married, the viscount wore buckskins and boots and sat in the saddle as if he'd been born there. Add to this the fact that he obviously shot well enough—

"We're not finished discussing this, Charlotte," he said.

She tried to go around him, but he countered her move. Twice.

"Running is for children," he said, as much a statement as a taunt, for the determination on his face was new, an expression she'd not seen in all their time together. Had she not been fiercely irritated, Charlotte might have found his continued persistence admirable.

"All right," she said with a sigh. "If you insist on continuing this discussion, why don't you start by telling me why you've chosen not to keep your promise?"

"Actually, I *am* keeping my promise." An owl's call split the evening air, and Alex paused to calm his skittish horse. "The same one you made. In the chapel."

"The same one we *both* agreed was temporary."

Alex sobered and glanced toward the horizon. "Can we talk about this back at the ranch house? It's getting dark."

Shadows did gather long and dark, and the blue sky wore a tint of deepest purple at the edges. But though the moon had risen above the horizon, there was still plenty of time to find home without losing the trail to lack of daylight.

Charlotte regarded Alex with narrowed eyes. Taking a stand might cause him to rethink his stubbornness. "What's left to say, Alex?"

"Let's go." He turned his horse toward the ranch, expecting her to follow.

But Charlotte had a stubborn streak of her own, and the light was quite lovely here by the river. There was just enough illumination to paint the landscape and the beginnings of a starlit evening above.

She dismounted and led the mare to a tree. Using extra care, she secured the apt-to-flee horse, then reached for her paints and stool.

"What are you doing?" Alex demanded.

Ignoring him, Charlotte made short work of setting up a serviceable outdoor studio and began mixing tints.

Her temporary husband looked down from his horse and shook his head. "You're a madwoman."

Again, she ignored him. The stars were popping out by the dozens. Soon the night sky would be filled with the pinpricks of light she adored to capture on canvas.

"You are my wife, Charlotte, like it or not, and—"

"I don't." She met his stare. "I do not like being married."

"To me or in general?" he asked.

She turned back to her work, unwilling to answer. Had she not been forced to agree to a sham marriage, Charlotte would have enjoyed life without Papa's rules.

"I think you don't like being told what to do."

Charlotte's gaze collided with Alex's stare. He'd practically read her thoughts, but she knew she must protest.

"You don't know anything about me, Alex," she managed before returning to her work.

"I know you're a menace," he said. "And I know you're quite talented at painting. And your persistence is legendary." He looked to her for a response. When she offered none, Alex continued. "And then there's your creativity. Goodness knows you've come up with some of the most interesting ideas."

She continued to pretend to ignore the Englishman as he listed a few more of her positive traits and a few more of her negative ones. Through it all, Charlotte held her tongue.

"But one thing I do not know about you is where you stand with your faith," Alex finished.

"Faith." She stabbed her brush into the holder and turned to face him. "You too? Have you been talking to Papa? Because my faith is just fine."

"I see."

His tone alone told Charlotte that he didn't, but she wasn't continuing this discussion, especially now that it had turned far too personal.

"And I'll thank you to keep your opinion of the matter to yourself," she said.

One dark brow rose as Alex adjusted his leather glove. "I've offered no opinion on the matter, wife."

The last word caused his lips to turn up into a grin, crinkling the corners of his eyes. A chill wind lifted his hair then skittered down Charlotte's spine. She shuddered and shrank deeper into the heavy coat.

"You're cold," Alex said.

He climbed off his horse and reached for her paints, but Charlotte grabbed them first. In her haste to close the case, the entire thing tumbled from her hands and landed in a heap at the water's edge.

"Oh no! Look what you've done." She hurried after her treasure only to stumble on the sandy riverbank, fall, and roll past them.

"Charlotte?" Alex called. "Are you injured?"

"Only my pride," she muttered as she climbed to her feet and swiped at her riding skirt. Charlotte took a step toward her paints and then another, edging around a rocky outcropping and across sand that was more shift than solid, carefully making her way up the bank. She could not lose her last link to her mother. She simply could not.

Almost within reach of the precious case, Charlotte heard the shriek of an owl.

Her mare skittered and kicked, causing Alex's horse to bolt. He held tight to the reins just long enough for the animal to yank his shoulder hard and cause the viscount to cry out. His horse disappeared into the shadowy prairie.

"Alex?" Charlotte called. "Are you all right?"

She turned, intending to climb toward him, but her foot slammed against a rock, sending her reeling backward into the sand. As she fell, Charlotte's arm knocked into the paint case, sending it skidding down the bank. She rolled to her side and grabbed for it, but she missed. Her fingers just brushed its edge as it plummeted toward the river. It landed with an awful plop and disappeared beneath the rushing waters.

"No!" she cried, still reaching vainly toward the water.

Alex somehow kept his footing as he hurried to her side. "Hold my hand and don't let go," he said as he scooped her into an upright position with his right hand. He held his injured left arm close against his side.

"My paints," she said through the haze of her anger and grief. "They're lost."

"Forget the paints. You've done enough for today. Let's go home."

"No." Charlotte pushed him away and started toward the river, determined to dive in if she must in order to retrieve her paints. "You don't understand. The box. It belonged to my mother."

Alex reached around her waist and once again hauled her against him. "I said forget the paints."

Her protests fell on deaf ears as the viscount stood stock-still and allowed her to flail against him. Finally, when she'd tired herself out, Charlotte gave in.

"All right," she said slowly. "Release me, and I'll do as you ask."

"Just like that?" he asked, his voice rumbling against her ear. He turned her to face him.

"Just like that," she echoed.

But when Alex loosened his grip, Charlotte slipped from his arms and dove toward the river. She managed to get hip deep in the frigid water before her temporary husband stopped her progress.

"I will buy you more paints, Charlotte," he said against her ear, "but I cannot buy you good health should you ruin it by catching your death in this river."

"Nothing can replace the box. Nothing."

Blind fury made her want to pummel his broad shoulders with her fists, but she knew it would have no effect. So she complied, once more allowing Alex Hambly to tell her what to do. She bit her bottom lip to keep from crying. She'd done enough crying in front of Alex.

He led her back to the spot where she'd left her stool and easel. Seeing where her paints should have been, Charlotte allowed the first angry tear to fall.

"Here," came the gruff voice behind her.

And in spite of herself, Charlotte turned toward the sound. Alex Hambly stood behind her, half-soaked and covered in mud. The handkerchief he thrust toward her with his uninjured right hand, however, was pristine.

"It's clean," Alex muttered as he took her hand and closed her fingers around the handkerchief.

"Unlike you." The words slipped from her lips before Charlotte could help herself.

"Thanks to you." He stormed toward the rise.

"Your horse," she called. "How badly did it hurt you when it ran?"

"I'll be fine," he said tersely. He folded her stool, then reached for the canvas and easel.

Charlotte watched as he loaded her gear with his uninjured hand. "You're *not* fine."

And yet when the time came to climb back into the saddle, he somehow managed to help her up.

"What will you do for a horse, Alex?"

He shrugged. "I figure that stubborn pony will get hungry and find her way home, won't she?"

"They usually do," Charlotte said.

"Then move up and we'll share." Before she could protest, Alex had unseated her from the saddle and fitted himself behind her. "I've a bit of a twinge in my arm," he admitted as she settled in front of him. "You take the reins. Just remember that should I be sent plummeting from the horse, you're going along with me."

Charlotte took the reins but made no move to set the horse in motion. Rather, she looked back at the spot where her paint box had disappeared into the river.

"Don't think of it," Alex said. "It's too dark to see now, and I imagine that river's deep in spots. You'll never know whether you're looking in the right place." He let out a long breath. "Tomorrow I'll come back and look for it. How's that?"

"All right." She returned her attention to the trail and urged the horse toward home.

The feel of the Englishman behind her, of his good arm wrapped around her waist and his chin resting against her cheek, set Charlotte thinking about what it might be like if they had a real marriage. A marriage like Papa and Gennie had.

As soon as the thought appeared, Charlotte dismissed it. Never would she find anything resembling a real marriage with Alex Hambly.

It made no sense at all.

33

A lady never tells her age or the amount in her bank
account. For the former must always be thought
lower than it actually is while the latter should be
thought higher.

—MISS PENCE

The throbbing in his arm dulled to an ache when Alex thought of the
woman leaning against him. His wife. He hadn't truly considered what
that meant until now.

He had fun calling her "wife" and watching her reaction, but to
actually consider her his wife? Likely Charlotte would not make a marriage to her easy, even if she did resign herself to never having the annulment. But doing the right thing often meant doing the more difficult
thing.

Alex swiped at the melting snowflake trickling down his cheek, then
turned his attention to Charlotte. Stubborn woman. Her wet skirts
slogged against his leg as a stiff wind blew from the north, and he could
feel the chill of the damp fabric. She was probably numb with cold,
though she was far too stubborn to admit it.

"Charlotte," he said against her ear, "are you warm enough?"

"I'm fine," she said, but he could not tell if her tone was bravado or
a blatant lie.

"Perhaps we should stop," he offered.

She angled her head toward him, and the silver light of the moon slid over her profile. "I'd much prefer my warm home to this cold trail."

As he could think of no good argument to that statement, Alex merely nodded. The mare picked her way down the nearly dark trail, missing the rocks that could cause them to tumble back into the river. A better plan would have been to turn from the bank to find another route back to the ranch, but any other route would need a full moon to illuminate it, and tonight they had nothing of the sort.

The breeze picked up. Flakes of snow began swirling through the air and caught in Charlotte's hair and decorated her clothing as the temperature dropped. Beneath the heavy Western jacket, Alex could feel her begin to tremble. Further evidence that her damp skirts would be her downfall.

Damp skirts that he, at least in part, had caused.

"Charlotte," he said against her ear. "I'm sorry."

She jumped at the sound of his voice. "What for?"

"Oh, all of it, I suppose." He paused. "But at the moment, I'm thinking of how you must be freezing and we've still got at least an hour to ride."

"I'm fine," she said.

"At least switch places so that I can block the wind."

She shook her head. "A waste of time."

He contemplated taking the matter into his own hands, removing her from the saddle, and fitting her behind him. Only his injury kept him from acting. He settled for wrapping his arms tighter around his wife and silently daring her to complain.

She did not.

As the snow fell harder, Alex began to look for shelter while the ever-contrary Charlotte spurred the horse on. If the lights of the ranch did not soon appear on the horizon, he would find someplace to get her out of the wind and build a fire for warmth.

The trail turned away from the river and wound through a stand of aspens. Though the light had grown dim, the horse seemed to know the path. Alex flexed his fingers and tried to move his injured arm, with moderate success.

Charlotte's shoulders and backbone slumped. For his part, Alex no longer felt his fingers, despite his gloves, and his feet were chilled to the bone.

"The cold comes on quickly here," he said. "Just this afternoon the weather was quite pleasant."

No response. When Charlotte's head dipped, Alex called her name.

"I'm fine," she snapped.

His wife was anything but fine, but he knew that further conversation would be of no use. He began to pray.

A few minutes later, they emerged on the other side of the forest, and Alex spied a cabin tucked up against the hillside. No trail of smoke could be seen from the chimney, and there appeared to be no lights in the windows. Likely the place had been abandoned.

"Up there," he said. "We're stopping."

"Don't be ridiculous," Charlotte said.

He snagged the reins from her. Her cry of complaint told him there was still a bit of starch left in her spine.

"Ridiculous would be bypassing perfectly good shelter." Alex tightened his grip on the reins. "Pride will only keep you so warm. After that, a good fire is required. Now, will you remain still until we reach that cabin, or will I have to slow this mare to deal with you first?"

She opened her mouth to complain, then thankfully thought better of it. When she nodded, he celebrated the not-so-small victory. Still he figured his hardheaded wife would eventually find her voice and object.

Alex decided to hurry.

Finding the best path to the cabin proved difficult, as the mare encountered more than one rocky patch along the way. Alex waited for the protest that never came. Instead, Charlotte leaned meekly against his shoulder and closed her eyes.

"Charlotte?"

No response.

He shook her. "Charlotte?"

Her murmur of complaint was barely audible over the sound of the horse's hooves. Her shivering, however, had increased to the point that Alex had to hold her as tightly as he could with his injured arm to prevent her from sliding off the saddle.

"We're almost there," Alex said. "Just hold on to me until I can get you inside and warm."

"No," she said through gritted teeth. "Home." She made a grab for the reins, but Alex easily thwarted her.

"Stubborn woman," he muttered. He urged the horse on until they had closed the distance to the cabin.

Alex gave the structure a quick but critical look and judged it, at least from the exterior, to be structurally sound. However, even with the moon rising and the sun long set, the place wore its lack of attention for all to see. Still, he allowed for the possibility that its owner might be about.

"Wait here," Alex said as he slid from behind Charlotte and swept the snow from her hair. "And don't even think about running off and leaving me."

Her weak smile worried him almost as much as her docile attitude. Apparently she was more chilled than she looked, and she looked awfully cold.

"Hello?" Alex called as he approached the cabin. He repeated the greeting, then slowly pushed on the door. It swung open on hinges sorely in need of oil, revealing a serviceable cabin empty of humans but—from what he could see in the deep shadows—decently furnished.

In one corner he could just make out a crudely made table and two benches set before the fireplace. He spied a lamp and matches on the mantel and made short work of illuminating the room. Though the cabin appeared to have been uninhabited for some time, there was a log in the fireplace that only needed kindling to be lit. A simple matter once he retrieved Charlotte.

The opposite end of the one-room abode held a wooden bed covered in a faded quilt. Several other blankets had been folded at the end of the bed, and Alex grabbed one.

"All right, wife," he said as he headed back outside, "I think this will do."

But though the horse was still tethered to the post, Charlotte was nowhere to be found. He called her name into the swirling snow but heard only the mare's whinny in response.

"Charlotte, where are you?" he yelled again. Then he saw a set of footprints in the snow.

It only took a minute to find her, as she'd not strayed far.

"Did you intend to walk back to the ranch?" he asked.

When she continued to walk, he halted her progress, then turned her to face him. Wide green eyes stared blankly past him as her lips, tinged blue from the cold, trembled.

"Need to go home," she managed. "So cold."

"I've a warm fire for you," he said, wrapping the quilt around her shoulders. "Or I will, once I get you inside so I can light it." She swayed and Alex held her against him to steady her. "Can you walk?" When she nodded, he forced a smile. "All right then. Let's go this way."

Charlotte did as he asked, a sure sign she'd soon succumb to the cold if he didn't get her inside and warmed up. Though his sore arm ached, Alex urged her forward, swiping at the snow on her face and in her hair, until he managed to get her inside.

"Sit here," he said as he settled Charlotte onto the bench nearest the fireplace.

She did, again without protest, and watched while he piled kindling around the log and then struck several matches until one finally lit. Tossing the match into the fireplace, Alex stood back and watched as the flames took hold.

When he turned around, Charlotte was gone again. This time, he found her moving slowly toward the bed, the ends of the quilt dragging behind her.

"Where are you going?" he asked. "The fire's just getting warm."

"No," she said without looking back. She reached out to grasp the bedpost, allowing the quilt to slide to the floor.

"Wait, Charlotte, your clothes are wet," he said as she yanked back the covers. "And you're still wearing your riding boots."

She looked back, the slightest spark of awareness in her expression. "But I'm tired."

"You're cold," he said, "and the only remedy for that is to sit near the fire where you can get warm." Alex reached for her arm and drew her toward him. "And you're going to have to get out of those wet clothes."

Obediently, she shrugged out of the heavy jacket and allowed the fringed leather to fall at her feet. Charlotte moved toward the fire, and

Alex ran to retrieve the quilt, then followed Charlotte to stand in the warmth.

"Here," he said, holding the quilt up by the corners to block his view of her. "You need to get out of those wet clothes. The quilt will protect your dignity, and I promise to close my eyes."

Even though you're my wife, he almost added.

He waited for a response and, hearing none, called her name.

She turned to face him, still fully clothed. "My faith is fine," she whispered, her lips only slightly less blue than they had been outside.

"I believe you."

"Papa doesn't." She looked as if she might continue, then shook her head and turned to stare into the flames.

"What matters is what *you* know to be true," he said gently. "The Lord sees the heart, Charlotte, and that's what's important."

She blinked twice as if clearing her focus, then regarded Alex with a serious expression. "I've been so selfish," she whispered. A lone tear traced down her cheek and she lifted her hand to wipe it away. "So maybe my faith isn't fine. But I want it to be."

How many times had he wanted to remember what he believed? To find faith enough to go forward? Too many times to judge Charlotte for any lapse now.

"Faith isn't a feeling," he said gently. "If it were, we'd all lose and gain it every time the winds changed." He mustered a smile as he spoke, not only to her, but to himself. "Faith is the knowledge that no matter the circumstances, you do not walk through them alone." He shrugged. "At least that's how I look at it."

"Yes," she said softly.

Alex allowed the silence a moment longer. Then he set the quilt on the bench and pressed his palms to her cheeks. "Charlotte, we can talk about this later. Right now, you've other things to think about. Like getting warm. You have to get out of those wet riding clothes. Either you can do it alone or I'll be forced to help. Which is it?"

Her fingers went to her bodice.

"First your boots," Alex said quickly. He knelt before her and, with extreme effort, kept his mind off her slender ankles and the curves of her legs that the damp riding garment only served to accentuate as he removed her boots.

"There," he said. "Now you can proceed."

Alex lifted the quilt to allow her privacy. Whether Charlotte noticed his discretion or not, Alex couldn't say, but after a moment, she stepped over a puddle of damp clothing and into the folds of the quilt. She held the blanket tight, allowing only a few inches of ankle and leg to show as she padded toward the bed.

"Good night, Alex," she mumbled.

"Wait."

He hurried past her to pull back the faded quilt and check for any unwanted creatures. Finding none, he allowed Charlotte to climb under the quilt. Before he could cover her with it, she had turned over and closed her eyes.

Only after Charlotte had settled into a slumber did Alex go outside and take care of the horse. When he returned, the cabin was nice and warm.

Stomping the snow off his boots brought no reaction from beneath the pile of blankets at the far end of the room. Nor did she rouse when he leaned over the bed to check on her. But when he brushed her cheek with the back of his hand, her eyes opened. Before he could move away, she grasped his hand in hers.

"Thank you," she whispered.

34

Sufficient rest is a lady's most precious beauty secret.

—*Miss Pence*

The sun shone orange against Charlotte's eyelids and warmed her face as she snuggled deeper beneath her blankets. Odd that the maid hadn't closed the curtains last night.

Reaching toward the bedside table, Charlotte groped for the bell and found only air. She reached further, and her fingers hit what felt like another person.

Her eyes flew open. Her temporary husband stared at her from a chair situated next to the bed. From the look of him, he'd slept there. The glow behind him was not the sun but a fire of decent proportion. She blinked twice to adjust her focus, then allowed her gaze to sweep the one-room cabin.

Meager furniture combined with dim light offered little to recommend the place. It was, however, quite warm.

"Alex?"

He scrubbed at his face with his hands, then shook his head. With slow, deliberate movements, the Englishman straightened his collar then regarded her through tired eyes.

"What happened?" she asked.

Her last recollection was of her paints sinking beneath the icy waters of the Cache la Poudre River. Instant anger flared within her, tempered by a less precise recollection of riding a horse and then, perhaps, of being wrapped first in something very cold and then in something very warm.

His gaze lowered and she followed his attention to see that she wore a threadbare, multicolored quilt trimmed in an odd shade of saffron yellow and nothing else.

Realization collided with dread and sent Charlotte scrambling to find her modesty. When she had covered what she could with the less-than-lilac-scented bedding, she fixed Alex with a direct stare. "Explain yourself, Viscount Hambly."

Alex lifted a dark brow. "Excuse me?"

"Well, isn't it obvious I'm..." Charlotte's heart fluttered as she considered exactly what she *was*. "I demand to know how I came to be"—the quilt slipped and she clutched at it—"how I came to be here."

Without sparing her a glance, Alex rose and raised his arms overhead in a languid stretch. "You came to be here," he said, turning his back on her to move toward the fireplace, "because you're a stubborn woman who refuses to listen to good sense. And it made *no* sense to wade into a river after a box of paints that can easily be replaced."

The paints. Of course.

Charlotte's temper sparked as she recalled the moment her mother's paint box tumbled down the embankment. She remembered reaching for the precious box only to push it farther away.

Watching as it disappeared beneath the water.

And it all began with Alex Hambly.

A glance outside told Charlotte the hour was late, or perhaps early. How long had it been submerged? Though the paints would be ruined, perhaps there was still hope of finding the box.

With Alex occupied stoking the fire, Charlotte took the opportunity to climb out of bed and adjust her makeshift costume. Her clothes had been laid across two benches and set in front of the fire. In order to retrieve them, she would have to step within view of Alex.

Taking a deep breath, she inched toward her goal, taking tiny steps to keep the blankets in place.

"Close your eyes."

Alex looked up from his work at the fire. "What?"

Charlotte froze and pulled the fabric up just below her nose. "I said close your eyes," she said, inhaling the musty smell of old quilts. She gestured to her riding garments and the embarrassing unmentionables on full display.

Alex followed her gaze, then returned his attention to her with a grin. "You intend to put on those wet things?"

Her bravado slipped slightly. "Yes." She squared her shoulders and moved toward the circle of warmth near the roaring fire.

"I see." He set the fireplace poker aside and dusted off his palms. "You might want to reconsider."

Ignoring him, Charlotte snatched up her clothing and moved to the other side of the room. "Just keep your back turned, all right?"

"Of course, wife." He punctuated the statement with a chuckle that stabbed at Charlotte's last drop of patience.

"Wife," she echoed as she began the difficult process of dressing while maintaining her modesty. "You *do* enjoy taunting me with that, don't you?"

He shrugged, but kept his back turned. "Only stating fact, Charlotte."

And then she recalled the rest of the cause for her anger: her husband's unreasonable refusal to allow the annulment. When she reached for her stocking, she caught Alex peering at her over his shoulder as he knelt by the fire.

Before Charlotte could scold him, Alex straightened and regarded her with a look that scorched through her blankets. She offered him her back and finished donning her undergarments without looking his direction.

"Charlotte," he said softly, "what have we done?"

Grimacing, she pulled on skirts soggy with river water and splotched with mud. "What?" she asked as she reached for the remainder of her ensemble. The bodice was less muddy but no less damp, making Charlotte wonder whether modesty was worth enduring the chill.

He repeated his question, this time from much nearer. Charlotte hurried to complete her dressing, then let the quilt drop. She turned to find Alex standing within reach.

"What we have done," she said as she felt the cold air hit her wet skirts, "is make a bargain that benefited us both."

Alex picked up the quilt and wrapped it around her shoulders. His hands lingered, smoothing the fabric over her collarbone and touching her chin with the back of his knuckles. Then he traced the length of her jaw line.

"Four years," he said softly, "and I never quite rid myself of thinking about you, Charlotte." His fingers stilled. "Why?"

Entranced with his touch, with the curve of his smile and the way his eyes slid shut as he caressed her jaw, Charlotte could only breathe a soft, "Because I'm a menace."

"No," he said slowly, "though I cannot deny that fact." His palm went from Charlotte's jaw to the nape of her neck. "When I considered the bargain I'd made to marry you, I never failed to be reminded of some irritating thing or another you'd said or done. And though I didn't intend it, before long I'd found a smile where I shouldn't have."

Dare she tell him the same had happened to her? But she'd made her choice, and marriage did not fit with her plans. After all, look what happened when Mama fell in love and married.

Papa left her.

The thought surprised Charlotte. She'd never considered it that way before.

Alex must have noticed for he shook his head. "What aren't you telling me, Charlotte?"

Look what happened to Mama.

Did she want to pursue her interest in business because she loved it or because she feared falling in love? She didn't have an answer.

Except, possibly, the faith that the Lord would send her in the direction He preferred if she let Him. And, perhaps, even if she did not.

"Charlotte?" Alex's voice caressed her name just as his fingers had caressed her jaw.

"Nothing." She shrugged out of his reach and moved toward the window. Ice covered the pane and snow drifted past. There would be no ride to the safety of the ranch tonight. Not until the sun rose and, Charlotte hoped, sent the temperatures soaring. She suppressed a shiver that even the quilt could not stop.

Footsteps moved her direction, and Charlotte steeled herself for whatever Alex might say.

"Wife," he whispered, "what does that expression mean?"

·She turned to rest her back against the cold windowpane, suffering the frigid feel of glass against her wet bodice rather than allow herself to stand any closer to Alex Hambly. Not when she longed to rest her head against his shoulder, to fall into his embrace and forget any thoughts of Mama and Papa.

And of marriage.

To anyone.

"Wife," he repeated. He grasped two corners of the quilt. "Come stand by the fire." He tugged gently on the quilt, moving her—as much by her own will as against it—into his arms. "Four years," he said, "and I never forgot your kiss."

Nor did I, Charlotte longed to admit.

"I can't be married to anyone," she whispered across his shoulder. "I just cannot."

Alex's chuckle rumbled against her ear. "Yes," he said slowly but deliberately, "you can."

And then he fit his lips over hers. Somehow her hands found his shoulders and then the back of his waist. She pulled him closer, deepening the kiss.

Perhaps she could be married.

Perhaps...

Alex ended the kiss far too soon, and Charlotte whimpered. She pulled him back to kiss her again, and he did not complain. This time when the kiss ended, he swept her off her feet and into his arms. The quilt fell away, leaving her wet clothing exposed. Had she not felt warm from the inside out, Charlotte might have shivered. But in Alex's arms there was no thought of cold. For that matter, there was no thought at all.

"It's time we were well and truly married, Charlotte."

He waited until she managed a nod, then stepped over the quilt. They reached the bed so quickly that Charlotte had no time to wonder what might happen next. She allowed her husband to lower her gently and give her a kiss that seared her heart.

"You're beautiful," Alex said as he stood over her. The orange flames danced behind her husband, and the golden glow played in shadows across his cheekbones. Indeed, Alex Hambly was something to see.

She almost told him. Instead, she entwined her fingers with his. At her tug, he joined her. Lying on his side, Alex propped himself up on his elbow and rested his head on his right hand.

A niggling fear slithered up her spine and lodged in the words that longed to be spoken. Words that would stop Alex's kisses. Words that would keep her heart safe.

She sucked in a deep breath. "Alex," she managed. "I'm afraid."

"Shhh," he said softly. He kissed her. "There's no need to be afraid. You've had my heart for years, though I've only just realized it." He obliged her with a kiss that was every bit as soft as it was urgent. "I will never hurt you. I promise."

And she believed him.

She pulled him down for another kiss.

"Charlotte?" someone called from outside. The sound of horses filled the previously quiet night.

She sat bolt upright. "Papa?"

Alex groaned and fell back onto the pillow beside her. "It appears we're being rescued, Charlotte." He slid her a sideways look. "Best attend to your hair."

She lifted her hands to her head and blushed at the mess of curls. When in the fog of kisses had that happened? Charlotte tried to remedy the damage, but her trembling fingers refused to cooperate.

"Here," Alex said. "Let me." His fingers combed quickly but painlessly through the tangles.

Footsteps outside quickly became boots on the porch, and then the door opened. The first member of the search party, Colonel

Cody, found the married couple sitting side by side on a bench in front of the fire.

If he noticed her mussed hair, the colonel did not say. He simply removed his fringed leather jacket and placed it around Charlotte's shoulders. "Show time," he whispered. He tipped his hat to Alex, then led her out onto the porch and into the waiting arms of her father.

"How did you find us?" she heard Alex ask.

"Knew there had been trouble when the horse came back without a rider," Papa said as he helped Charlotte up into the wagon. "There are only so many line cabins out this way, so Bill and I took the ones to the south, and the other boys headed north." He paused as Alex climbed up beside Charlotte. "So, how'd you end up unseated, Hambly?"

"Actually, I—"

"It was my fault, Papa," Charlotte interrupted. She tucked her trembling hands into the folds of Colonel Cody's coat.

Papa laughed. "Of course it was. Never suspected anything else." He paused. "Though I do have to wonder if—"

"Excuse me, sir," Alex said. "I believe we've already discussed what sort of questions regarding our marriage are not allowed. Might the one you're about to ask fall into that category?"

"It just might," Papa said with a chuckle. "So I'll not ask."

But Charlotte blushed all the same.

When they arrived home, the first rays of the morning sun peeking over the eastern horizon, she hurried up to her room and shut the door before Alex could follow.

By the time his knock sounded at the door, she had shed her wet clothes and donned a nightgown. He knocked again and called softly, "Charlotte?"

Charlotte opened her mouth to respond, to whisk him into her bedchamber so that she might once again find her fears gone. But losing her fears to Alex Hambly's embrace only seemed like a good idea when logic was not involved. And now that she'd found her own bed, she'd rediscovered her good sense as well.

When he knocked one last time, she ignored his call.

The words *look what happened to Mama* chased her into sleep. But Alex Hambly caught her in her dreams.

35

A lady always packs well, and with assistance.

—*MISS PENCE*

September 8, 1891
Fort Collins, Colorado

Charlotte instructed the maids to pack everything, including her canvases and brushes. Where she was going she wouldn't need most of these things, but it felt right to empty the room that had been her refuge and prison at the same time. And though she had no paints, she liked knowing the other tools of her hobby were available should she decide to pick them up again someday.

Moving to the window, Charlotte allowed her attention to slip past the breathtaking view of the Rocky Mountains to the cornflower blue Colorado sky. She would miss the West with its broad expanses of open land and bracing fresh air. While a storm could take her by surprise on the Continent, here in Colorado Charlotte could see one approach from miles away.

She let out a long breath. If only she'd seen her feelings for Alex before they'd surprised her in the cabin.

"No," she whispered as the fear rose. "I'm sorry, Mama. I can't."

Charlotte wrapped her arms around her middle and closed her eyes. This fear was new, strange, and in direct opposition to the loss of independence she once worried about. And yet everything about knowing for certain that giving in to a marriage meant allowing for the same loss her mother suffered felt true. Right. Terrifying.

A knock sounded, and she turned to bid the maid to enter.

"Beg pardon, ma'am," the girl said, "but there's a problem with one of the trunks. Might we leave it here until a replacement is found?" When Charlotte nodded, the girl gestured to someone behind her. "Bring it on in."

A lad, not much bigger than the damaged luggage he carried, struggled to gently set the trunk in the center of her room. A nod and a poor attempt at a bow later, both servants scurried away.

Absently, Charlotte returned her attention to the sky and then to the trunk sitting squarely between her and the writing desk. Apparently the latches had given way, for the top was askew and one side bore a crack that reached midway down the trunk.

She opened it. No wonder the latch had broken. The trunk was full to the brim with books and papers and letters. One of the servants needed a lesson in packing.

Charlotte reached over the mess to the writing desk for the bell to call the maid, but she stopped when she spied an envelope from Uncle Edwin wedged partway inside the copy of *Sense and Sensibility* Uncle Edwin had given her at her wedding.

Odd that she hadn't opened it when she opened the gift. Especially with her uncle helping Grandfather run the company, as the missive could contain important information.

A glance at the mantel clock told her there was nothing to be done for it now. After the reception, Charlotte could read and respond to the almost-missed correspondence. She set the letter on top of her writing desk and penned a note to the maid.

Then it was time to submit to the hairdresser and the small army of servants it took to remove all vestiges of the woman who'd awakened in her bed this morning.

Finally they finished, and Charlotte stood back and looked in the mirror. Miss Pence would have been proud of her transformation.

"Shall I fetch the mister?" the maid inquired.

"The mister," Charlotte echoed. "No."

Though she knew making an appearance with Alex by her side would be required of her, Charlotte planned to delay the inevitable as long as she could.

She touched the pearls roped around her neck, the pearls Alex had given her aboard the *Teutonic*. When her fingers found the bejeweled locket at the end of the rope, she opened it to reveal the time.

Already guests were assembling for what had been predicted by society columnists at both the *New York Times* and the *San Francisco Chronicle* to be one of the must-attend events of the year. Papa had outdone himself, sparing no expense as he hosted the Old West's version of an elegant celebration.

Though she'd avoided all pretense of interest in the proceedings, it had been impossible to miss the barrels, crates, and wagonloads of party preparations arriving daily for the past week. Great tents had gone up where the horses once roamed, each furnished with enough gold, silver, crystal, and fine furnishings to fill a palace drawing room. But then, that was the intention.

To top it all, Gennie had pressed Papa's old friend Colonel Cody to linger a bit longer before returning to Scouts Rest Ranch for the winter. He responded by commanding his best performers to join him in preparing a private Wild West extravaganza in honor of the newlyweds.

It was all too much.

Charlotte set such thoughts aside. Tomorrow the ruse would be over. No more playing blushing bride to Viscount Hambly, and no more avoiding Gennie and Papa when her husband was in their company.

She released the watch, allowing it to slide into place in the hollow of her neck. But something about the evidence of a memory she shared with Alex against her bare skin made her uncomfortable. Shifting the pearls around, she moved the bauble until it swung from the longest strand.

"There," she said softly as a ridiculous tear threatened to fall. "No need to keep track of the time tonight."

And yet she knew she would.

When the knock came, she composed herself. Crossing the room with her head held high, Charlotte opened the door to find not Alex but Papa.

"Might I come in?" he asked.

"Papa," she said on an exhale. She moved back and allowed him to enter her room. "Yes, of course."

He went to the window, where she'd stood some hours earlier. Rather than admiring the view, he too looked deep in thought. When she shut the door, he turned to face her.

"You might be fooling Hambly, Buttercup, but you have not fooled me."

Her heart sank. "I've no idea what you're talking about." The truth, she realized, for she'd shared very little with her father these past few months.

Papa's gaze bore through her. "You love him."

The accusation stunned her. How had her father guessed when she had barely acknowledged the fact to herself?

All attempts at pretense fell away. "How did you know?"

"I didn't," Papa said. "Until just now."

"Oh, Papa. What am I going to do?" She fell into his arms, not caring what the embrace and the tears that came with it did to her carefully constructed exterior.

"There, there," he said. "Is it so awful?"

Look what happened to Mama.

Charlotte bit her lip and tried to will away the thought. The fear. She failed miserably on both counts.

"What is it?" Papa demanded. "Has he treated you poorly? If he has, I swear on my life I'll—"

"No, he's been nothing but a gentleman." *Most of the time.*

"Then if the problem isn't Hambly, it must be..."

"Me." Charlotte slipped from her father's embrace and wrapped her arms around her waist. "It's completely me." Slowly she lifted her eyes to meet Papa's stare. "I'm...afraid."

He shook his head. "Of what?" Then his brows lifted. "Ah, well...perhaps you should have a conversation with Gennie regarding the wifely..."

Papa coughed as his face reddened. Had she not been so heartbroken, Charlotte might have giggled.

Instead, she shook her head. "No, that's not it at all."

Papa's look of relief was short-lived. "Then you'll have to tell me, Buttercup. I'm all out of ideas."

She took her father's hand. "For reasons that are mine alone, I can't marry Alex," she said. "Not now. Not yet."

"Darling, you *are* married."

"You've the connections to remedy that," she said. "As does Alex. Only he refuses." Charlotte paused. "There are valid grounds to annul the marriage. Do you wish me to state them?"

"No." He shook his head. "I can guess."

Charlotte tightened her grip on his hand. "Will you help release me from this marriage?" She paused. "Please?"

Papa looked away, then slowly returned his attention to Charlotte. "Not without knowing exactly the why of all this." He held up his hand to prevent her response. "If you love him and you've got no compunction about performing the, um, requirements of a wife, then I need to understand why you want out of a marriage you've already been in this long."

"All right." Charlotte swallowed hard to dislodge the lump in her throat. "I won't allow what happened to Mama to happen to me. I won't...I won't let myself love someone only to have them leave me."

Her honesty appeared to take all the starch from Papa's spine, for he quickly found the nearest chair. Leaning forward to rest his elbows on his knees, her father sighed. Slowly, he lifted his head to find her.

"Come here." He gestured to the chair nearest him.

She complied, though her feet nearly refused to move. "I'm sorry, Papa, but you required an answer, and that is the only true response I can give."

"Well, I suppose it's time we got around to the truth, you and I." His shoulders sagged as their gazes collided. "It's not fair to you that I've refused to speak of your mother. It just seemed simpler that way."

Had she been able to find her voice, Charlotte would have told Papa exactly how complicated his simple solution had been.

"Until I met Gennie, your mother was the only woman I ever loved. It's not right to find a love like that at so young an age." He shrugged. "I was a fool, but I've no regrets. Were I to go back to the day I chose Georgiana for my wife, I'd do it all over again." He sat back and waited for some sort of response from Charlotte. When none came, he shrugged. "I suppose you're looking for more than that."

Charlotte cleared her throat. "Yes."

"All right." Again he leaned forward to rest his elbows on his knees. "Your mother was the prettiest girl I'd ever seen. Just looking at her caused me to lose all good sense. It was a good two weeks before I could speak more than a sentence or two in her presence without stuttering."

At Charlotte's smile, Papa continued. "Georgiana wasn't without suitors. Chief among them was my brother."

The breath went out of her. Uncle Edwin and Mama?

"But she loved you," Charlotte offered.

"I thought so." Abruptly, he rose. "Charlotte, I don't feel comfortable going any further with this." He moved toward the door. "Suffice it to say your mother loved you and never wished to cause you any harm. Now, if you'll excuse me, I'll be going and so should you. Our guests will be wondering where the bride and groom are."

Charlotte stumbled to her feet and blocked his path. "With all due respect," she said. "I deserve more than the crumbs you've just offered."

"Crumbs?" Papa gave her a look of great offense. "Have you any idea what you're asking of me?"

"I think I do," she answered though she truly did not.

"All right, then. If you wish me to admit it, I shall." His gaze fell to the desk and he retrieved the letter from her uncle. "Oh, perfect. You've correspondence from Edwin." He held it up. "Why haven't you opened it?"

"I only just found it," she said. Papa thrust it toward her. "I assume you'd like me to do that now?"

"Why not?"

She tore open the envelope and allowed the page to spill out into her hand. But instead of a letter, what landed in her palm was some sort of legal document. She tossed the envelope aside and unfolded the page to read it. "It's a birth record." She handed it to Papa. "Mine."

He took the document. "I'm sorry you had to find out this way, Buttercup. I've loved you as any father would. You're my world. My very life."

Charlotte shook her head. "Of course you have, Papa. But why would Uncle Edwin give this to me? Don't you find it odd?"

He looked away from her, down at the birth certificate. Slowly, a smile lifted his lips. "You're mine," he said softly. "Right here it says I am your father."

"Of course it does," she said. "What else would it say?" Her father didn't answer, and a sick feeling bloomed in Charlotte's stomach. "Papa?" she whispered.

He shook his head. "It doesn't matter, Buttercup. It doesn't matter at all." He gazed again at the birth certificate. "Where did you find this?"

"It—it was in the book Uncle Edwin gave me at the church on the day of our wedding," Charlotte said. "Somehow I never noticed it before now."

"Yes, well, fortunate you found it, isn't it?" Papa said the words with cheer, but Charlotte knew her father, and something was gravely wrong.

He retrieved the envelope and turned it over. "This isn't from Edwin. It's from your grandfather."

"Papa?" She ran her hand along his arm, then entwined her fingers with his. "If you loved Mama so much, why did you leave her?"

Her father seemed not to hear the question. Or perhaps he merely wished to avoid the answer.

"You wished to open this discussion," she reminded him. "I find it quite unfair to close it before it's done."

"Unfair." He nodded and tore his eyes from the certificate. "All right. You said you fear what happened to your mother might happen to you. Exactly what happened to her? When I left, she appeared quite happy to see me go."

This she hadn't expected. "She missed you terribly."

"And this you knew as a child of what, three? Four?" He shook his head. "Keep in mind that Georgiana did not bother to mention the existence of a daughter until she arrived on my doorstep in Denver."

"I—I had no idea." Charlotte wrapped her arms around her waist and willed away the awful thoughts swirling around her. "But she spoke of you so often, and I always assumed..."

"Never assume." Papa clenched his fist around the certificate. "I loved her. What in all the years of growing up in my home has told you otherwise?" He paused only to take a breath. "And what in my behavior toward you has ever led you to believe you were not a child who was well loved and cherished?"

"Nothing," she whispered.

"Then listen carefully, Charlotte," he said in a tone that only vaguely resembled the man she knew and loved. "What happened to your mother was due to her own actions. Had she wished to come with me to America, she could have. She *chose* to remain behind, promising to follow when I sent for her."

"Then why didn't you send for her?"

"I did," he snapped. "I sent multiple letters to..." His eyes widened, and his face fell. "Because I assumed she was still living at Beck Manor in Northumberland, I sent the letters in care of"—Papa shook his head—"of my father." He turned away. "Could it be that Georgiana never received my letters? That she loved me and not…"

He appeared to ask this more of himself than of Charlotte.

"Papa," she said gently, "my mother loved you until her dying breath. Why else would she seek you out even when she felt you didn't want to see her?"

Her father's eyes grew moist. "I asked her about the letters. Demanded that she explain why she'd waited so long. She claimed no knowledge of them, but by then I was certain that she and Edwin…" He looked away. "I dismissed the truth and believed a lie."

Charlotte looked at the birth certificate crumpled in his hand. "Oh, Papa."

She reached for her father and tumbled into his embrace. The years fell away, and she felt five years old again, newly arrived in a strange land. Then she was ten trying to be twenty, proving that while Papa was putty in her hands, he still loved her enough to say no to her schemes. And now, today, she was a grown woman, not newly married but about to be truly married.

A knock sounded, and the maid slid the door open just a crack. "Begging your pardon, but Mrs. Beck is looking for you and your pa."

"Coming," Papa called. "Tell my wife we've been slightly detained, but all is well." When the maid closed the door, Daniel looked down at Charlotte's tear-stained face through tears of his own. "All *is* well, isn't it, Buttercup?"

"Yes," she said softly. "All is very well."

36

Living happily ever after is a lady's best revenge.
—*Miss Pence*

Despite her complete disinterest in the celebration, Charlotte couldn't help but notice that workmen had been busy building bunkhouses, refitting wagons, and generally doing Gennie's bidding ever since her return from London. Now the bunkhouses were filled to capacity with party guests, as was every spare bedchamber in the main house and the caretaker's quarters. In addition, Papa had claimed every room in the best hotel in Fort Collins. While Charlotte hadn't seen the official guest list, she'd heard the servants whispering that there would be several hundred in attendance.

The massive old barn and attached stables had been completely refitted for the occasion. From the outside, no evidence of the opulence of the interior could be seen. The rough wooden exterior had been left exactly as if it was still one of the many abandoned buildings on Papa's property.

Guests dressed in the required buckskins and baubles—mostly diamonds or pearls—were greeted at the bunkhouses assigned to them and taken to the barn on horseback or by wagon. Stalls where Papa's prize horses once languished still contained straw, but on top of the fresh layer of straw lay rugs imported from the finest shops in Istanbul and Persia. And rather than horses in residence, the walls between the stalls had been removed to allow for a chuck wagon and tables laden with the finest cuisine Gennie's favorite French chef could prepare.

The walls in the stable had been covered in tapestries more fit for a British castle than a Colorado outbuilding, and crystal chandeliers hung from ceilings where bridles and tack were once stored.

All of this Charlotte had heard about but not seen, though she would soon make her entrance and view the extravaganza for herself. Papa escorted her down the hall and into the main foyer where the rustic décor had been bedecked in elegant finery and scented with the fragrance of huge arrangements of white roses and orange blossoms.

"Isn't it lovely?" Gennie hurried toward them. Dressed in an outfit that could best be described as a cross between Annie Oakley and House of Worth, and wearing a tiara on top of her Stetson, she appeared to be taking the theme of the party seriously.

"Yes, lovely," Charlotte replied.

Her stepmother gave Charlotte a sweeping glance then turned to Papa. "Didn't you explain the theme? I know I certainly tried."

Charlotte looked down at her gown and then back at Gennie. While she hadn't intended to go along with the silliness of the theme, the fun of it began to appeal to her. "Perhaps I could find something else."

"Along with you, then," Gennie said. "Your father and I will wait."

"No need," Charlotte tossed over her shoulder, already hurrying up the stairs. "I won't keep you from the guests any longer. Just please send Alex up if you see him."

She hurried up to her bedchamber and found the desired additions to her outfit. By the time she'd donned the boots and slipped the fringed jacket over her gown, Charlotte heard a knock.

"Alex?" She hurried to open the door.

Her husband greeted her with a bemused smile. Impeccably dressed in formal attire, her British groom wore boots and, instead of a top hat, a black Stetson. In his hands he carried a large, beautifully wrapped gift.

"Well now," he said as his gaze swept across her. "Don't you look…interesting?"

"Do you like it?" She twirled on her toes, and the pearls clattered. "Perhaps you remember the jacket?"

"I do." He set the gift aside to admire her. "As I recall, the last time I saw it, I was taking it off of you."

Charlotte paused to take a deep breath. "Alex." She touched his sleeve. "I'm counting on that happening again."

"Are you?"

Was it her imagination, or did her husband's voice contain a slight, hopeful tone?

Her fingers moved from his sleeve to the back of his arm, then slid up to find the nape of his neck. "I am."

Alex cleared his throat. "Charlotte, what are you up to?" He held her at arm's length. "I won't fall for your scheming."

"This is no scheme, Alex. I've just realized that…" Charlotte paused to consider her words. "I know now that I was wrong." Her eyes never left his as she slid from his grasp to move closer. "*We* were wrong." She heard him sigh and tried not to smile. "Marriage is a sacred promise," Charlotte continued as she once again found the nape of his neck with her hand. She carefully removed his hat and cast it aside.

"It is," he managed.

"And until today, we had grounds for ending this marriage." Her eyes locked with his as her fingers traced the line of his jaw.

"Until today?"

"That's right, husband." She stepped back and let the fringed jacket fall, leaving only the Parisian gown and the cowboy boots she'd borrowed from Gennie. And then, with trembling hands, she touched the first button on her gown. "Until today."

Alex placed his hand over hers. "This is no game, Charlotte, and I'm no one to be toyed with."

"I do not wish to toy with you," she said evenly. "I wish to amend my part of the bargain and be the wife I promised before God in the chapel. Is that agreeable to you?"

"Y-yes." His fingers tightened over hers and he pressed his palm against the small of her back. "Are you certain?" The question drifted across her ear on a warm breath.

She looked up at her husband and, with complete assurance, nodded.

"You're a menace," he said as he hauled her against him. "You've gone and broken something again."

Charlotte tilted her head to better see his expression and found him smiling. "And what is that?"

"My will," he said in a rough voice. "You've completely taken me by surprise. Though it is quite the pleasant surprise."

His kiss was soft, sweet, and ever so welcome. Charlotte's lips sought his, and the kiss deepened. She rose up on her toes to press closer.

"Wife," Alex said, "we've a ranch full of guests and we're in danger of missing our celebration." He held her at arm's length.

Charlotte offered a pout that seemed to have no effect on her husband. "All right, then," she said, "but might we make our escape as soon as possible?"

"We might," he teased in response.

This time there would be no interruption. No rescue by a concerned father or his famous friend. Alex saw to this when he stationed guards outside the door with instructions to allow no one in under any circumstances.

This time, he wasn't worried about the trunks he'd seen leaving the house this morning with her name on them, for they were headed far from Colorado and any lingering concerns Charlotte might have about their marriage. First, her trunks would join his aboard ship, and together they would take that long overdue wedding trip to Italy, France, and whatever other locations struck their fancies.

And then they would return to England, but not to the Hambly home at the Heath. Though his mother might complain, Alex intended to begin his life with this woman in a home of their own. A proper palace in which to install his princess. And while he'd continue his work at the Observatory, and not at the University of Colorado as he'd been tempted to do, Charlotte could pursue whatever captured her fancy in the business world.

Once the babies began to arrive, things would likely change. But together they would figure it all out.

Together.

He and his wife. She was truly breathtaking, this wife of his, and he struggled to keep his composure without frightening her. For as much bravado as Charlotte wore, as she looked up at him, he saw uncertainty.

But he also saw love.

"Charlotte," he said against the warm skin of her neck. "I love you. Do you know that?"

His wife bit her lip then nodded. "Yes, I think I do."

"You think?" His palm slid down her arm to entwine her fingers with his.

"Well, no...I know you love me. And I love you," she said slowly. Her gaze scorched the length of him.

He released her hand and stepped back. "Before I forget, I want you to open the gift I've brought."

She shook her head. "Now?"

"Yes, now." He retrieved the wrapped box he'd brought her before their reception, gestured for her to sit on the bed, and set it in her lap. "Go ahead. Open it."

Her fingers tossed aside the bow, then tore at the wrapping. "Alex," she said in a trembling voice as she examined the gift. "How did you find one so like…"

"Like the paint box you lost in the river?" He shrugged, allowing himself the slightest bit of pride for the reaction his gift had elicited. "Actually, that is your paint box."

"What?" She ran her hand across the surface then looked up at him. "It can't be. Mine was lost."

"Yours was found. It took some doing, but I managed to locate the box and have it restored." He removed the paint box from her hands and set it on the bedside table. Soon enough she would open the paint box and find the treasure trove of jewels he'd had made for her. For now, however, there were more pressing things to discover. "Back to the matter at hand—the fact that we are in danger of losing grounds for ending our marriage."

"Yes, I believe we are."

"This inconvenient marriage of ours has begun to appeal to me, Lady Hambly," he said. "So put any thought of annulment out of your mind."

Charlotte lifted her head to meet his kisses. "Stop talking, Viscount Hambly," she said against his lips. "Or I shall be forced to do something to get your attention."

"Such as what? Pick my pocket?"

Her giggle was smooth as silk. Smooth as the skin of her neck beneath the palm of his hand.

"Silly viscount," she said, her gaze direct and her intentions obvious, "you won't have any pockets to pick."

"Quite inconvenient," was the only reply he could manage.

Acknowledgments

Wrapping up the Women of the West series and saying good-bye to the Beck family is bittersweet. Charlotte Beck has lived in my mind and heart, first as an impish child in *The Confidential Life of Eugenia Cooper*, and then as a young lady longing for adulthood in *Anna Finch and the Hired Gun*. I hope I've met the challenge of giving Charlotte a story with her spunk.

The making of any book is no solitary endeavor. First and foremost I want to thank my fabulous editor Jessica Barnes for taking my lump of coal and polishing it to find the diamond beneath all that dust. Thanks also to Shannon Marchese for your encouragement and mentorship and to Amy Partain and the copy editing team for a job well done. To the rest of the WaterBrook team: I am in awe of all you do!

And to my fabulous agent, Wendy Lawton, thank you for perfecting that combination of task master, psychologist, and confidante. You're the best!

In preparing to write this novel, I traveled to London to scout locations for scenes. I could never have made that trip if my amazing children hadn't made me cry once again at Christmas by giving me a round-trip ticket to London. Thank you, Josh, Andrew, Jacob, and Hannah! I love you guys!

Also while in London, I met the lovely Vanessa Miter, who gave me invaluable insight into Victorian England. From one history buff to another, I am in your debt, Vanessa. And to my cousin Susan Cunningham and her husband, Mike, thank you for hospitality. If only I could have managed to somehow set a scene at Crazy Homies.

Finally, to my husband Robert Turner, whose encouragement and penchant for punctuality and detail got me through those moments when I was tempted to rename this novel *The Never Ending Story.* Thank you, sweetheart, for understanding that a writer sometimes must work, even on her honeymoon. Mission accomplished! Next time we go to Hawaii, I promise to leave my computer at home.

Romantic, enchanting, and adventurous

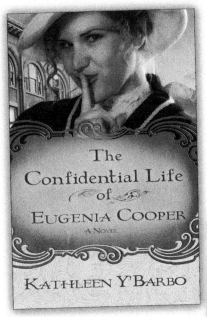

A New York socialite sets out to experience the adventurous life portrayed in her favorite dime novels—and finds herself up to her bonnet-strings in Wild West danger and romance.

When an aspiring reporter and a Pinkerton detective get tangled in gunslinger Doc Holliday's story—and each other— sparks can't help but fly.

Read an excerpt at WaterBrookMultnomah.com